I0588748

A London Affair

1st Edition

ISBN: 978-0-6451986-6-9

Copyright © 2023 Monica Ritz

Cover Design by Brand Artisans Australia
www.brandartisans.com.au

Follow the Publisher:

Facebook: www.facebook.com/monicaritzauthor
Instagram: www.instagram.com/monicaritzauthor

Sales and Distribution enquiries to Brand Artisans Australia
Email: info@brandartisans.com.au

brandartisans.com.au

"She took the leap and built her wings on the way down."

Kori Yamada.

Contact Monica Ritz

Website: www.brandartisans.com.au/monicaritz
Facebook: www.facebook.com/monicaritzauthor
Instagram: www.instagram.com/monicaritzauthor

A LONDON AFFAIR

MONICA RITZ

"You don't have to be great to start, but you have to start to be great."

Zig Ziglar

– PROLOGUE –

I met Shelley at a small but stunning resort on Koh Pha Ngan Island, Thailand, a fellow Aussie also on her way to London. The resort had a dozen basic dark-wood and thatched huts, elevated by thick wooden logs, just enough so they did not require multiple steps to enter. Inside was a wet area with a hand-held shower which was also used to fill a bucket to flush the toilet. There was no hot water, but as it was summer and hot, the heat on the exposed pipes warmed the water sufficiently. Each hut was a one or two bed, air-conditioned or not. Mine was a two bed, not air-conditioned, but no one who stayed here complained about the lack of luxury. This was part of the experience we came to Thailand for. All the huts were fully occupied by couples and friends from all over the world.

Shelley's two-bed air-conditioned hut was more like a caravan, which I first experienced the night I needed refuge from a monster-sized spider scurrying across my ceiling. Even though it hid somewhere, I was not taking any chances. Just the thought of it made me shiver. It was bigger than any huntsman spider I had ever seen, and size *does* matter when it comes to spiders.

The resort had a large communal area complete with wooden decking, brightly coloured cushions, and a view of the beach you could never tire of. This was where the residents became friends, and continually exchanged stories. It was obvious we were all here for the same reason, the 'Full Moon Party'.

After just one afternoon, it felt like we were on tour together and had known one another for months. It did not matter that English was not the dominant language nor that there were couples, friends, or singles. We were a like-minded group with a single focus, and we communicated easily.

When it came time for the party, the girls followed the normal getting-ready ritual, scurrying between huts, giggling in pairs, and experimenting with products from around the world. The boys rolled their eyes and focused on their beers. It became clear that no matter where you are in the world, girls will be girls and boys will be boys.

The Full Moon Party took residence on the pristine beach of Haas Rin, a twenty-minute drive from the resort. By the time we arrived it was dusk, and the party had already begun. To feel the energy shift in sync with the rise of the full yellow moon, as it cast its glow across the still waters below, was truly magical. As the music rose into the air, the entire length of the beach exploded into a dance frenzy. The young, the old, the residents, the tourists all responding to the DJs at their decks pumping out the tunes.

There was music for all tastes: techno, dance, drum and bass, Latin, and Reggae. We were seduced by the moon, the music, the simple vodka Red Bull, and the 10,000 people engrossed in one of the world's best parties. There was more than just vodka feeding the frenzy and it was not hard to find the chemical cocktail your heart desired. A pill, some powder or to be smoked, its consumption took you on a journey, emotionally, spiritually, surrendering completely to the environment, embracing everything good with humanity.

My journey took me towards another singleton from the resort. We had no need to talk, literature was all around us. We kissed, we touched, we danced, we indulged, we stumbled through the sand, we kissed some more. We were having our own party. I cannot remember ever feeling freer from the world, and what happens on tour stays on tour.

There was no concept of time, the atmospheric pulse the only indicator. With my head resting on his shoulder, I knew the party was winding down. More and more party-goers moulded into the sand, exhausted but exhilarated, resting aching legs from endless hours of dancing and moving through fluffy sand.

Most of our group sat quietly together, watching the sun rise over the rippling water, enchanted by the sight of the boats coming to shore to retrieve their staggering party-goers. Others were acting on their desires, with no concern for how exposed they were, leaving nothing to the imagination for those close by.

With daylight, it was easier for the rest of our group to find us. Together we tackled the unenviable task of attracting transport back to the resort. There was no boat for us. These needed to be pre-booked and none of us had thought to do that, we were relegated to what can only be described as an army truck consisting of two rows of seats facing each other. No seat belts, no traffic lights, no road rules. On our mini road trip, we passed two similar trucks toppled over, but there were no passengers to be seen.

Thankfully, we arrived safely to our hosts cheerfully greeting us, handing out bottles of water and taking our breakfast orders. They knew this routine well.

Our mouths were coated with the sweet residue of our drinks; our eyes were on stalks from the pills and powder consumption; and our physical need for sleep was fighting our brains that still desperately wanted entertainment.

The smell of bacon and eggs frying was the best smell in the world, and when it was ready, we quietly and eagerly consumed every last crumb. There were no leftovers.

With our bellies full, we stumbled towards our beds. We did not think about who belonged in which hut, we all crashed wherever we landed, and I landed in his cabin.

We ripped off each other's clothes and did not care that the grit from the sand was exfoliating our skin as we moved passionately as one. The build-up of hours of seduction fuelled our aggression of wanting more of each other, before crashing into a deep, heavy sleep. When we woke, I dressed, mumbled a thanks, gave him a final kiss, and returned to my cabin.

My holiday fling left the resort later that day. There was no exchange of numbers, or empty promises, just a mutual acknowledgment that we had had fun.

It took me days to recover from the party and I was thankful that I still had time on the island to do nothing. I gave up my spider ridden hut and moved permanently in with Shelley.

Once we had recovered enough to pack, we spent our final days in Koh Samui, and then we were London bound.

- CHAPTER 1 -

It has been four weeks since leaving Thailand, the memories now replaced by new ones as I settle into London life. My days currently mimic those of a student: jobless, falling into pubs, getting up late, and doing random activities with friends in the same situation. Today's random activity is to provide moral support to Shelley while she tries to rent a flat, which is not an easy feat. All the flats we have seen are either awful and affordable or perfect and expensive, so when we pass a pub with a beer garden, we are easily lured in. I justify this choice to myself that soon, when I have a job, I will not be able to do this in the middle of the day, and besides, the sun is out.

There is only so long you can apply for jobs without becoming thoroughly discouraged. I have submitted numerous applications for jobs I thought I could easily do, and even ones where I did not really understand what they wanted. I am convinced there is a big black hole that job applications get sucked into, never to be seen again, making me question whether these jobs are even real. Maybe I have underestimated my skills. I am not receiving any responses, not even to say that I am unsuccessful, which would be helpful to know, so I could change my tactics.

At last count, I had applied for twenty-two jobs. I have meticulously kept track, to give me some feeling of order in my otherwise less-than-orderly life. This is the first time in my career I have been rash enough to leave a job without another job lined up, with no idea when I will have an income again.

I am usually optimistic, regardless of how grim things seem, but I am starting to struggle to think positively. The pessimism is creeping in at the thought of having to return home after only six weeks away. That would be a monumental failure.

Looking at my job application list again with no dates or times for interviews, I hit a real low. I'm hoping my savings do not run out. Staying out of pubs and limiting random activities would help this, but every time I walk out the door, there is something to buy: coffee, or beer, or a new top. Clothes, handbags and shoes are becoming a problem, as the London fashion is a squillion times better than anything I can buy at home. I keep telling myself that the worst that can happen is my funds run out and I am forced to go home, but at least I would look fabulous doing it. In the meantime, I focus on enjoying the sunshine.

I cannot understand why Londoners complain about the weather, however, I have not experienced a winter yet and I am still very much a tourist. Today is the perfect example, as spring has hit London. I have been told that anyone who has survived a year in London knows that winter is the dominant season. Spring is just more of the same, only with extra daylight hours and the need for fewer layers of clothing. The weather can be erratic, just like Melbourne, sometimes catching everyone in winter gear when it suddenly turns hot. Today this city is bathed in glorious warm sunshine.

In true English tradition, when the sun is shining, London's population appears to double. Its habitants are drawn out from their caves, their hibernation replaced by the desire for all things outdoors: parks, cafes, restaurants, but the most popular... pubs. There is hardly anyone indoors, except for those at the bar. People claim any available outdoor space, even those parallel to a busy road. On days like today, the punters have right of way.

Shelley's desire is to live in Putney, south of the river, and that is where we are today. It is a new area and a new pub for me. Surprisingly, everyone seems equipped for the heat in flip-flops, shorts, skirts, and tank tops, but I know discreetly tucked away are the cardigans and jackets.

I am enjoying an icy-cold beer, one of the few, as most have been warm at best. Many Aussies complain that English beer is not cold enough, and I wholeheartedly agree.

"I can't believe I cannot find a job," I say to Shelley, watching the condensation form on the outside of my glass.

"I can't believe how crappy the flats are and how much they want for them," Shelley says with a sigh.

"How long can you stay with your friends?"

"They said I can stay as long as I need, but they don't have a big place. I just need my own space."

"I understand," I say, nodding in commiseration, "but you haven't been looking for long. Maybe you need to broaden your search to other areas. I know Putney is a cool place but that's probably why it's expensive. Look around, everyone is well dressed so it must be an upmarket area."

"It's just so hard," she says dejectedly. "In Australia, some of the places we saw today wouldn't even be allowed on the market, and if they were, they'd never attract tenants."

"Yes, I know, but we are no longer in Kansas, Toto," I reply, which makes us both laugh. "If you don't want to stay where you are now, could you find a place with another friend? Or even look for a flat share instead?"

"It is good in theory, but I need my own space."

"Well, I have heard that if you soulfully tell the universe what you want, then the universe will provide."

"Do you really believe in that hippy stuff?" Shelley asks, rolling her eyes.

"No, not really, but you never know," I shrug, then take another gulp of my beer. "But seriously, what is wrong with me? I just need a bloody job."

My phone rings. We both look down at it with curiosity before I pick up the mystery call.

"Hello? Cari speaking," I answer in my best professional tone, mouthing a silent "sorry" to Shelley.

"Hello, is this Cari Jackson?" An unknown male voice asks.

"Yes, it is," I respond, my heart beating a little faster.

"My name is Andy Smith and I work for RecruitMe. I would like to talk to you about the Senior Project Management role you applied for. Are you still available for new roles?" He asks.

I am flapping my arms at Shelley, so she knows this is one of those calls I have been waiting for.

"Hi, yes I am," I say, wondering whether he can hear my heart pounding through the phone. This is my first call about a job, although I have no clue which of the twenty-two jobs he is calling about.

"Is this a good time to talk?" Andy asks.

"Sure. Yes. Absolutely."

"Have you had any interviews recently?" He begins.

"Not recently. There are a few positions I'm interested in, but I am still waiting to hear back from them," I answer truthfully.

"Excellent! I have your application in front of me. Apologies for only calling you now, but the position was put on hold due to a funding issue. This has been resolved and they need to move fast to make up for the lost time. They believe you have the skills they are looking for and would like to interview you."

"That's great. When?" I answer promptly, maybe a little too eagerly. More arm flapping at Shelley.

"Today, this afternoon, they want to complete the first round by close of business today. I apologise for the short notice, but the agency only just contacted me and, as I said, they need to move fast on this placement. They are a top-five UK agency, and these opportunities do not present often as they usually recruit from within," he says.

He does not need to convince me; I was ready to say yes as soon as he introduced himself. This is my first and only opportunity to secure a job, and I do not care who it is with.

"Yes, that's fine. Where do I need to go for the

interview and what time? I'm out at the moment, and not dressed for an interview," I respond with a little more control.

"They are only offering phone interviews at this stage. Can they call you on this number?"

"Yes."

"There will be at least two people interviewing you," Andy continues. "Is three o'clock suitable?"

"Yes, that will work for me, thank you."

I am not only tipsy but ill prepared. I have no information on this company as I do not even know who they are. The recruiter did not mention it and I did not want to ask. To add to this testing situation, I have only twenty minutes to find a suitable location for the interview, and this pub is not it. It is full of animated punters enjoying the sun and making a lot of noise.

A few doors down is the last real estate agent we visited, so we decide to take a gamble and ask if I can borrow a room for the interview. It is the only option I have, so when we spot the agent who serviced us, we do our best to convince him, over-exaggerating the importance and insinuating it is a life-or-death situation. He either believes us, or takes pity on us, or wants us out of his face, and directs us towards a set of stairs.

I bound up the stairs with purpose, believing I will find a private room at the top. Instead, we are confronted with an open plan office with, at a quick count, twelve people sitting at their desks doing whatever real estate office workers do. I explain why I am in their office, and they look as if they are about to be sprung on candid camera.

On the stroke of three o'clock, my phone rings, sending a jolt of nervous energy through my body. As I navigate through the busy office towards an empty desk, I answer the call and introduce myself. The two people who are interviewing introduce themselves in posh English accents. I do not tell them I am performing in front of an audience. I am sitting metres away from the office workers and even closer to Shelley so I need to concentrate hard to block out my onlookers.

The interviewers take turns asking in-depth questions relating to my application and the various roles I have listed. They give me a lot of information about the role, the project, and themselves, but not who they are and it did not seem appropriate to ask.

The interview lasts for twenty-five minutes and yet it feels like hours, so I am relieved once it is over. Jumping to my feet and eager to leave, it is clearly written on the faces around me that I have provided some light entertainment for this poor crew stuck inside. I do my best to remain composed, thank my audience, and skip towards the stairs to make my exit.

Yes, I skip, and I mean... I literally skip. While most people would depart quietly, my tendency to make uncomfortable situations worse, makes me decide to choose skipping as my stride of choice, which I do all the way to the exit, where I turn gracefully and wave.

We leave the real estate agent and head back to the same pub. Within minutes, the recruiter rings to ask how the interview went. I replay the odd scenario, which amuses him, however am confident in saying that even though it was distracting, I thought I'd answered their questions well. Andy wishes me luck and informs me he will be in touch as soon as he receives their feedback.

All my hopes are pinned on this one and only interview for a mystery company I know absolutely nothing about. Again, I should have asked Andy but this time it did not cross my mind.

Two pints later, Andy calls back to invite me to attend a face-to-face interview, tomorrow morning at nine. This is our cue to leave the pub, as we have consumed too many beers for what has suddenly turned into a school night.

*

The early start is a shock to my hungover body. The interview location reveals the job is for an advertising agency called Tyn-T.

At nine o'clock on the dot, I am escorted to a room to meet the panel. Each position at the table has a glass of water provided but I wait to be invited to sit, before I claim the empty chair. There are three faces staring back at me, the original phone interview pair and a third. It is nice to put faces to the voices, although they look nothing like I had visualised. The phone interview duo look older than their voices implied, whereas the third is younger and has the most amazing, alluring, distracting blue eyes.

They introduce themselves, provide a brief description of their functions in the agency, describe the available role, and then the questions begin.

"Why should we award you the position?"

What an opening question, are they trying to frazzle me? Do I start witty? Would they find it funny? The older one looks bored, and it is only the first question. What I want to say is, 'because I need to stop spending my days in pubs and to re-join the real world', but as this is serious, I take a deep breath and regurgitate a pre-rehearsed answer I have used several times before.

"With my experience in both similar and quite different industries, I believe I can fit seamlessly within a team, offering familiarity as well as something new." I pause and they look pleased. I am desert mouth thirsty and would like some of that water. But what if I grab the glass and my hand is shaking and they think it is because I am nervous? Probably better than realising I am hung-over. I really do need a job to inject some normality into my life. I need to stop the boozy nights usually ending in a lock-in, and stumbling home at stupid o'clock completely wasted.

"Yes, I have had experience working with client service teams," I reply to their next question. "In fact, one of my good friends is an account director. I believe a good project manager– account director combination is almost unstoppable," I claim, another great answer if I do say so myself.

Even though my tongue is sticking to the roof of my mouth, I continue to leave the glass on the table, while hoping

I still look presentable. I check my skirt has not ridden up to expose an unacceptable amount of leg, my blouse is still buttoned up...but what is that white splat on my black blazer collar? I freeze, my heart beating in my head, temples pulsating, about to explode. To make matters worse, my burning red face attracts all three sets of eyes to that particular spot. This is an interview in a prestigious agency for a senior role and I have what appears to be toothpaste on my blazer.

Losing control of my brain–mouth connectivity, I start confessing that it must be toothpaste dribble from brushing my teeth this morning. 'Toothpaste dribble' were the exact words that flew out of my mouth. It is obvious by the uncomfortable shifting in their chairs that the panel members are disgusted.

It no longer matters that my mouth is a desert as I can no longer feel my face. Get me out of here!

Much to my relief, the awkwardness is interrupted by a phone ringing, which for a brief second, I thought was mine. It belongs to the older man dressed in a suit. I can't even remember his name, despite the fact they introduced themselves at the start of the interview. Three names, three roles, a hangover, and nerves thrown in for good measure has mixed everyone up, so I am playing 'Guess Who'. Suit man picks up his phone, apologises and walks out the room, we are now down to two.

Once I regain control, the interview hums along and during the more technical-orientated questions, the suit man re-joins the panel. He grabs what looks like my application from in front of his colleague and studies it as if it is the first time he has seen it. He looks at me, pauses and then asks whether I think clients are fickle.

Boom! This is not a question I have been asked before. The existence of agencies like this one is conditional on clients and their purses. This could be their knockout question. Depending on how I answer, this could potentially be all they need to know about me. The shock of the question stifles my brain–mouth connectivity again and "yes" comes flying out. I panic, believing this cannot be a good answer, and my reaction to this panic is to just keep talking.

"With diminishing budgets, higher expected returns on investment and a fast-moving market, clients have to respond with little or no regard to how they originally briefed their agency. This then relies heavily on strong management to make it work for the client and the agency, so the fickleness is more about how they need to operate to remain competitive in their markets," blah, blah, blah, yawn! What a boring answer, but much better than yes. I didn't really yawn, at least, I don't think I did. Oh gosh, what if I did?

I need this to stop, I cannot take much more. This feels like the longest interview in history.

It does not stop. There are more questions, standard ones like what are my strengths, what are my weaknesses, more questions referring to my application, mostly from the new interviewer, the man with the blue eyes, who then asks a question that tops the fickle question. Another question I have not had before.

"If in your team you had a very strong character who was senior within the agency, and that person did not get along with the client, what would you do? Would you recommend termination?" He pauses and all eyes look searchingly at me. This question seems to have a hidden depth, possibly a scenario that I would have to deal with if I got the job.

"No, I would not recommend termination without reason. That person is probably still valuable to the delivery of the project and contributes significantly to the agency overall. I would manage the situation, ensure their contact with the client was limited, but continue to work as usual in every other way."

The panel exchange looks with one another, and the female invites me on a tour of the building to meet some of the team. This must be a good sign, but I do not want my positive thoughts to jinx it.

We exit the elevator on the fourth floor and enter one of two large rooms. My eyes are drawn to the walls plastered with brightly coloured designs, and then to the hammock hanging from the ceiling surrounded with oversized cushions and bean bags. Loud indie music infiltrates the quietness that would otherwise be filled by the tapping of keyboards and office chatter.

The music must not be to everyone's taste, as many are wearing massive headphones and seem to be in a world of their own. Since leaving the interview room, I have been silent, and I wonder if my guide has noticed. Having spent two hours answering every probing question thrown at me, there is nothing left. My mind is blank, but I'm hoping this tour means I am still in the running.

We only stay a short time in this room before moving into the next, which also has walls littered with brightly coloured designs. However, the walls are not this rooms most identifiable feature, that award goes to the corner filled with an arrangement of cactuses. I count at least nineteen, all different sizes and a few different colours, but mainly summer-grass green with well-defined spikes. Why cactuses? I wonder. It is common in offices to have a collection of some sort, snow globes, postcards, even gnomes, but I have never seen cactuses, and according to Feng Shui they are not considered welcoming.

"They are travelling cactuses," my guide claims, pausing to let me digest this information. "When someone goes away, they are challenged to find one and bring it back. Not the easiest of things to find, or bring back," she continues, as if reading my mind.

"Wouldn't chocolates be easier?" I respond, which makes us both laugh.

"Chocolates are not creative enough for this team."

My mind is processing the hammock in one room and cactuses in the other. But that is not the extent of the oddities. There is also what looks like a fireman's pole. I hope it is a fireman's pole and not a stripper's pole. Note to self, must read contract carefully, especially the extra duties section. I do not want to find out the new girl is expected to provide the Friday afternoon entertainment.

"Why is there a fireman's pole in this room? I assume it's a fireman's pole and not meant for pole-dancing?" I ask boldly but with an amused tone.

"It is most definitely a fireman's pole. Many years ago, this part of the building was a fire station. It adds character, don't you think?"

"It certainly does," I respond.

This room has a different vibe to the other room. Both rooms are equipped with the same standard computer equipment and nice pens, same brand on all desks in an array of different colours. This serves my mild obsessive-compulsive disorder towards pens, possibly to all stationery in general. My pens must be good quality, write well, be ascetically pleasing, and any different colours must be of the same brand, belonging to the same set. If there are odd pens that do not belong to the set, they must be bunched together and set aside, away from my working set.

"Hi, my name is Kelly," a woman says, popping up from nowhere and holding out her right hand to greet me. A second person is holding what looks like a beer. It is starting to feel like a Sunday afternoon at the pub, not a Friday afternoon in the office.

"Yo, I'm Craig." Craig is barefoot, has unbrushed hair and is sporting a trendy t-shirt with three monkeys, see no evil, hear no evil, speak no evil. An ultra-cool pair, Kelly and Craig must be designers.

As we move around the room, I start to feel self-conscious as this office is not what I am used to. No one is wearing a suit except me. The only other suit was on the panel, and he did not join us for the tour. It is obvious I am the topic of conversation.

My guide manoeuvres us to a small group and explains that if I am successful in winning the role, I will be working with this team. They share the same look of eagerness and utter exhaustion. This group is surrounded by different shades of green, red and blue plastered on every available space. There are designs, magazine cut-outs and different materials such as paper, fabric and boards.

Leaving the cactus room, returning to the elevator and heading to the ground floor signifies the end of this tour and hopefully, this interview process as I have nothing more to give. To make matters worse, my feet are now killing me. Since leaving the Australian shores I have worn nothing but trainers and flat shoes and now I think my feet have spread.

The conversation remains light and is about the construction of the two rooms. Each room has approximately thirty or forty people who have been arranged into project teams, two project teams in the hammock room and three in the cactus room. This is how I like teams to be arranged and I believe this place will be a good professional fit, although I am questioning whether I am hip enough.

I finally leave the building at twenty past one and head straight home. That was the most brain-intensive thing I have done since landing in London. I forgot how tiring and stressful interviews can be.

I change out of my suit, rolling my eyes at the

toothpaste splat, and head out for an espresso from my favourite local coffee shop. In London, coffee shops are as popular as pubs. There is one on every corner and the masses are equally divided between Costa, Nero and Starbucks, and once you have been seduced by the incentive of accumulating points for a free beverage, the consumer stays loyal.

Pleased about my productive morning, I settle back to enjoy the rest of the afternoon. The interview showed promise, but I am determined to keep my excitement at bay in case I am disappointed.

Like most solo coffee house dwellers, my phone is my companion and I check for missed messages of which I have two. One is from the recruiter, enquiring about the interview; and the second is a cryptic message about another job. I respond to this message first.

"Good afternoon, thank you for returning our call. We would like you to attend a screening session this afternoon," a lady says, startling me as I did not get a chance to introduce myself and she did not introduce herself either.

"Hello, who am I speaking to?" I ask.

"I am calling regarding a job that might be of interest to you, and we would like you to attend an initial screening this afternoon," she repeats. Obviously another one of those twenty-two jobs I applied for.

"What does an initial screening consist of?" I ask.

"It's a standard psychometric test. They are common practice in the industry. Can you make three-thirty?"

"It depends where it is, as I am not home and would

need to get changed into something more appropriate." This feels like deja vu, and I would prefer not to revisit my suit, or contemplate this test today.

"Come as you are, the address will be texted to you." She hangs up.

At least from the address I should know which job it is for. It is reassuring to know another application has made its way out of the black hole. I return Andy's call and give him my version of events. He says he will be in touch as soon as he has heard back from Tyn-T.

The texted address for the psychometric test is not easy to locate. I find myself on a long, curved street, lined with identical buildings with only big gold numbers identifying them. They look like residential dwellings and not businesses, and nothing is sign-posted. I find the correctly numbered building and enter a few minutes late. I am asked to sit in a small reception area which is empty except for the two identical dark brown leather lounges, flanked by two single chairs in the same leather. No cushions, no rug, no table, no magazines, and no personality.

These are the only thoughts I have before I am escorted to a room. This room has the same amount of personality as the reception area. White walls, no windows, one chair, and a large wooden table supporting a laptop. I am instructed to commence the test by pressing the start button, and I have to answer all questions as quickly as possible, because it is timed. I am not fully recovered from the last interview so this is going to be a challenge. I hope my instincts kick in and drive me through the process, either that or the two coffees I just consumed.

As I complete the last question, number one hundred and seventy, I lean back to catch my breath and refocus my eyes. According to my timing, it took around one and a half hours.

My breather is interrupted by the receptionist entering the room to escort me out. She says nothing other than that they will be in touch. I leave the building. How did she know I had finished the test? There were no obvious cameras in the room. The only logical explanation is that she was notified as soon as I completed the final question. My phone rings, snapping me out of my daze.

"Hello, Cari speaking."

"Hi Cari, it's Andy, I have some good news for you."

"Have you heard back from Tyn-T?" I reply.

"Yes, I have, and they would like to offer you the role."

"Really, wow that is good news, when do they want me to start?"

"Monday, I hope that's okay? If not, we might be able to negotiate another day, but they are keen to get you in asap."

"They really are in a hurry, I can do Monday, but what about the paperwork that usually needs be signed before starting a job?"

"I will send our paperwork to you over the weekend. You can print it Monday and send it back to me."

"Okay, I am really surprised how quickly this has happened, but I am so happy I won the role, thank you."

"No need to thank me, you did all the work. You will be happy at Tyn-T as they are a good company to work for. Good luck for Monday, and if you need anything, you have my number."

"Thanks Andy, seeya." I hang-up and immediately call Shelley. "Shelley, it's Cari."

"Hey, how are you?"

"I'm great!" I tell her excitedly, "you will never believe it, but I got that job."

"That is awesome! I knew you would. When do you start?"

"Monday. I'm so not ready for it." I admit.

"Yes, you are, this is what you asked the universe for."

"Yeah, yeah, but now that it's here..."

"Now that it's here, it's time to celebrate, and this time we actually have a legitimate reason to drink."

"Absolutely," I agree. "Where are you now?"

"Just finishing with a client."

"A client, why do you have a client?" I ask, surprised.

"I am a personal trainer, remember? I used to dabble in it back home, but there seem to be a lot more vacancies here."

"When you say dabbled, are you qualified? You're not going to hurt someone are you?"

"I have a certificate. I don't plan on injuring anyone, but it does hurt." Shelley states, laughing.

"That's awesome, we have a double reason to celebrate! I cannot believe you are training people," I say laughing out loud.

"You are so funny," she laughs. "Actually, it will be a triple reason as I have found a flat as well. I'll meet you at Barns and Brooks pub in twenty minutes."

"This is going to be huge. See you soon."

- CHAPTER 2 -

My Monday morning alarm does not interrupt my relaxed holiday mode. I am in no hurry to respond, and in my hazy morning fog, I wonder why it is ringing at all. Then I jolt upright. Today is my first day at Tyn-T!

Holiday mode is suddenly replaced by first-day nerves. I need to make a statement both mentally and physically, but in the right way. I need to show them they made the right decision and that I fit in perfectly. This has me walking around in circles throwing one clothing item after another onto my bed. Something must make it onto my body, and it needs to be something confident but cool.

I go down the colourful route, subliminally inspired by the brightly coloured walls of the cactus room. A frilly red, A-line ballerina skirt, teamed with a blue silk blouse with yellow spots, comfortable blue shoes, not too high as I am tall enough and I do not want to tower over everyone. I complete it with nude tights. Colourful and creative, perfect for an advertising agency, I think.

I pack a new pen set and notebook, plug in my headphones and I am on my way. Music is an essential part of travelling around London. This is a very noisy city, an orchestra of buses, cabs, cars, horns, roadwork drills, building construction, children screaming, and people competing to be heard on their phones. I never leave my flat without my headphones. On my way to the train station, I text Shelley to let her know I got up on time and I am on my way to day one. She replies with 'good luck', and that she is on her way to meet a client in the park.

Of what I know about Shelley, she is not really the park type or a morning person, but I guess as a personal trainer you cannot always pick your locations or timings.

Entering the train station, I see that it is jammed with commuters, which explains why the streets are not as busy as I expected for this time of morning. This is a new experience for me as my derelict ways saw my mornings start much later. For a while there, noon was the new nine.

Rows of commuters line the entire length of the platform, everyone patiently waiting, almost drone-like. There are several trains worth of people, I could be late on my first day. The first train pulls up, the doors open, and an impossible number of people disembark. With the train almost empty, every single person waiting on the platform moves forward to board. How is that possible? It is a well-rehearsed jigsaw puzzle.

I panic when I cannot reach a handle to hold onto, but as the train departs, I realise I do not need one as we have human handles front, back, left and right, we are each other's support mechanism. There is no sense of personal space. I can see the pores on the face of the lady to my right, the wrinkles on a man's neck in front of me and the dandruff on the suit jacket to my left. I hope I do not inhale any. I lower my head and concentrate on my music.

My destination station is popular too and the majority disembark with me. I now compete with the foot traffic, moving at a ferocious pace. Before long, the dusty odours of the tube station are replaced by the seductive rich aroma of freshly ground coffee beans seducing passers-by. It works on me, and I enter the small but charming coffee shop with aged wooden floors, exposed wooden beams and a collection of unusual produce. I order a long black takeaway and know this will be part of my daily routine.

Even with the coffee stop, I arrive earlier than I expected. I have often been told that my obsession with avoiding tardiness can be annoying, but I do not like people waiting for me any more than I like waiting for others. Enthusiastically, the caffeine kicking in, I introduce myself to the receptionist.

"Hi, I'm Cari Jackson. It's my first day. I think I'm meant to be meeting Gillian from Human Resources?"

"Please take a seat and I'll let her know you're here. While we get your pass organised, can you please make sure you carry this temporary one at all times?"

I clip on the pass and sit on a red cube which is one of many different coloured cubes stacked in an almost square and almost rectangle formation. Above the reception desk, a television screen shows a series of clips, some of which I recognise as television commercials, others from magazines. Clearly it is showcasing Tyn-T's work and I focus hard to remember as much as I can.

Gillian greets me with a handshake and asks me to

follow her size zero frame for a comprehensive tour of the building. She did not actually say 'to follow her size zero frame', but her strut was obvious, and she was proud.

"Anthony Briggs would be interested to know you were sitting on his installation," Gillian claims, a little sarcastically.

"Sorry, what do you mean by installation?" I ask, beginning to fear the worst.

"What you were sitting on is an art installation by a local artist Anthony Briggs. The seating area is there," she offers pointing to what is quite obviously a seating area.

"Oh really, I didn't realise, there aren't any signs," I say, feeling the blood rush to my head.

"Mr Briggs is well known for his cube constructions. You will find them spotted throughout London, in buildings situated in the more creative parts of town," she educates.

"I'm really sorry, I haven't been in London long enough to know the local artists or the creative parts of town," I explain. "There are a lot of people arriving, how many work here?" I ask, changing the subject hoping to restore my face to a normal colour.

"Tyn-T is considered medium sized, we have about 250 full time employees and about 30 contractors."

"It's much bigger than I expected. Are all the floors made up of project teams?"

"There are six floors but not all of them are occupied by projects. We have administrative teams like Human Resources, Account Management and Communications, which occupy space on these floors as well," she explains.

"Of course," I agree with a nod.

"Right," says Gillian as we reach the cactus room, "this is the end of our tour, and here is Jake, your line manager." I smile at the blue-eyed man from my interview, who apparently is now my line manager. Gillian in her business-like demeanour, reminds me to get the forms back to her by the end of the day. She turns and, clickety-clackety, away she goes. Sheesh, that women definitely needs to increase her calorie intake.

I offer Jake my hand, and he takes it.

"Hi Cari, I'm happy you've joined our team," Jake welcomes.

"Hi Jake, thanks for having me," I say as I try to avoid gazing inappropriately into those bright blue eyes. The last time I fell for a pair of eyes did not end well, but it did contribute to the person I am today.

It is not just his striking eyes either. He is tall, about six-foot two, with broad shoulders and dark yet sun-kissed hair. He is speaking but I am lost, so I just nod and smile. He may already be regretting the decision to hire me.

While explaining my agenda for the day, he shows me to my desk so I can leave my bag. He points out the ladies' room and the kitchen, takes me to the photocopier, art room, and human resources. I do not let him know that Gillian has already given me the tour of these areas.

We then get comfortable in a small breakout area, and he tells me his expectations of me as a Senior Project Manager on his team; the projects I will be managing, emphasising project Toadstool; the processes Tyn-T follow; and some of the larger-than-life personalities. The descriptions explain why that question was asked during the interview.

My new home is in the cactus room where I first met the team which now includes Kelly and Craig. I take my seat and, following the login details left on my desk, gain access, change my password and find I already have twenty-four emails. I have only been here two hours!

My next session is with the Senior Account Director of project Toadstool, Sheree. Sheree is American and stunning. She is of average height but wears significantly high heels. Thin but not size zero thin, and by the looks of her toned muscles I would say a disciplined yogi. Sheree takes me through the project structure, not a normal task for an Account Director, especially a senior one. However, I do not question it and absorb as much information as possible, hoping my brain can bring order to the jumbled facts being shoved into it.

I am finally left on my own to familiarise myself with my new role and the project. I snoop around my computer to see what I have access to. Surprisingly, I have everything I need. I start trawling through the project folders, pretending to look focused and interested when the reality is that my brain is already full. The first few weeks at any new company are agonising.

A bubbly girl interrupts my pretense. "Hi, I'm Charlotte." Charlotte is Australian and has the familiar wired but exhausted look of everyone else around here.

"Hi, nice to meet you. Where in Australia are you from?" I ask. Her accent is really pronounced, and I am betting that she's from the east coast.

"Queensland, you?"

"Adelaide. How long have you been in London?"

"Two years but they've flown, it's like time is on speed here... or maybe it's just the speed," she giggles.

"The speed?" I ask.

"Fast," she responds making an aeroplane noise with matching gestures.

"How long have you been at Tyn-T?"

"Almost the entire time, well, a year and a half and now as penance, I get to show you all the boring bits of our job, timekeeping, resourcing, finance tracking and planning."

We get stuck in and after only a short time, I have a distracting need for more caffeine.

"Grab your bag and follow me," Charlotte instructs, as if reading my mind. It is refreshing to know we can leave the building at any time with no questions asked. "How are you finding it?"

"There's a lot to take in, but it seems like a great place to work," I respond.

"It is and it's really social too. We have been known to party Monday through to Thursday, usually at The Brandstead just around the corner. If we went past there now, we'd see a few Tyn-T'ers indulging."

"How do you manage to get work done?" I ask in surprise.

"It helps with the creativity," Charlotte laughs. "Oh crap, I'm going to be late, I'm really sorry, I have to go to a meeting, you should stay and finish your coffee and I'll talk to you later. Cheerio." And poof she disappears.

As it is mid-afternoon and this is my first break, I stay out, surprised I am still standing. I check my phone to find messages from the place where I did the psychometric test, inviting me to ring back.

"Hi, this is Cari, you left a message for me to return your call."

"Good afternoon, Cari. We would like to meet with you tomorrow," says an articulate woman.

"Oh, right, um well you should know that today I started a full-time job so there's no need for me to continue with this process but thank you for the invitation."

"I understand. We would still appreciate seeing you tomorrow and we can work around your schedule, can we say twelve-thirty?"

"Really? Um, okay, but is there any reason to continue if I already have a job? I doubt I will be able to do another job on top of this one," I respond trying to get my point across.

"Cari, please consider continuing with this process, twelve-thirty?"

"Okay, fine, is it at the same place?"

"We will text you the address." Before I have the chance to ask any more questions, she hangs up. Maybe this is a consultative role, or maybe it is a recruitment company screening for future jobs. I am interested in my test results, and I assume this is the only way of getting them.

This has been a full day and it is not over yet. Back at

the office, I wish I could make myself invisible so I can cruise through my final hours uninterrupted. Scrolling through my ever-growing list of emails, I find a meeting request from a Tod Chambers, subject line "Project Toadstool Technical Build", four-thirty today. What is so important to discuss on my first day? I guess I will find out soon.

I eventually locate the cosy meeting room seconds before Tod wanders in. He does not look happy or awake.

"I know you're new, but..." Surely there are no problems I need to deal with yet? "I'm not sure whether you've been briefed yet, right, but I'm hoping you can fix project Toadstool, right? We can't deliver by the date given to the client, right? And you have to negotiate extra time, yeah?"

I sigh deeply but silently. Tod is one of Tyn-T's technical directors. He's of average height, he wears his salt-and-pepper hair long, needs a good dose of sun, and I can imagine him happiest when locked in a room surrounded by an array of computer monitors and only looking up for pizza and beer.

"Tod, I hear your concerns, but I was not responsible for setting the delivery date. I do know there are market influences and a spectacular launch dependent on this website so we have to do what we can to deliver." I am impressed that my brain has managed to make some sense of the information that has been crammed into it today. I continue, "The client expectations have been set, the team has been moving towards this date from the start of the project, and I am not about to, either on my first day or any other day, change it without a good reason."

Clearly, Tod is not impressed. We continue discussing what could be done to achieve the delivery date, and by the end of the session, I have agreed to look at the scope and timings. He has agreed to nothing. I add the new tasks to my list and head off to find Mr Blue Eyes to quiz him about Tod.

Mr Blue Eyes, Jake, aside from being beautiful, has an air of mysterious confidence about him. He can turn on the charm in an instant and I am sure he knows the power of those eyes. He must attract a lot of attention; I would like to give him my attention.

"Hi Jake, do you have moment?"

"Sure Cari, what's up?" He gestures towards a meeting room for privacy. "Is everything okay?"

"Yes, I think so, I wanted to ask you about Tod. He just cornered me to tell me his team can't deliver Toadstool on time and that we need to push the dates back."

"This is normal for Tod, however I'm surprised he got to you so quickly. Were you okay to handle him?"

"I reminded him of the market pressures and of the launch being dependent on the website completion, and that these dates were not sprung on him. I did say I'd review the project plan to see if there is anything we can do to alleviate some of his pain and find some breathing room."

"He would not have liked that but it's a good response, especially on your first day. As I said, this is typical Tod behaviour. He's been making these claims since the start of the project, even though we based all our development timings on his estimates, and then added contingency. He feels it's his responsibility to shout about it under the pretence of protecting the agency."

I am shocked at Tod behaving this way when he was involved from the start. "So, Tod believes he's the only one who cares about delivering projects on time? That's actually funny," I chuckle.

"Apparently so, but don't feel singled out, he does this for most projects even though we do everything we can to support him and his team. Even more so for this project, as there are penalties if we are late."

"Penalties? What penalties? I didn't know there were penalties."

"It's your first day and I wanted to make sure you would come back tomorrow," Jake joked. "Tyn-T agreed to something it generally tries to avoid, penalty clauses."

"So, what are the penalties?"

"If we are two weeks late then we surrender two percent of the fees, three weeks three percent, four weeks five percent. But it only applies if there was no prior agreement, and the delay falls outside the tolerance level. But we won't have penalties, will we Cari?" He says cheekily, his eyes twinkling.

"Not if I can help it, but penalties do add a new dimension to this project. Is Tod going to behave like this throughout, does he know about the penalties?"

"Yes, he knows, and yes he will continue to state his case, but don't worry, this is his style of working, don't take it personally."

"Are you calling annoying a style?" I question jokingly.

"You will find many different styles of working at Tyn-T, but it somehow works." His eyes are sparkling.

"Good to know, I think. Thanks for your time, I should let you get back to it, it's been quite a first day, I'll sleep well tonight."

"It's been a pleasure, don't let Tod get to you, he's just one little cog in the big Tyn-T wheel. You will be coming back tomorrow?" He asks.

"Sure, why not, and besides, if I don't, I'll never get to see these other cogs," I laugh.

"Glad to hear it, and feel free to come to me any time, that's why I'm here."

"Thanks Jake."

"Pleasure." We leave the room and go our separate ways; my way is home.

Day two and I feel a lot more settled than yesterday and I already have a new work routine. I arrive earlier than most of my colleagues and relish the almost silent surroundings. While logging into my computer, I think about the interview I agreed to attend later today.

My email list is long. I have five from a Brett Ferguson about the advertising industry, company news and the latest Tyn-T blog post. Being new to Tyn-T and to the advertising world, I read each one expecting to find some insightful information. Wrong! Delete, delete, delete, delete, delete!

I spend the morning trawling through project plans, financial statements, and contracts to determine whether project Toadstool is on rocky ground and needs an injection of life. My initial perception is correct and, more alarmingly, Tod was correct. Project Toadstool will require some creative thinking and juggling to get it across the line, but any mitigation strategies need to wait for now. I need to leave for the interview.

Even though it is the same location, the reception area furnishings have changed.

"Hello, I'm Cari and I have a twelve-thirty appointment. You've changed your furniture, it looks better, more inviting," I offer.

"Welcome, please follow me," says the receptionist, ignoring my comment as she escorts me to a room labelled 'C'. She knocks, I enter, and she closes the door behind me.

I remain by the door and say, "Hi". A man is sitting at an empty table with an empty chair opposite, there is nothing else in this room. I continue to stay by the door until the man, who has not taken his eyes off me, points to the chair. He is expressionless and says nothing. This is eerie, I am uncomfortable and have a strong urge to laugh.

"Hi," I say for the second time.

"How are you enjoying London, what's it been, seven weeks?"

"How do you know I've been here for seven weeks?" I respond, thrown.

"Are you planning to stay?" He continues, ignoring my question.

"Yes, that's the plan. Can you tell me what this job is

for?" I ask politely.

"Are you on your own?"

"Sort of, I came here with a few friends."

"Partner?" He keeps firing questions at a ferocious pace. It makes my heart race. My hands are clammy, and the urge to laugh has been replaced by the urge to run as far away as I can.

"No."

"How long are you planning to stay in London?"

"I don't know," I answer panicked.

"You don't know?" He replies.

"I haven't really thought about it. I guess as long as things go well, I'll stay. I've just taken a permanent job so I'm not planning on leaving any time soon," I answer, believing this response might change the direction of his questions.

"Do you have any travel booked?"

"No."

"Have you been anywhere recently?"

"On my way to London I spent two weeks in Thailand."

"We know about Thailand, where else?"

"How do you know about Thailand? Who are you, and why do you know these things about me?" Something is not right. "I have a job so I don't need to continue with this, can I please go now?"

He pauses, "We are aware of your job status, but what we do here is not conventional and can work within existing commitments. I would appreciate you staying and seeing this through, it won't take long," he reassures slowing down the pace, but no change to his expression.

"What do you do here?" I ask.

"I cannot disclose that now. This is a conversation to see whether we feel you would be suitable."

"Suitable for what?"

"A role with us."

"But what is the role? I already have a full-time job."

"Yes, I understand. Can we continue?"

"Sure," I say, feeling a little less freaked but positive I would not be a good fit no matter what the role is.

"Do you have any future travel booked?" He picks up exactly where he left of.

"I don't have any travel booked, I just started a new job, but there are lots of places I want to visit." It is obvious he has his own agenda and is clearly sticking to it.

"Can you tell me about your family?" His pace is speeding up again.

"What do you want to know, and why do you want to know about my family?"

"Just answer the question."

"I have a mum, a sister, a brother in-law, two aunties and two nieces in Adelaide, plus I've some family in Austria." The speed of my responses are matching the speed of his questions.

"You didn't mention a father, and who lives in Austria?"

"My father passed away many years ago and it's relatives on my father's side who live in Austria, an aunty, an uncle, a few cousins and their children."

"When did you last see your Austrian family?"

"Years ago in Adelaide, I was still studying at uni, but I'm planning to see them as soon as I can, especially as I'm only a short flight away from them." Maybe this is his version of being friendly before he starts asking about my professional experiences and education.

"Where are they in Austria?"

"An hour out of Graz. Why are you interested in my family?" I ask.

"Thank you for coming in, you are free to go." Abruptly, he ends our 'conversation'. I follow his instructions to leave and head towards the door, but just before I turn the handle, I ask, "I'm sorry if I missed it, but who are you?"

"You didn't, thank you for your time. Goodbye." His demeanour is unchanged and he has no interest in telling me anything.

"Can you at least tell me what this is all about?" I try one final time.

The door opens.

"Goodbye, we will be in touch." The door opening is my cue to leave. The receptionist escorts me out of the building. Has she been waiting outside the door the entire time?

I head back to the office on autopilot, filled with nervous excitement, an extra spring in my step, recalling every word from the interview and trying to find a clue about what this job could be. How did he know how long I had been in London? And how did he know about Thailand? I ring Shelley to tell her about this freaky encounter but there is no answer, so I leave a message. Maybe this is just the British way, and what a stiff upper lip means!

- CHAPTER 3 -

I am excited to be a part of the final stages of the pitch presentation which, if successful, will secure Tyn-T a new piece of work from the same client as Toadstool, solidifying the account. The team has been cobbled together from across Tyn-T and have been working relentlessly for weeks. Every hour spent thinking, writing, and preparing the presentation is absorbed by the agency, taking resources away from paid work and more often than anyone likes, overextends the already overworked.

There is an air of excitement as they prepare this final run-through before the live presentation tomorrow morning. They will take the client on the same journey the team went through to ensure they want to buy the idea. When the presenters are ready, we settle in to observe. They perform with precision and accommodate our interruptions to tweak areas that are not quite right and to reorder others. By the end, we are relaxed, and confident that we are ready.

The next morning, the client contingent arrives on time, and everyone is smiles. Two are from the local office and three flew in from America. The pitch process is cruel on the pitchers. If there is not already a solid relationship with the client, then this is the only way to win work and seduce a client out of millions of dollars, or pounds when in England. Even though agencies are at the mercy of the client, this process has been around as long as advertising has been gracing our newspapers, billboards, magazines, and televisions. It has moved through the ages, paper, typewriters and computers, and without its buyers the agency cannot survive.

As we enter a different meeting room from the one we rehearsed in, I feel a knot form in the pit of my stomach. I try getting the attention of one of the managers, but he is engrossed in conversation, all I can do is follow the team inside. I am relieved to see the presentation material on the walls, but nothing in this room is suitable for this type of presentation. It is cold and clinical, nothing like our original room which had the relaxed ambiance of a lounge room, helping to make the clients more susceptible to our manipulation. A lounge room implies we are friends and can be trusted, a boardroom is business and beware.

There is an uncomfortable distance between the presenters and the audience, but when the managing partner introduces the team it makes us sound like superstars, and I relax. When the floor is handed to the presenters, I freeze. One half of the duo is strong and sticks to the material that was rehearsed. He articulates the path taken to reach the final idea and explains some of the earlier thoughts and why they would not work. He is also clean-shaven and wears trousers and a casual shirt. The other half misses his cues and is dressed like a surfer dude. He has scruffy hair, is unshaven and proudly displays the top of his underpants with every movement. After all the blood, sweat and tears, the way he's presenting makes it appear as if we do not really care. How did it change so dramatically from the rehearsal and why isn't the Managing Partner or Account Director trying to salvage it? There must have been conversations after the rehearsal, and this a deliberate pivot from script.

I am fighting to stay engaged, as are the clients who frequently glance at their phones. The presentation ends and no questions are asked, not even about price. I am mortified, embarrassed and questioning how any work can possibly flow through this agency.

While the Managing Partner escorts the client contingent out of the building, we hang back to debrief. We have a lot to talk about.

"Woohoo, that was great," one of the dynamic duo claims, "I think we nailed it."

"How can you possibly think that?" I ask, shocked. "Why did we spend all that time rehearsing and agreeing to a format when you changed it all?" My mental sledgehammer rises to the surface.

"It's our presentation and we thought we would change it up to make it feel younger and edgy, we nailed that."

"You can't seriously think that went well?"

"What do you mean?"

"From where I was standing, which was next to your audience, it did not go well. They were not engaged and spent most of their time looking at their phones," I articulate.

"We didn't get that impression, we thought it went really well. It flowed, we covered all the material and we behaved more like their customers."

"But we are a business trying to win their business, they want to know we are capable and take it seriously. I don't think they thought we were serious."

"That's exactly how we came across, we nailed it."

"Not sure how you could have even known since you spent most of your time with your back to them," I point out. "Sheree, surely you agree with me?" I prompt as she has not said a word.

"It would have been better if we stuck with the original format, but it wasn't that bad, I think we are still in the running," Sheree responds not sharing my sentiment.

"Well maybe I am overreacting, and this is the way things are done in London, but I really believe we lost that work. Anyway, time will tell. Seeya, have a good day," I say my final piece and make my exit.

So that was that, end of my first pitch in London and I am quite confident we will not be awarded this piece of work.

I return to something I have control over, project Toadstool and the mitigation strategy to revive its health. I start reworking the project plan to determine how to deliver what is promised in a different way but on time and on budget. I am confident that adding two more developers will help. The only obstacle to this plan is to prove if we drop the margin slightly, we can afford it, and the only person I must convince, is Mr Blue Eyes.

Just the thought of seeing him makes me nervous. I touch up my makeup, check my teeth for food and perform a quick breath test. As soon as I see him, I grin girlishly and my cheeks flush. His expression tells me that neither has gone unnoticed and I launch into my request. After listening to my reasoning and verifying my numbers, he agrees and explains the resource booking process, advising to check for progress with the resourcing team daily.

The resource booking process is straightforward. When a project requires additional resources, they are booked through the Tyn-T Human Resource team who balance the resources across all projects. Each request is assigned a Resource Manager. The Resource Manager looks for free capacity and if there is none, then people are either juggled between projects, or an external contractor is hired. My requirement can only be filled by external contractors, and my Resource Manager, Gregor and I discuss the requirement at length to ensure I get the right skills for this project.

During the following two weeks, I check in daily with Gregor, who assures me everything is on track. At one point, I was even given names, which is why I am floored when the developers on the day they are due to arrive, are nowhere to be seen and Gregor is denying all knowledge of this request. I hang up the phone and bolt to the resource department.

"Hi, so where are my developers? They were booked in to start today and you didn't seem to know what I was talking about."

"As I said on the phone, there are no new starters today for yours or any project." Gregor replies.

"Hang on. On Friday when we talked, you said everything is still on track, and they would both be here

Monday, as in today, right?"

"I'm sorry Cari, I don't know what you're talking about. I do not recall seeing a request for developers on your project. We have a process we have to follow and if you need resources you will need to complete a resource request."

"Are you kidding me? You know I have completed a resource request. We discussed the requirements at length and agreed to hire two contractors."

"I don't recall. If you would like to complete a resource request now, we can make it a priority."

"Every day for two weeks we chatted about this, you said you had two developers. That was either a lie, or you thought I was talking about another project, so which is it? How can this happen? Are you seriously going to stand there and claim you know nothing about my requirements?"

"We have a process to follow."

"So, who are G Stratford and M Fuller, the names you gave me? You can't claim you don't know what I'm talking about!"

"I've never heard of those names." He claims starting to shift around uncomfortably, feeling the noose tightening, continuing to shift the blame my way.

"You're an idiot. I'm going to take this up with Marty." I walk away. There seems to be something amiss with this place. Resource Managers are meant to resource, nothing more. If they do not do resourcing, then what do they do?

"Hi Marty, do you have a minute, I have a resourcing issue with one of my projects. Before you say it, yes, I followed the process and worked closely with one of your team, Gregor to be precise, but it hasn't worked out. Can I have the name of the recruitment company you use so I can contact them myself?"

"No, you can't contact them directly, you have to go through our team. That is company policy, and the recruitment agency will only deal with me or my team." Marty states.

"I already tried to go through your team, and it didn't work, what do you suggest I do now?" I am trying to keep my temper at bay.

"You need to complete a resource request and submit it to my team. We will..."

"Stop! I've already completed the request, had Gregor assigned to me, we discussed in detail the skills I need, and had daily catchups to ensure we were still on track, and I still didn't get my resources. So now what do I do? We needed them to start today."

"I take offence to your tone. You know the process and you should have followed it, you are blaming my team and that is not acceptable."

"ARE-YOU-KIDDING-ME? Have you not heard a word I said? Look at this," I almost shout, waving the completed request form in the air, "what do think this is? It's your stupid request form that I filled in two weeks ago! I also have an email trail of the daily check-ins with Gregor or if he was not around another member of your team. Every time I was told we were on track. He even gave me the names of the two developers being hired. So, tell me how this is my fault.

You're just as ridiculous as your staff. I refuse to talk to you anymore." I storm off. This is insane! I need to tell Mr Blue Eyes as this is a problem for all of us. It takes a few attempts to find him and I eventually corner him in the kitchen. "Hi, can I talk to you for a minute, privately?"

"Sure." He quickly finishes making his coffee and follows me to a meeting room. I can see from his expression that he knows something is not right. I close the door behind him and go for it, even standing so close to his brawny beauty cannot lessen this rage.

"Remember how we spoke about getting two developers to help deliver Toadstool?"

"Sure."

"They were meant to start today, which was crucial to the delivery, but they haven't arrived. I'm not even sure if they were booked."

"Did you not follow the resource process and submit a form into the central resourcing team?" Mr Blue Eyes asks looking a little confused.

"Of course I did, I put my request in two weeks ago straight after you approved the margin drop. I sat with my resource person, Gregor, and explained in detail the type of person I needed for this project, and the twat said they had no one available internally so we agreed to hire contractors. I stressed the urgency and then I did exactly as you suggested and checked in with him every day."

"And, what happened?" He is very calm compared to my impending explosion.

"Good bloody question. Nothing happened. I spoke to him every day either face-to-face, by phone or by email and every time he said everything was on track. He even gave me the names of the developers he had booked. And, I still can't believe this. This morning I chase him down to see what time I should meet with my contractors as today is meant to be their first day, and the idiot claims to have no idea what I'm talking about. I can't even begin to comprehend how he can deny all knowledge!" I blurt angrily. "But wait, it gets worse. Then I went to see Marty and he implied I didn't follow the process and that it's my fault. He said I should have filled in a resource request form, and even though I had it in my hand when I was talking to him, he still didn't accept responsibility."

Mr Blue Eyes puts a hand up to stop my barrage. I think I forgot to breathe.

"Are you saying that both Marty and Gregor denied any knowledge of this request, or any of the communications you had with him or his team? I assume you still have the emails?"

"All of them, and this is the original request, and yes, they are both denying any knowledge of the request or anything that has happened in the last two weeks." I wave the request around and then hand it over to him. I pace with purpose around the table in the room, ranting like a mad woman about how either this place is mad, or it is me. Maybe I am the mad one for working here.

"You're going to have to leave this with me. If the team is denying all knowledge, it will need to be escalated beyond

Marty. But I must give Marty a chance to explain first. He will have to accept that there were conversations and that the process was followed."

"How can he deny that there was a request submitted when I had it in front of him? There's something wrong with the resource group, I have never seen such behaviour in the workplace and absolute denial when the proof is right in front of their noses!" I am in utter disbelief, but relieved that Mr Blues Eyes acknowledges something is not right.

"You've done everything you can to get the developers, following the process and checking in regularly. Unfortunately, this is not the first time this has happened. I will deal with this. Marty is not going to be sheltered from this one." His serious side brings a darkness to his eyes, which hovers on the scary. I would not like to be a recipient of him dealing with it.

"Are you going to be okay?" He asks.

"Yes, I'm okay now. I feel a bit relieved that it's not just me, but it's crazy. How can this happen? If a resource team doesn't resource, what do they do, and how am I supposed to get my developers? Sorry for unleashing on you, but this sort of thing makes me so angry that I lost it. Imagine what the client would think if we don't deliver due to an internal administration screw-up. How embarrassing."

"No need to apologise, I understand your frustration and it shows that you care. We will get you the developers. By the way, do you remember what their names were?" He places a hand on my shoulder. I feel the electricity ricochet through my body and his eyes return to their bluest best.

"I think their last names were Stratford and Fuller, I don't think I was given their first names, maybe their initials. And thanks, I guess I should let Tod know he won't get his developers today. That'll be a fun conversation," I say, rolling my eyes.

"Stratford and Fuller?" He questions curiously. Something shifted in his eyes, only slightly but I caught it.

"Yes, have you had these developers before, are they not good?"

"Why do you ask?"

"It was as if you had heard those names before and that maybe they were not a good choice or caused problems before."

"No, I don't recall them working at Tyn-T before. Leave it with me. Let Tod know we will get the developers we need. I'll let you know when I know more and hopefully a starting date."

"Thanks Jake, I'm sure you don't need this in your day."

"No, I don't, but it's not your fault, and that's why I'm here. Don't let it get to you, it'll be sorted."

"Until the next time I need a resource! Thanks again." During this fiasco, I missed a call from the other job requesting me to call back. What could they possibly want with me now? I am not in the mood, although after dealing with some of the characters and witnessing recent events, jumping ship might not be a bad idea.

"Hi, this is Cari returning your call, sorry I missed it, I

was in the middle of a crisis," I know that was more information than necessary.

"We would like you to attend the next stage of the process."

"Really?"

"Yes, really."

"I don't understand why. I've already told you that I have a full-time job and that I haven't been doing it long."

"Thank you, I understand your situation, but as previously stated, this role can be performed alongside other commitments. We would like you to attend the next stage of the process."

"What sort of job can be performed alongside other commitments?" I asked, not really expecting an answer.

"We would like you to attend the next stage of the process."

"What is the next stage of the process?" What is it with people today? Am I speaking a different language?

"A medical and a physical test," she replies, as if it is the most normal thing in the world. I, on the other hand think this is crazy. I still do not know what this job is, and now they want to do a medical and physical. The only time I had a medical was when I was applying for a job in a defence department and that was a full-time position. Tyn-T is more than I can handle as it is. Dealing with the people is a full-time endeavour let alone delivering projects on time and on budget. I have no capacity left for a second job. I am not going any further until they tell me.

"A medical and a physical is a bit extreme when I don't even know what this job is, so I'm not agreeing to either unless you tell me, or explain how you think I can do two jobs at the same time?" I state firmly, feistiness in full swing.

"The job will be explained during this session," she responds.

"Are you sure? So far, no one has told me anything other than it can be performed alongside existing commitments, whatever that means, and I was only told that when I was going to leave the interview. How can I be sure things will be different this time?"

"I can guarantee you will be fully briefed," she says convincingly, even though I am still sceptical.

"Okay, I can't do anything this week. How about Monday lunchtime, how long will I need?" I ask.

"Two hours."

– CHAPTER 4 –

Everything feels slightly off-centre at Tyn-T, but this could be perfectly normal for the advertising industry. Their people do have skills, but they apply them like trying to fit a square peg into a round hole. This behaviour makes me constantly readjust my approach and expectations. As it is my first job in London, I can only assume this is how it flows.

One thing I am familiar with are company parties, and I am about to enjoy my first one. The excited events team, easy to spot in their matching Hawaiian gear, are recruiting extra hands to arrange the catering, set out the glasses, fill troughs with ice and alcohol, and put-up decorations to transform the balcony and adjacent office space into a relaxed, Hawaiian themed party place. The summer party is the result of months of planning and now, on this Thursday evening, the team is taking it very seriously. I do not understand why this office party is held on a Thursday evening. Surely, the following day is a write-off, and the productivity levels will be low by those well enough to make it in.

According to the flyers littered throughout the building and pinging our inboxes, this soiree will start at five with drinks on the balcony and a CEO address. At eight, the party will adjourn to the main venue, a club within walking distance of the office.

Five ticks over and it feels as if a switch has been turned

on. Those who still have tasks to complete grab a drink and take it back to their desk. I am one of them. An enthusiastic events team member provides hats, oversized sunglasses and leis to anyone who wants them, and there is even an indoor bouncy castle crammed into the limited space available.

I attempt to grab a second drink by stealth, but instead I am dragged into a conversation about football codes. This brings out my inner Australian Football League bias and I attempt to squash the argument that soccer is the superior code.

This marks the end of my working day. Being my first London work event, I am a little reserved but know the alcohol will provide mental freedom, possibly a little too much. I may dance, make declarations about saving the world, or even worse, proclaim love to the person I happen to be babbling to.

It has just gone seven and I am all smiles and rosy cheeked. The champagne has hit the spot and I am ready to party. Looking around, I realise I have gravitated to my own team, which seems to be the trend.

"Yeeha! Put your hands in the air like you don't care!" I am all party.

The bouncy castle is getting crazier by the minute. Arms and legs flail in every direction, accompanied by hysterical laughter, spontaneously spreading to the onlookers. The castle supervisors try to coerce the participants out of the castle to allow the party to move to the club. As they are being ignored, they deflate it regardless of the fact that it's still occupied. The castle-jumpers soon get the point.

Inside the club it is easy to spot our crew, as they are still kitted out in Hawaiian gear. The crowd is clearly fuelled, and being topped up with the free-flowing cocktails, wine, champagne, and beer, allowing for some lethal mixes to be consumed. A space clears in the middle of the dance floor, and to my surprise, two middle-aged men start break-dancing. This is exhibit 'A' of what mixing your drinks can do. Sheree jumps to my side and asks if I want something a little stronger. I am intrigued and follow her out of the club, where Shelley is just arriving.

"Shelllllleeeyyy," I animatedly announce as she appears from out of nowhere. "Youuurrrreee heeerrrrreeee. What are you doing here?" I ask, welcoming her open armed.

"You nut, you told me about the club you were going to and convinced me to join you."

"Did I, that's awesome, paaaarrrrtttttttyyyyy?"

"Are you leaving already? The club is that way," she says pointing to where we just came from.

"The night is still young, we are going back to the office to freshen up, maybe refreshments, refreshments to freshen up, freshments to freshen up yeah, freshments to freshen up yeah." I conga tune out, Sheree joins in.

"Refreshments? In the office?"

"Yes, you'll see, come with us," I demand and link arms with her.

We head to our floor and into the ladies'. There are so many reasons why I should not be doing this, but my party side has control. Sheree rolls a note and creates two perfectly sized lines of white powder on her purse. I am thankful for her consideration. I would not want to consume anything that has been on any bathroom surface. Shelley opts out of this party favour, alcohol is the only thing she needs since she has a training session early in the morning and has to set a good example to her clients. There are so many things wrong with that statement but right here, right now my focus is elsewhere.

The beauty of a class 'A', is that it can dampen the effects of too much alcohol, but still give you the confidence boost without the heavy head. Half left, half right. I take a moment, waiting for the initial rush to pass before checking for residue, tidying my hair and applying fresh makeup. My pupils will be my only giveaway. Luckily, the party is in a dark basement club. I feel liberated and best of all, I have no thoughts of tomorrow.

Instead of heading back to the party, Sheree, Shelley and I sit and chat at my desk about where we were before Tyn-T; people we know in the industry; and some general bitching. Not wanting to show that side of myself just yet, I let Sheree do all the talking to see what juicy information I can pick up, and she does not disappoint. She has a lot to say about certain people at Tyn-T and is well connected both in the company and the advertising industry.

Kelly and some of her designer friends pull up chairs and join us. Shelley tries to recruit us for personal training at her club. Sheree explains yoga is enough for her, I explain physical exercise does not rate highly on my list of things to do, and I am about to do physical exercise as soon as we get back to the club, and it is called dancing. Kelly's friends do not stay long and we promise we will not be far behind them. When an office party is close to the office, there are always people venturing back.

From out of nowhere, Gillian appears, looking completely hammered, which is not surprising for her size zero frame. "Where, where have you been Sheeerrrrrrreeee? I love you!" Gillian stammers, holding her arms out for a hug.

"We needed a breather," Sheree replies, awkwardly embracing her.

"Lots of peeps are looking for you, we thought you'd left. Don't leave, we love you!" It is always amusing what an office party brings out in people.

"We miss you and we want to dance," Gillian claims, jigging like a stick insect dancing.

"Why are people looking for us?" Sheree asks, slightly paranoid. I say nothing, as my visual of Gillian as a stick insect is amusing me.

"Ok, let's go back," Sheree says, so we get up and head towards the elevators.

The elevator doors open to reveal Mr Blue Eyes. He acknowledges us and has noticed the stranger, Shelley, but asks me if he can speak to me for a few minutes, assuring the girls he will not keep me long. When the elevator doors close and they disappear, I follow Mr Blue Eyes to a secluded area of this already empty office. I am buzzing and jigging to tunes only I can hear in my head.

As we choose a set of seats and get comfortable, Mr

Blue Eyes starts, "I know you haven't had the smoothest introduction to Tyn-T, but I wanted to let you know that you fit perfectly and we really appreciate what you have done so far."

"Thanks, that's really kind."

"Do you have any concerns that might make you question staying with us? I'd be really disappointed if there were, especially if you didn't give me the chance to fix it," he continues more slowly. I pause, searching for the right answer, but before I can get anything out, he leans in and kisses me on the lips. It's passionate, but at the same time soft, with the perfect amount of tongue, his hand caresses my face and my hair. Then he slowly moves away, his eyes fixed on mine, deep pools of perfect blue lusciousness.

"Um, no, nothing, I've, interesting, I've found it interesting." I make no sense. My words do not join to form sentences and I cannot take my eyes off him and now those lips. He moves in again but is startled by a noise from somewhere on the floor. He gives me a quick peck on my forehead and disappears. I stay, feet planted, lost in the moment and blushing. I am sure I did not imagine this. I am pretty sure it was not a hallucination. It was either the best kiss I have ever had, or this substance has supercharged my senses. I am rattled, confused and high as a kite.

I return to the club, and finding my friends brings me immediate comfort. I feel the urge to sing, 'I just kissed Mr Blue Eyes, do da, do da!' but decide to keep this one to myself. I am grinning from ear to ear. Mr Blue Eyes will be at the party somewhere and I inconspicuously glance around for him, half of me wanting to find him, half of me not.

Shelley delivers me a drink and I am back in full party mode, forgetting all about Mr Blue Eyes. I dance like there is no tomorrow, surrounded by hats and oversized glasses. Photos are being taken and I voluntarily pose for them, ignoring the small voice in the back of my head reminding me I will regret every single one of them when they make their way around the office in the morning. Everything is blurring, the drinks, the cocaine, the dancing, more posing for pictures, accessory swapping, pizza, and more breakdancing. We are being seduced by the DJ who is reading his crowd well.

I hit my threshold, and my self-preservation mode kicks in. I need to leave immediately. I do not say goodbye to anyone, all I can do is stop, find my belongings and leave. I never realise it is happening, and do not remember anything until the following morning.

I always wake up in my bed, on the couch or in the bathroom half changed out of my evening clothes. Each time it happens I wake panicked, realising I do not recall how I got here, but relieved that I did, and that this time I am alone. Apart from waking to the odd random man, or one of my friends who needed refuge, the worst I have ever woken to was a half beaten donkey piñata, in the bed, on a pillow, under the covers. Still to this day I have no idea where or how that happened. I have always assumed the half beaten was done by me needing a snack, but again, who knows!

This time I wake up on my bathroom floor in my

pyjamas, which are inside-out, and regurgitate the evening's substances, twice. I now recall eating pizza.

Once I am empty, I feel I can move off the floor, so I clean my teeth, grab a bottle of water, crawl into bed and pass out.

Several hours later, I wake to excruciating pain in my head, my stomach, my eyes, and every other muscle in my body. How much dancing did I do? My head and body try to settle on what I need to alleviate the pain. Stodgy food, no food, a banana, a sports drink or, wait, maybe another trip to the bathroom?

This is a common conflict with an alcohol and cocaine hangover. I am craving fish fingers on a toasted bagel, but this is never going to happen on a Friday morning.

Even though I know I am going to be late, I stay snuggled in bed. Then the flashbacks start, the first being Mr Blue Eyes and that kiss. Being Friday, I will inevitably cross paths with him in the office. What am I going to say to him? I keep shaking my head and move my duvet up over my face. This is why it is never a good idea to cross the line with a work colleague, especially when that work colleague is your boss. I broke one of my own golden rules.

Then I remember the cocaine and that I have a medical next week. My heart is pumping faster than it should indicating it is still in my body, I am one big bag of mess. What was I thinking or more accurately, why wasn't I thinking? Maybe I can ring and ask what the medical consists of, claiming to be squeamish with needles. If I take the test and they are looking for precisely that drug, what could happen to me? Could I be extradited?

I calm my catastrophising and settle back to fish fingers and Mr Blue Eyes.

I force a bottle of water and a banana into me, which stops my brain from rattling in my skull long enough to coax myself into the shower. I arrange something that looks sort of fashionably correct, and crawl to the train station. I am over an hour later than usual, evident by the considerably fewer people on the platform. I have a double seat to myself but have to concentrate hard to ignore the hangover fuelled motion sickness, making this train feel like it is going really, really fast.

I make it to my coffee shop and into work without any mishaps. My inbox is filled with emails from people claiming they are sick, working from home or taking a short notice annual leave day. Why did I not think of this? The office has arranged a breakfast, a variety of sandwiches and rolls with bacon, bacon and egg, egg or sausage. Perfect, this will do nicely, except for egg, I am still a bit squeamish, and the thought of eating a chicken egg makes me shudder. Halfway through my sandwich, the project Toadstool client, Alex calls me. So much for thinking an empty office will mean an easy day.

The call starts cheerily and upbeat, asking about the summer party and saying that he was sorry he could not make it. Then he begins briefing me on some new functionality he needs for the system we are currently building for him. He continues in great detail, then pauses, expecting a response.

During his spiel, I open the relevant documents to understand the timing and cost impact, and still manage to nibble on my sandwich.

"The existing requirements are going to be a challenge to deliver on time let alone adding this new functionality," I explain.

"We cannot afford to be delayed. As you know, we need it for the launch, and bookings have been made. Also, I am not expecting to be billed for this work," he states bluntly.

"We're doing everything in our power to deliver the initial requirements on time, but this new work will impact it. I recommend delivering as a phase two," I respond, tackling one problem at a time.

"Okay, but I would really like it with the initial launch but if it's going to impact then it can go in after. Can you get back to me on the timings?"

"Yes, I can do that, but expect it to be post launch and I will also provide a cost estimate to complete this work."

"I don't think you heard me, I am not paying for this work."

"Why not?"

"Because I'm paying enough already and you get the benefits of my brand," he says.

"It's a new function that requires more resource across all disciplines. While we're certainly happy to be working on such a great brand, we have to at least cover our costs. You're already on a discounted rate card but I'll see if there's any additional room to move," I say. Considering my hazy head, this is a good response.

"Why would I consider that acceptable! My company gives you a lot of business already and as you know, there is more work coming your way. I thought we could land on a mutually satisfying agreement."

"If it were a smallish change then we would absorb it, like we've already done several times already. But... hello... hello...Alex?" He has hung up.

I have never had a client hang up on me. How can he expect Tyn-T to do a whole phase of work for free? I need to ring my Account Director.

"Hi there, how are you feeling today?" Sheree asks. "Are you in the office?"

"Unfortunately yes, and I feel like death. Where are you?"

"I'm still at home, can't decide whether to make an appearance."

"I think you should come in. Tyn-T has provided sandwiches and there are loads left as not many people have made it in. Anyway, the reason I called is that Alex just rang. He wants some changes done. When I said there would be a cost associated with it, he hung up on me! I'm really sorry if this is going to cause a problem."

"Don't worry about it, he's already rung me, and he was gloating about it."

"He was gloating?"

"Yep, he's odd like that, he found it amusing."

"What sort of person hangs up on someone and then

gloats about it?"

"A depraved one! Don't worry, Tyn-T isn't into charity and Alex was just trying it on as he knows you are new. You did the right thing, so thank you. How on earth did you manage that call?"

"With great difficulty. I feel really ill. Hurry up and get in here, I need moral support." We both laugh.

That was an experience I could have done without, at least I have not seen Mr Blue Eyes, but he is based on a different floor and could be suffering quietly at his desk like the rest of us. Feeling immensely fragile, I do not dare move from my seat and opt to email him. His auto response advises he is not in today but is contactable by mobile.

He has a lot to answer for.

Before the kiss, he was just Mr Incredibly Beautiful Blue Eyes, someone who was the perfect distraction whenever I needed distracting. Now I need to know more, but most importantly, where did that kiss come from, and then all the things that start you down the slippery slope of falling. Is he single, does he have a family, and does he kiss women regularly catching them off guard? Maybe that is his thing, his party trick, and I was not the only one for that night.

Finally, it is Friday afternoon. Apart from the phone call with Alex, my day has been as unproductive as I predicted. Everyone who made it in is doing the absolute minimum. Everything takes three times as long and there is no guarantee the quality will be up to scratch. The pressure is lifted for those working on accounts where their client also attended the party.

The pixels penetrate my eyes and are like pins into my brain. What I would give to be able to put on my sunglasses.

Everyone else's attention is on which pub to go to for more comfort food and for a hair of the dog. While a pub visit would be a welcome relief, my thoughts are mostly about my upcoming medical and Mr Blue Eyes, in that order. I have not made the call to cancel the medical but know the sooner I do, the better I will feel.

Sheree finally makes an appearance, but instead of taking off her coat she informs everyone she is headed to the local Brandstead pub with most of the others.

"Just got to make a call, Sheree. I'll join you down there shortly," I tell her as I walk to an empty meeting room to make the call.

"Hi, I have a medical and physical test Monday lunchtime but I'd like to cancel it please."

"And why would that be?" the usual articulate woman responds. Why did I not think to prepare an answer? Stupid, stupid, stupid!

"Work is really busy, and two hours is a long time, people will wonder where I am."

"Ok, we can make it one hour, see you Monday."

"I really don't think I need to continue with this process as I have a job and really do not need anything else taking up my time."

"Yes, we know about your employment status, see you Monday, twelve thirty as scheduled." She hangs up. Must be a Friday thing.

It is time to put aside this looming appointment and go to the pub.

I stay at the Branstead for the rest of the afternoon with the contingent that made it into the office. All the conversation was recapping the previous evening, dissecting gossip, sharing photos and playing videos. To my horror I have featured in many and look as drunk as I recall being. I try not to look guilty when the conversation turns to 'hook-ups'. To my relief, nothing is said about my rendezvous, and we all sneak back to the office at five to check our emails and shut down our computers.

I am looking forward to a weekend of recovery, being a tourist and a fish finger bagel.

- CHAPTER 5 -

Monday morning starts like any other weekday. I am up early, prepared for the train crush, and I collect a coffee on the way to the office. But today there is something new, a feeling of utter dread. The fear of my first post-party encounter with Mr Blue Eyes has my stomach tied in knots. Nothing can settle it, nothing can distract me. I focus on my inbox to find a meeting request from Mr Blue Eyes starting in thirty minutes, and it is only the two of us. I accept and start hyperventilating, trying to convince myself that this cannot be as bad as I think, even though my heart is reverberating in my ears.

"Hi, how are you?" I ask casually as I enter the room, convinced he will see right through my façade.

"Hi, how are things with you?" He grins back at me.

Keep it together, I tell myself, he is just a work colleague, he is just a work colleague.

"Good thanks." I have a stupid grin on my face. Deep breaths, think professional thoughts.

"I have a new project brief I want to run by you. It's with the same client you're working with on project Toadstool, but it's a new piece of unrelated work," he says matter-of-factly.

"I don't suppose you heard that Alex hung up on me Friday morning and then rang Sheree to gloat about it?" I want to make sure he knows that my relationship with Alex might be strained.

"Yes, I heard, and you did exactly what I would

have done. He always tries to push the boundaries. Just keep working the way you are, you're doing a great job."

"Thanks. So what's this new project? Is it to do with the recent pitch?" The work talk is allowing my heart rate to return to normal. Who needs cardio when you have a work crush?!

"No, it's nothing to do with the pitch. We are not due to hear about that for a few weeks yet, and we may need to do a follow-up round. This brief has come directly to us."

"Oh okay, so what's it about then?"

"Redesign of an existing site, it's smaller than project Toadstool and we only need to do the design. Another agency will do the implementation, but as we are the lead, we need to coordinate it all."

"Sounds interesting."

"Alex as per usual wants this yesterday, so give it a read and let me know if you have any questions or concerns." He hands me the brief. "How did you pull up on Friday?" He asks as we get up to leave.

"I felt the same as the rest of the agency, like death, a very tough day to get through. You were lucky you had a day off," I grin, wondering if he is going to mention that kiss.

"You really got into the spirit of the night, it was good to see you enjoying yourself," he responds with a stunningly beautiful grin that makes me melt.

"I really must have needed it. The fact that everyone got into it made it easier to let loose. Did you enjoy yourself?" I probe.

"It was exceptional, should be more nights like that."
He ends the conversation, smiles, gestures goodbye, and we go
our separate ways. There 'should be more nights like that', what
did he mean? Was he referring to the kiss, or maybe other stuff
he got up to? I should stop overthinking it and put it down to
an office party encounter, just a bit of flirty fun, for both of us.

Now that we have moved past the initial encounter,
my brain is clear to concentrate on the new brief. It is short
and concise and seems straightforward but will require a
briefing session with Alex. The recent hang-up by Alex will
make this an awkward meeting, but not as bad as the first post-
kiss meeting with Mr Blue Eyes.

It is approaching midday which means it is time to
venture back into the unknown job. Today I feel gullible and
vulnerable, knowing I have allowed myself to blindly follow
this process without demanding an explanation or to have any
of my questions answered.

I arrive late, apologise and the articulate woman
directs me to the waiting area. The furniture in the waiting
area has been swapped back to what it was originally, the dark
brown.

I am soon following an unfamiliar young man down
a familiar hallway to a new door. The room beyond reveals a
sterile, stark white, box shaped area. He asks me to take a seat.
The chair he points to is diagonally opposite another chair,
with a small table separating the two. Against the opposite
wall is a bed with a tray of instruments. Another wall holds
a solitary cabinet with frosted glass. There are no posters or

plaques on the walls, and hence no hints on what this place is.

This man appears to be emotionless, cold and forgettable just like everyone else I have met during this process. He explains what tests he will be doing and then asks me to roll up a sleeve so he can test my blood pressure. It's probably off the scale.

Then he listens to my lungs and heartbeat, draws some blood, checks my knee reflexes, does a chest x-ray using a machine he pulls down from the ceiling, and asks me to provide a urine sample. For this, I am taken to a bathroom. Even though I am on my own, I cannot shake the feeling I am under surveillance.

On my return, I ask sheepishly why all these tests are necessary. A chest x-ray seems a bit extreme. More to the point, I ask why they have all this equipment here. Is this job for a medical firm? True to form, the medic does not answer any of my questions or react to any of my small talk. I even asked him if he knew that a cashew nut is not a nut? I think by now he thinks I'm a nut.

Once the probing is over, I am directed to another room which is huge in comparison to what I have seen so far. This room could compete with any commercial gym and is equally equipped. There is a treadmill and a rowing machine, both separately wired up to some sort of computer. In a separate section, there are free weights, kettle bells, medicine balls, weight machines, and other equipment I have never seen before. This room is decorated in pastel blues and greens, a contrast from the starkness of the other rooms I have seen.

For such a big room with so much equipment, it astounds me that the only people here are my next handler and me. He presents me with a bag and points to a door.

"What am I doing with this bag?" I ask.

"Changing into its contents," he replies.

"Why?"

"You will be more comfortable."

"More comfortable for what?"

"For your physical."

"I'm not doing a physical." I surprise myself, folding my arms behind my back and refusing to take his bag. "Not until you explain what's going on. I've had a psychometric test, a weird interview, and I've just endured a series of intrusive medical tests. Every time I ask anyone a question, I get blanked, and now you want me to do a physical. I'm done, no more. I was promised that today my questions would be answered, and I would be told what this job is for, so either you tell me or I'm leaving." I now cross my arms in front of me to show I mean business.

"Usually the tantrum comes at the beginning of the medical," he says. Another emotionless response. This does not help my current mental state. I am now fighting back the tears from feeling stupid as I realise I should have made a stance much sooner.

"So are you, or are you not, going to tell me what this is all for? I'm not doing anything else without knowing what this job is and who it's for. I really mean it. I already have a job that is doing my head in, I don't need another one."

"Please sit down," he says, and locks the door. "Before I continue you must read and sign a confidentiality agreement, there is no compromise on this. Agreement is only by signature. If you do not sign it, the process stops here, I explain nothing, you won't do the physical and you are free to go." He sternly hands me a piece of paper and a pen. "If you sign the agreement, we can talk, but be aware, like all confidentiality agreements we take breeches seriously. There will be consequences. Do you understand?"

"Yes," I obediently reply, pausing for a moment to consider if I will be able to keep it to myself, and would they even know if I did? As I have come this far, the need to know takes over and I accept the paper and pen, let out an exaggerated breath and start reading.

The document fills a single A4 sheet of paper and is precise. It states that no details regarding the location of, including directions to and from, room layouts, people, procedures, or conversations are to be spoken about, written about, or communicated in any form whatsoever under any circumstances, and there are absolutely no exceptions. Breach of any item stated will lead to serious consequences.

"What are serious consequences?" I ask.

"Breaches of such are dealt with based on severity, but there is no case where there is no consequence."

"Like what?"

"Keep reading."

I do as I'm told. Most of it seems reasonable but as for the 'consequences', there is no explanation and could be anything from a fine to being fired. I re-read the document, trying to find hidden meanings, sign it and hand it back to him. He signs it and places it inside a folder.

"This is an interview and a series of tests including a background check to determine whether you are a suitable candidate for what we like to refer to as an industrial researcher. There are certain people who are placed in companies under false pretences, for a purpose other than to serve that company. It is our job to find out what they are doing, why they are doing it, and how far-reaching it is, with the aim of putting an end to it. Officially, we are part of the government, but a department whose work is not made public. Our work is important, and it is funded appropriately," he explains.

I suddenly feel the urge to laugh but I hold it in just in case something bad happens to me as a result. How can someone like me be a good candidate? This is not even my country, and I am not even a citizen. I look around to see if there are any cameras, or someone about to tell me I am part of an elaborate prank initiated by Shelley. He continues.

"Our recruits investigate these people based on a profile we have developed. The physical is to ensure you can protect yourself if needed. Staying physically fit means you are mentally fit, and this is a mandatory requirement of all our recruits – without exception." He pauses, waiting for a response. No words come out of my mouth, which is gaping. My heart is pounding right up into my temples.

"Quite a normal reaction to a not-so-normal situation," he responds. "Take a moment, but I do need an answer."

"What do you need an answer for?" I question, bug-eyed.

"Whether you want to continue with this process," he answers.

"Is this for real? What makes you think I can do this? I already have a job. What sorts of things are these people doing in these companies, and how is it that no one in the company catches on that they're not doing what they're supposed to be doing? I'm not even a citizen!" Then I do start laughing, I cannot help it, these things do not happen to me... come on. As if. He stares back at me stone faced.

"This is not a laughing matter, we take it very seriously. You came onto our radar in Thailand, and then when Tyn-T was interested in hiring you, due to the speed they were moving we had to move fast to catch-up. That is why your interview seemed 'weird' and was focused on personal questions," he reveals.

"Why did I come onto your radar in Thailand? I was there on holiday before coming to London."

"Yes, we know, and it's not important."

"I thought I was going to get my questions answered?"

"The island you were on, the group you were with, had a person of interest to us."

"So, why was I on your radar?"

"We needed to make sure you were not connected."

"Well, that's stupid, as if. You know I'm not, right?" Crap.

"Yes, you have been cleared."

"So what is it about Tyn-T that got you interested? They're just an advertising agency and I'm working on real projects. Although some of the people are questionable."

Things might actually be starting to make sense.

"Again, a person of interest, and as you were already traced and cleared in Thailand, and we were watching Tyn-T, we decided to put you through the process to see if there was a chance you would be a good candidate."

"And, am I?"

"You are still in the process and that is yet to be determined."

"Oh, right." But really, me? This feels weird, and I am still half expecting someone to jump out with a 'gotcha'.

"So why put me through a medical and a physical if you're still not sure about me?"

"This is part of the process, and it also depends on when people like me are available. We all know the steps that need to be completed, the order doesn't matter. As the candidate passes a stage, we continue. We have to be thorough in all aspects of our screening as people of interest can be involved in serious operations."

"Like what?"

"Fraud, embezzlement, money laundering, drugs, corporate spying, fronting for another business, you name it. Even a few terrorist plots. It's a different world with different types of people operating with different rules. We can never be too careful or too prepared."

"Are you serious? How do you think I can do this? I

don't know the first thing about any of this and to be fair, I can be quite gullible at times." I am starting to believe this might be real. Maybe it is a test to see how gullible I really am.

"You haven't completed the process yet but if you are successful and you accept the terms, you will be trained and allocated a mentor who will develop you physically and mentally," he answers.

"O-M-G, really? Seriously, this can't be happening, can it? Can this really be true?" I say softly to myself. I cannot breathe and I move my head between my knees.

He does his best to reassure me that my reaction is normal and that there has been worse. Then he continues explaining that working for them can be an exhilarating experience, and is definitely a unique opportunity, not to mention the financial reward.

"Financial reward?" I ask, as I raise my head slightly above my knees. Until now, money has not crossed my mind.

"It is level based but there is a very attractive base rate, all expenses are covered and there are other bonuses too," he explains.

"So what is the base rate, and is this paid additional to my day job salary? And what about tax?" I enquire, momentarily forgetting what this is actually about.

He responds with a figure that I ask him to repeat, and I lower my head back between my knees. As I rest my head, I do the arithmetic. Then the little voice in the back of my head reminds me that no one gives out that sort of money for nothing.

I pull myself together, take another deep breath, accept the offer to continue the process, and get up to leave.

"Where are you going?"

"Back to work. I've been gone too long and they'll start to wonder where I am."

"You still have the physical to complete." He points to the door again. This time I take the bag on offer, through the door and into a change room. The bag contains a full training kit and surprisingly, everything fits perfectly, even down to the size ten trainers.

The physical is tough, uncomfortable and performed under constant stress. It is hard enough being pushed to the limits, but being hooked up to machines at the same time feels intrusive. I am pushed to a point where my lungs are burning and my muscles spasm. I have become very unfit.

Once the torture is over, I have just enough energy to freshen up in their fully equipped shower room. I take advantage of their shampoo, conditioner, moisturisers, and deodorant.

Leaving the building, I feel as if I left a different world and this one has now shifted. I feel dazed and wired at the same time. This is the strangest day I have ever experienced, not just in London, but ever. How many people could say they have been in this situation, asked to be an industrial researcher?

Signing that confidentiality agreement, agreeing not to divulge any of this is already getting to me and here is my first test as I answer my ringing phone.

"Hey stranger, how did you pull up after the party?"

Shelley chirps.

"OMG the next day was tough, when did you leave?" I ask.

"Quite late. I left you doing some weird moves on the dance floor. How has your day been?"

"It has been one of the most interesting days yet," I claim honestly.

"What's made it so interesting?"

"Just work stuff."

"Like what?"

"New projects, old projects. Tyn-T is a very interesting place filled with larger-than-life personalities," I reply, dying to tell her, but knowing I can't. I do not want to find out what those breach consequences could be.

"Okay, cool. I gotta go as another eager client awaits. Speak to you later."

"Seeya," and we hang-up.

The rest of the day, I plug in my earphones to appear busy and unapproachable. The adrenaline has worn off and I need time to process the earlier events, especially about people working in roles under false pretences to commit corporate crimes.

I now look at this agency and its employees through different eyes. He said there was a person of interest in Thailand and maybe there is someone at Tyn-T too. Surely this place does not employ anyone that I would need to research? Please no, I am not ready, I would not know what to do, I have not been trained. What if I get caught? What if it is someone

I already know?

I suddenly feel physically sick and hope food will help. I leave the building in search of snacks.

Once I have eaten and replenished my caffeine levels, I focus on the job I know, but I cannot stop my head replaying the conversation. I remind myself I have not completed the process and I am not employed by them. I still do not know who they are, a question I forgot to ask. All I know is that they are a government department. Once they analyse my fitness test and see my medical results, I doubt I will progress any further. But what if I do, what could be next?

I need to focus on tomorrow morning's meeting with Alex and gather as much information as I can so there is no excuse to pull this piece of work from Tyn-T, or have him question my ability to deliver. I have not met him face-to-face and I do not like that he thinks hanging up on me was a rock-star move.

The next day, Sheree and I arrive at the client's office and wait at reception. The office looks like a gentleman's club. The walls are lined with dark wood panels and are dotted with exquisite art. I expect to see gentlemen wielding cigars, but all we see are people working, like any other office.

Eventually the receptionist ushers us into a meeting room, also styled old-meets-new. The most surprising is a Playboy poster boasting magazine covers from past decades.

We are offered refreshments and I decide on the safe option of water. It is a further twenty minutes before Alex arrives, and as we have a full agenda, I expect to start straight away. Instead, his focus is on the chairs surrounding his table. He does not like two of the same coloured chairs next to each other and starts re-arranging them.

As he gets closer to us, we jump to our feet and remain standing until he sits, and we begin. He offers no apology or explanation for his tardiness. He is the most eccentric person I have ever met. He is wearing what looks like a dressing gown, as if he just got out of bed and wandered downstairs, which could be true, as from the outside the building does look like a residential townhouse.

The meeting is going well until Alex suddenly stands up, claiming he needs something from his office, and we are left sitting on our own, once again.

Fifteen minutes pass and I head to the receptionist to ask when Alex might be re-joining our meeting.

"Alex has left for the day," the receptionist replies, chirpy and upbeat.

"Sorry? We were in the middle of a meeting. Has he definitely gone for the day?"

"Yes, he has left for the day. He is a busy man. Shall I call you a cab?"

"Yes please," I say, and return to the meeting room for Sheree.

On the way back to the office, I arrange a meeting with Mr Blue Eyes, keeping the conversation short and professional. At the office, we go directly to meet with him and I explain what happened. As Sheree is now late for her next appointment, she excuses herself and we are left alone.

His face changes from business to pleasure, and his dreamy eyes return. I feel a blush spread across my face but do my best to catch it before he sees, and my sentiments are known.

"How was your weekend?" Mr Blue Eyes asks, catching me by surprise.

"Um... it was fine thanks. I did the touristy thing. How was yours?"

"Mine was good thanks. How long have you been in London?" He asks surprised.

"Not long enough to stop doing the touristy things," I respond cheerfully.

"Are you here on your own?" He asks. I pause long enough to let him know this is not a question I feel comfortable answering. I hope he is not implying that I am the sort of person that would kiss someone else if I was already in a relationship.

"Yes, well no, but yes." Hearing the words come out make my cheeks glow red again.

"Yes or no, do you not know?" He responds playfully.

"I mean, I came here with friends, not a partner."

"It's good that you have some support, it must be tough moving countries and London isn't the friendliest of cities."

"That's certainly true. I've had a lot of fun and need to remind myself this is not one big continuous holiday." I laugh.

"That's London, there's always something happening somewhere. I'm really sorry, I have to go now. I'm late for a meeting."

We get up and move towards the door, and just before we get there, he turns and stares meaningfully at me.

"Is there something you wanted to say?" I prompt.

"I just wanted to let you know that I haven't forgotten you, me and the summer party," he says in a tone I have not heard before, switching his gaze from my eyes to my lips then back again, and then he leaves.

Great, just as I come to terms with the kiss being a party thing and nothing more, he says that. Now I think maybe it was more, maybe it meant something to him. This is not fair. It is like being dangled on a line. I want to know what it was, and what it meant to him. Is this something? What does he want? I want that kiss and more.

The rest of the day is uneventful, other than Tod moaning about the aggressive delivery dates and me reiterating that it is not just his reputation on the line.

I receive another call from the articulate woman asking to set up an appointment. I think 'asking' is an understatement, it is more like a pleasant demand. I am surprised they want to see me again. They clearly saw how unfit I am, gullible and a bit crazy, and there is still the issue of my medical results. I have resigned myself to the fact that there is no way I can avoid it, and they now probably know more about me than I do.

"Sure, what is the appointment for?" I ask with a bit of a cocky undertone.

"Next steps. We would like to see you Tuesday at nine and you will need two hours," she states firmly.

"Two hours! I'm not sure that I can get two hours off

work." Everything is in two-hour blocks.

"I'm sure you will manage. Nine, Tuesday. I will text you the address."

"I've been there a few times now and remember where it is," I say, a little more cockier.

"I will text you the address," and she hangs up. How am I going to get two hours off work?

Suddenly there is a lot of movement and packing up going on around me. I ring Mr Blue Eyes and he apologises for not letting me know earlier about the office restructure, which has just now been confirmed. You would think an advertising agency would be strong on communication.

He tells me the agency has decided to rearrange the seating. No longer will project teams be sitting together, instead, teams will be arranged based on accounts. Account directors, account managers, project managers, designers, developers, analysts, client services representatives, anyone working more than fifty percent of their time on the account will now be seated together.

While the new team get acquainted, it is obvious who knows who. I gravitate to the new Project Manager, Lita, who has been working at Tyn-T for a little over two years. During our conversation we exchange stories and there is an instant connection. I may have finally found my true confidante at this agency. Mr Blue Eyes is also her line manager which means she must know him quite well. I will leave this line of questioning until I get to know her better.

Now that there are two project managers on this account, I decide to do the right thing and share this information with my new neighbours and extended team.

"Hi everyone, sorry to interrupt, but I just wanted to introduce you to the new project manager on this account, Lita. I for one am grateful to have her expertise."

"Hi everyone, I know a bit about this account already and look forward to working with you all." Lita introduces herself. There is an uncomfortable silence, not the reaction I was expecting.

"Is everything all right?" I ask.

"Well, we usually have a say in resourcing projects," the new account director informs me.

"Really? This is not a resourcing decision, I was just letting you know that Lita is a project manager and will now be working with me on this account," I respond.

"Well, we are usually consulted first before any resource decisions are made," she continues, as if I did not understand the statement the first time.

"This is a project management resourcing decision. Why would client services have a say in that?"

"We want to make sure that we have the most appropriate people on the team. We know who's good and who's not." I take a sideways glance towards Lita who is still sitting next to me and has said nothing more since her introduction.

"Are you saying that you don't want Lita on this account? And are you also saying you want to know which designers and developers are assigned to each piece of work, and approve or not approve them?" I ask, put out by this conversation, especially when she has aired it in front of everyone.

Lita pings me an instant message with an animation of a boxer making a knockout. I quickly type a reply to Lita, 'If only it wasn't a sackable offence (rolling eye emoji)'.

"Generally, we know upfront who is allocated to which project so we can arrange for someone different if we don't think they are appropriate for the particular piece of work," she continues like a dog with a bone, complete lack of emotional intelligence.

"We don't know who is working on the project until they are booked, and even we don't have a say in that. It's obvious to me, based on what you are saying, that your concern is about Lita and that you don't think she is appropriate for this account. Please correct me if I have this wrong?"

"Oh, no, that's not what I'm saying at all," she retracts sheepishly, looking at Lita.

"Does your interest in the project management of Toadstool mean you are directly involved with this project?" I enquire, wondering where Sheree fits in all of this.

"No, I'm not working on it, I'm just helping you to understand how it works considering you are new to Tyn-T," she claims. I am a bit baffled as to why she felt the need to stick her nose in when she has nothing to do with the project.

"I can assure you I know exactly how to run and resource projects at Tyn-T. If there is a problem with anyone's performance on my project, I will sort it out. You can stay in your lane concentrating on the client relationship and new business."

"We need to be across everything, and I would like a say in all resourcing decisions," she continues, like a bull in a China shop.

"It has nothing to do with you. You have nothing to do with this project, so let it go. Even if there were problems with resourcing on this project, I would take it to Sheree, not to you." I am starting to raise my voice.

"I am still part of this account, and I am responsible to the client. You are just the project manager," she snaps.

"I don't give a damn if you're on the same account. You're irrelevant to anything I'm working on. Your lack of understanding astounds me. Firstly, I am responsible for the delivery and all aspects that go with it. You will find during a project I speak more to the client than the account director and I always know more about what's going on. If you think this is not right, you should take it up with the discipline leads. I'm sure Jake and Bill will have an opinion about this," I bark. I can see Lita is trying to hold back a smirk.

"No, it's okay, we don't need to take this any further. I was just saying, that's all," she caves looking a little surprised that I've stood up to her. Maybe she is used to getting her own way.

"Good, glad to hear it and I don't want to be having this conversation again."

As soon as Lita sees that the show is over, she springs from her chair claiming there is an emergency that needs our attention in the studio.

She leads me past the studio and exits the building. Once outside and out of earshot, she tells me the mouthy account director comes from a print background and does not know much about digital. Why would three non-digital client services reps be allocated to this account when Sheree can more than handle it?

"So what are the others working on?" I ask, not entirely sure how Lita would know the answer to that.

"Other projects on the same account, briefs and pitches I guess," she responds.

"So we now have four client service reps and only two project managers," I confirm, realising this team has no balance.

"Yep, bonkers. It's following a direct marketing structure." I have never worked in a direct marketing or print environment and am glad to have avoided it.

"I think there's going to be a power struggle between them and us. I hope they don't think we report to them. My priority is to deliver, and I don't need issues from within our own agency. I have already experienced my fair share of personalities."

"Yes I know," Lita says, "they tend to think they're the important ones," she laughs.

"I have an idea, let's give them pet names so they don't know when we are talking about them. I am pretty crap with real names anyway and fake ones seem to stick better with me."

"OMG that would be so funny, let's call Julie, Sparkles." Lita declares.

"Why Sparkles?"

"Have you not seen the eye makeup she wears? That glitter is only suitable for a night club and even then, it's questionable."

"That's perfect, Sparkles it is. Let's call the mouthy one Noddy, to reflect the lack of intelligence she portrays," I add.

"And Gonzo can be the one with the big nose," Lita completes the trifecta.

"That's so funny, a bit mean, but funny, I hope no one catches on," I claim laughing out loud.

When we arrive back at our desks, everyone smiles so I play along and get back to work chuckling about Sparkles, Noddy and Gonzo.

– CHAPTER 6 –

The promised text message arrives and reveals a new location, nowhere near the previous one. The waiting area is inviting, with soft seating in the shape of a rectangle, with a coffee table in the middle. Against the wall is a small glass-door fridge revealing San Pellegrino, orange juice and Diet Coke. The receptionist invites me to help myself, and I do.

Before I can take a sip, I am asked to leave my drink on the table and follow her. We stop at yet another unmarked door. She knocks, and it is opened by a young woman I have not met before. The room has a chunky table and a state-of-the-art laptop with a large monitor attached. The same man who interviewed me is sitting behind the desk. I instantly feel tense, and a knot develops in my stomach. I am instructed to sit in the empty chair, and I move my gaze from him to the woman, and continue this motion feeling like I am watching a tennis match.

"I want to remind you that you have signed a confidentiality agreement which still applies and always will," he says, sounding exactly the same as when we first met.

"Yes, I remember." I nod.

"Nothing about this session can be disclosed to anyone outside this room, do you understand?" He asks.

"Yes, I understand." I nod again.

"We have your test results and would like to discuss

the next steps." I suddenly remember the blood test and what it might reveal. Please do not let it show up, I silently implore, feeling beads of perspiration forming on my top lip. "Your fitness levels are below average for someone of your age, significantly in some areas, which is not a comforting result. However, the psychometric test, interview and the background checks show promise."

I do not like hearing I am below average. The 'show promise' statement reminds me of school reports saying, 'could do better'. I am not a marathon runner, but I cannot be that bad. Living in London I walk a lot more and I can dance for hours.

"Do you have any questions?" He asks.

"Who are you? I mean not you personally, but what is this place called? Is it true you're an industrial research company working for the government? Why are you looking to recruit me? I know nothing about this sort of thing. I have a full-time job so how can I work for you too? And why do a medical?" This is as much as I can get out before the man raises his hand to stop me. I think I forgot to breathe.

"We are an industrial research company under the government umbrella. We are looking to recruit you as you showed promise through the testing process. It takes a certain type of person to work this job and I can assure you, it is possible to do both this job and your placement."

"My placement? Is that what you call my actual job, a placement? It makes it sound like you had something to do with it. Did you?"

"We can, we have, but not in your case, not this time."

"Not this time? So you can be responsible for me leaving Tyn-T and getting a job somewhere else?"

"Yes."

"Huh! So, you think I can do this based on one interview, a medical and a physical, in which you say I tested below average?"

"With regards to the medical, we have to ensure any potential recruits are healthy. We run a standard set of tests, screening for HIV, hepatitis, cancerous cells, blood sugar level, cholesterol, and blood typing." He is obviously used to these sort of questions and remains very much in control.

"And am I healthy?" I ask, air quoting 'healthy' and surprised the tests covered so much.

"Healthy yes, fit no, your choice of recreational stimulants is probably contributing to this." And there it is, the bombshell. They know about my class A indulgence.

"Um, well, yes, it was a one-off." I stutter, shifting uncomfortably in my chair, my palms start sweating. Oh crap, crap, crap.

"It will be. Despite the results we would like to bring you into the team."

This is not what I was expecting.

"Even with everything you know about me and how unfit I am?" I ask nervously, believing there must be some repercussions for taking cocaine. The perspiration is now moving up my body and has reached my forehead. I can feel drips running down my back. "And what is the team exactly, am I really the right sort of person for this, and what about my other questions?"

"There are no circumstances under which recreational stimulants are tolerable. If you accept the job, this behaviour will stop. I have a contract in front of me and I would like you to read it, and please read it carefully. If you choose to accept, you will sign it in this room, now."

"What if I have questions?"

"I will answer them."

Hmm, we will see about that.

"So, are you offering me the job?" I want to be clear.

"Yes, but first you must read the contract and accept the terms. If you choose to accept the terms by way of a signature, then it will be official, you will be part of the team."

"What happens if I don't want to sign it?"

"Then this session will be terminated. You will be escorted out and you will never hear from us again, but you will still be held to the confidentiality agreement."

He slides the contract across the table, accompanied by a pen.

I must read it in this room without consulting anyone other than this man and maybe this woman, who has not said a word, but has not taken her eyes off me.

"Okay," I agree nervously. I move the contract directly in front of me, put my head down and give it my full focus. The first thing I notice at the top of the page, is the word 'Caitem'.

"Is Caitem the name of this company?"

"Yes."

"Does it stand for anything, like an acronym?"

"No."

Now that I know what this place is called, I feel a little more settled and begin to read. The next thing I notice is the obvious omissions from a standard employment contract.

(1) There is no official name or address for this company other than Caitem at the top.

"Why is there no address, and why are we at a different location from where the first interview and physical were held? Are there multiple offices?" I am going to use this opportunity to ask anything that comes to mind.

"For security reasons we keep our locations fluid," he replies.

"Why does the furniture keep changing in the reception area?" I know this is not an important question, but I am curious.

"It's not relevant, please keep the questions in relation to the contract."

(2) There is no place of work listed, instead, it states 'based on field requirements.'

"What does 'field requirements' mean? Are you saying there might come a time I have to leave Tyn-T because Caitem says so?"

"That might be a possibility but it's nothing to be concerned with for now. We try not to move people unnaturally."

"So, if the need arises, I could be doing this job at Tyn-T?" Again I employ the air quotes.

"Yes."

"How will I be able to do two jobs at the same time at the same location?"

"You will be trained. We do not put recruits into situations they cannot handle."

He is doing his best to reassure me, but he gets me wondering what sort of situations I could find myself in.

(3) There are no standard working hours declared, only again, 'based on field requirements.'

(4) Job Title = Level 0

"What does Level 0 mean?"

"It's your classification and it reflects your experience. As you gain more experience, you will be reclassified. All new recruits start at 0 unless they have a specialty."

"What level are you?" I ask cheekily.

"Keep reading." He responds as expected.

(5) There is no holiday entitlement section. All holidays and travelling must be, without exception, cleared by Caitem first.

"Does this mean any holiday? What if Tyn-T wants to send me somewhere?" I ask.

"Both will need to be cleared by Caitem first, there are no exceptions."

"In reality does this mean travelling will be difficult?" I need to know how much of an issue this could be as I want to travel as much as possible.

"It's not difficult, but Caitem must come first, and travel requirements must accommodate its needs."

"But what if Tyn-T needs to send me somewhere and

I can't get out of it? Would Caitem ever need me to travel? If so, how do I work that with Tyn-T?" I doubt I can just drop everything and go on a holiday.

"If Caitem needs to deploy you and Tyn-T are reluctant to let you go, then we will step in."

What could they possibly do to make things happen? Do they have that much influence?

"Step in, what does that mean?"

"If it is critical for you to be in another place and Tyn-T does not release you, we have the ability to make it happen."

"How?"

"This is not relevant, keep reading."

"Are there people at Tyn-T who already work for Caitem? How many people work for Caitem?"

"This is not relevant, keep reading."

(6) Absence from work – all forms of absenteeism must be cleared by Caitem first. This includes sickness, training courses or annual leave.

"Do I really have to clear absences with Caitem first? What if I am really sick and have to stay home?"

"Yes. You clear it with Caitem first."

"But what if I am really, really sick and can't possibly get out of bed, would you still make me go in?" I want to know just how forceful they might be.

"It could happen, but we are realistic, and we do look after our team." He puts me at ease, but only a teeny-weeny bit.

(7) There is no normal pension, notice period or termination clause.

"So, what happens if I decide to join and then want to leave at some point as I feel I really can't do it, or change my mind about wanting to do it?"

"This is not an easy question to answer, as not many people leave. Generally, they go into hibernation, which could last anything from a day to a year."

"Hibernation? Are you saying that you can never leave?"

"Yes. A recruit can be inactive for a long period, but we still track their movements, as there may come a time when Caitem needs their services again."

"Does it work the other way, can I get fired from Caitem?"

"This is rare, but there could be an extreme situation that leads to a termination. This is not pleasant for either party."

"Like what exactly?"

"There are no rules around this. It is dependent on the individual and the circumstance."

"But there must be something. What about the last person who was let go? What was the reason for that?" I do not really care as much as it must seem. It is my stubbornness kicking in because they never give me real examples, only rules.

"It is not important. All you need to know is it could happen but it's rare. Continue reading."

"How do the salary payments work? Won't it look suspicious having two income streams going into my account?"

"No, we handle it with a specific tax code."

"Specific tax code, what does that mean?"

"Caitem has its own tax code, and the processing is automatic. You will have full access to a separate account and there are no alternatives."

"Does this mean my account is tracked, and what happens at tax time?"

"Neither are of importance right now, but when and if a tax return is required, you will be informed."

I read every word again before I pick up the pen and sign the contract. I have a mixture of feelings gurgling through my body. Sick, excitement and nerves, feelings I now associate with Caitem. The man also signs it followed by the young woman. He types something into the laptop then walks around the desk towards me. I freeze.

"Welcome aboard, I'm Michael. Company policy does not allow my identity to be revealed until the contract is signed. I specialise in psychiatry, and I am a level six." He offers a hand, which I accept. His entire demeanour has changed, he almost looks like a different person, maybe his specialty is being a chameleon. "This is Poh, she will be your mentor and personal trainer. We need to address your fitness and get you on a healthier routine. First, we need to explain how you and Poh will meet. Agencies are generally associated with a fitness centre offering corporate packages and Tyn-T is no different. FitUs will soon be doing a membership drive at Tyn-T. Poh is already an instructor and personal trainer with FitUs. You will attend this session and sign up with Poh in front of your colleagues. The fee will come straight out of your Tyn-T pay, but we will reimburse it in full, directly into your Caitem account."

The change in Michael into a human with his free-flowing speech has thrown me for a six. I am still frozen.

"Are you okay?" Michael asks.

"I'm not sure, I'm a bit thrown about how much you've changed. You even look like a different person."

"This process can be daunting but it is deliberate. Your reaction is normal and a positive."

"How can that be? I feel sick."

"We have done this before. This is not a normal job or process, but we do not deal with normal situations either. You have to continue to trust us, listen to what we say and follow instructions," he says with Poh nodding in agreement.

I might have names now, Caitem, Michael and Poh, but it feels like I may have to pay a price for it.

"Okay, so I have to join Poh's gym and sign up for personal training? I'm sure I can manage that. When will this happen?" Directing my question to Poh.

"You will see an invitation in your email. Don't miss this session. There are no acceptable excuses." Michael answers.

"Why can't I just go to FitUs directly, and then mention at work that I've got a personal trainer? Wouldn't that be easier?"

"It's imperative it looks legitimate. It's important this is done in front of people. We know what we're doing. If you are spending time with a company affiliated to Tyn-T, even if it's a gym, there are always fewer questions asked."

"Surely no one will question me going to the gym – unless you think I'll be there a lot?"

"Everything we do is with precision, and you will need to remember that. No improvising. You will have a regular and sometimes a demanding schedule to keep with Poh, and we cannot afford to have anyone at Tyn-T question this time."

"Okay, once I've signed up with Poh, when will it start?"

"Immediately, and just so you are clear, the personal training sessions are not a cover, you will be training."

"As in proper hard-core training?"

"Yes, as I stated before, your fitness levels are poor. The training will be physical and will include Caitem training. Poh is a level four, and she will be your only contact within Caitem unless circumstances dictate differently."

"How long has Poh been with Caitem?"

"This is not relevant."

"So why do you think I'm a good candidate? Do I have a specialty?" I know what the answer will be.

"Not a specialty, but qualities that make you a good candidate. Firstly, there was Thailand and your close proximity to a person of interest that could become useful, but more importantly, as a project manager you can move in and out of different companies quickly and legitimately without raising suspicion. If need be, we can move you every six weeks. As you are new to the United Kingdom, you're not in all the systems, and your anonymity is useful to us. We will discover if you have a specialty over time."

"Who was this person of interest in Thailand?"

"If this becomes important you will be informed."

"Are there other Caitem people at Tyn-T?" I ask again.

"That's not important for you to know. If it does become important, or relevant to an assignment, then you will be informed through the proper channel."

"But wouldn't it be better for me to know?"

"Quite the contrary. If you knew someone from Caitem, you would automatically alter your behaviour towards them."

I know he is right. There is no way I would look at them or treat them the same way.

"I look forward to working with you and seeing you soon," Poh says.

Ah, she speaks.

There is obviously a pecking order and I take it as my cue to leave. As I pass the receptionist, I say goodbye and get nothing but a quick glance up. She obviously has not got the memo that I am one of them now.

"Hi Shelley," I ring her as soon as I think I am far enough away.

"Hey Cari, how are you?"

"Good thanks, I have a quick question. Do you think I can handle personal training?"

"Why do you ask?" She laughs.

"I'm thinking of getting fit and think this might be the best way for me to achieve it."

"Really?" She laughs a little harder.

"Yes really. So how hard do you push your clients?"

"As hard as I need to with no mercy." She replies as a matter of fact.

"Crap, maybe it isn't for me."

"It is probably the best thing for you," she teases.

"I am going to die, aren't I?"

"Yeah, probably. You are not that fit, but you will get used to it, and you never know, you might even grow to love it."

"So why didn't you offer to train me?" I ask.

"Would you have said yes?" Shelley laughs.

"No."

"Then there is your answer, I have to go, I have a client waiting, talk later."

"Seeya."

Armed with my phantom dentist appointment excuse, I head to the office and straight into Mr Blue Eyes, who is loitering in reception. He greets me with a cheeky 'good afternoon' even though it is quite clearly still morning.

"Good morning to you too. I had a dentist appointment," I remind him, and smile like a horse, showing him all my teeth.

"How did it go?" He asks, grinning at my foolishness.

"As good as any dentist appointment can go, but I might need to go back and get a filling replaced."

I must plant this seed just in case I really need a dentist appointment, or if I am called back to Caitem.

"They couldn't do it this morning?"

"No way, José. The only way I'd let that happen is if they knock me out and wake me when it's done."

"That's a bit extreme," he responds with a chuckle.

"Not when you have an irrational fear of dentists. It was bad enough going in for a check-up. I almost left twice from the palpitations."

I hate lying, yet here I am doing it as if it is the most natural thing in the world, and to him of all people. Maybe this is a quality that Caitem knew I had, that I am a natural liar. I have only been with Caitem for an hour, and I'm already compromising my own morals. I need to refocus.

"While I've got you here, can we have a quick chat?" I ask and start walking towards an empty meeting room expecting he is free and will follow.

"What's up?" He asks, shutting the door behind us.

"With the new seating arrangements. I met one of the new account directors and had a strained conversation. When I told her how project Toadstool was going to be split between Lita and me, she was not happy. She claimed that client services should have a say in all resourcing decisions. This can't be right, can it?" I ask.

"Not this again," he reacts strongly, catching me off guard. "Sorry, but every so often the client services team announce they need to have the final decision on everything, trying to take control without any of the responsibility. They look at project managers as their back-office administrators. It's definitely not the case, it is your responsibility. Stand your ground even if it gets heated. I'll always support you and I can resolve it at the right level."

His forceful response surprises me. It's so different from his normal, calm demeanour.

"I'm glad this isn't the first time. I thought it was a lack of confidence in me. Thank you, it's hard when you start somewhere new, and you have to learn how everything works. I stood my ground, but I needed to check with you that it wasn't the way Tyn-T did things."

"It's not the way any place does things. You're doing a really good job and it's been noticed by the right people, so keep it up." His puppy-dog eyes are back and trained on me. "I'm going to arrange a Project Managers' night out, to bring my team together. We all work on our own projects and rarely get time together. It could help strengthen our relationships and realise we can support one another. I expect you to join us." He smiles.

"Sure, sounds like fun. What will we be doing on this night out?"

"Something interesting, like the Summer party where we can let loose for a few hours away from the office."

I feel my colour rise. Did 'interesting' refer to the kiss, or to the event as a whole?

"Yes, the Summer party was fun, with one surprise in particular." I am trying to match his level of coolness.

"Yes, it was a surprise. It was everything I expected and more, a lot more." He stares at me, unblinkingly. I have no words as I return his gaze, realising he has me well and truly caught. "And I want to do it again," was all he got to say, before someone walked past our room interrupting our moment. He glances at his watch, tells me to keep an eye out for the invite, and then leaves. I float back to my desk to start my day.

I scan my emails for one from FitUs, or about FitUs, but there is nothing. There are a few from someone called Brett Ferguson again.

"Does anyone know who Brett Ferguson is, or what he does?" I ask the team in general.

"Why?" Lita asks, as some of the others look up from their screens but offer nothing.

"It seems like all he does is email. Does he do anything else?" I ask light-heartedly.

"I'm not sure who he is, but why don't you reply to one?" She offers mischievously.

"I might just do that! Or should I know who he is?"

"If that was the case, you would have met him already. Go on, it'll be fun, plus he might be really nice."

"Or it might just be embarrassing. What if he sits only a few desks away?" I look around at all the new people in our room, but I am pretty sure I know most, if not all, of them.

"Go on, let's do it now, c'mon." Lita is determined and she wheels her chair across to my desk. I reply to his most recent email, 'Why affiliates work'

Hi Brett,

I hope we do not offend you by this email.

It is in response to your many emails filled with nuggets of information. It seems not many people know who you are or what you do. Although from your emails we do feel we have a good understanding of what you like and dislike about the digital world. It would be great to put a face to these broadcasts to determine whether you are indeed an actual person, but if you are a computer then, nano, nano \\ //.

PS: going on first-hand experience, I believe affiliates, if used correctly, can drive campaign awareness. And one more thing: I think you meant to say 'public', not 'pubic'. Sorry, could not let this one go :-o.

Look forward to hearing from you,

Cari + Lita

Toadstool Project Managers

Lita and I re-read the email almost removing the 'pubic' comment but decide to leave it in. I hit 'send'. Instantly we hear an echo of dings and I see the same email flash up on my screen. Oh no! I hit 'reply all', not 'reply to sender'. This email went to the entire company, including the CEO and Mr Blue Eyes!

OMG, OMG, OMG, panic. How do I un-send?

I scramble around Outlook looking for damage control trying to get Lita to help, but she cannot see past the laugh induced tears streaming down her face. Finally, I find the un-send option and aggressively hit it. I hear echoes of laughter from every direction. People are looking at me, making remarks and holding up their hands in a salute to 'nanu, nanu'.

Emails start filling my inbox, 'Yes Brett, who are you?' 'Could the real Brett Ferguson, please stand up?' 'Is this a game like where's Wally?' And even worse, 'Brett, put your pubes away!'

I need to hide. Nervously laughing I try to distract those closest to me.

"Does anyone know of a good gym around here?" I ask.

"There are a few, depends on what you're after," says Lita kindly. "The closest is FitUs and I think we have a corporate deal with them, I'll send you the link." Then to keep the amusement going, she adds, "Why don't you send them an email?" Her hysteria returns.

"It's not funny, I'm not going to hear the end of this and I'm not sending any more emails today." I laugh and remind her, "don't forget, your name was on the email too."

"Yeah, but it came from your email address, and no one will read past the pubes comment. I bet you still won't find out who Brett is. If I were Brett, I wouldn't reply, he could have some fun with this!" Lita wipes away the tears.

"I don't want to know who he is now. What if he makes a comment about his pubes?"

This conversation is not helping me calm down.

"Oh, I so want to be there when you meet him."

"You need to find out who he is and point him out, so I don't get surprised by him."

"No way, this is too much fun."

"You have to. If he turns up at my desk, it's going to be embarrassing. Stop laughing, I need to get some work done."

Lita is adamant she is not helping me find Brett, but reminds me that tomorrow everyone will have moved onto something else. I try to keep my presence in the office at a minimum and ignore the responses that are still coming in. I look for something to do, Toadstool finances, boring but safe. The only thing I want to do is leave and never come back. This is not the way to remain anonymous. I wonder what Caitem would think about this, what if they somehow see this email?

- CHAPTER 7 -

"Has anyone seen my project Toadstool timeline?" I ask, shuffling through papers on my desk.

"No!" everyone around me choruses.

Odd, I clearly remember seeing them yesterday with my notes scrawled all over it. I continue searching in vain, eventually giving up and printing a new one. This time I will keep it more secured.

A few days has passed since signing up with Caitem and nothing more has happened, until an email alert pops up with the subject line 'FitUs for a fit new you'. I stare at it waiting for my heart rate to return to normal. The email is an invitation to meet the FitUs instructors on Tuesday. I wonder if Poh will be there, and if I will recognise her.

I accept the invite. Until now, everything to do with Caitem has been surreal, and a process I did not expect to amount to anything, despite signing the contract and being officially employed by them.

Remembering that I had asked about a gym, Lita also forwards me the email. A second invite arrives from Mr Blue Eyes. This email gives me butterflies. It is the 'Project Managers Night Out' on Thursday evening. I would prefer Friday, but the choice of night is understandable as Mr Blue Eyes no longer works on Fridays.

'Dinner and drinks with a surprise', he announces. I hope it is not bowling or karaoke. Neither show my best side.

The thought of going out with Mr Blue Eyes, even as part of a group, makes me want to improve my appearance and get rid of the pale complexion I have developed under London's grey skies. I have heard antipodeans often suffer from 'seasonal depression', a legitimate ailment caused by the lack of sun and vitamin D. A recommended solution is a sun bed, so I search online for one near the office.

Out of the corner of my eye, I see Tod heading my way, and he is not looking pleased.

"Do you have a second?" He asks without saying hi, looking concerned and a bit pissed off.

"Sure, now?" I respond.

"Yes, can we go somewhere else?" He asks as his gaze is set on the client services team. We head to the first available meeting room and before I can even sit down, he launches.

"You know this project is hard enough to deliver, right? So why do we have to make changes so late into the project, after everything's been signed off, yeah?" He speaks fast, inserting random words in random places, and I wonder how he ended up in a senior position when communication is clearly not his strong point.

"Sorry, I don't know what you're talking about. What changes?"

"The account manager from your team, right? What's-her-name, the young one helping Sheree. She's made some design changes, right? To parts of the system we're coding now and we've almost finished, yeah? Which means we have to refactor it, and we don't know how long it will take, right?"

The more he talks the more he is winding me up.

"Hang on, stop, what changes? There have been no changes that I'm aware of. I wouldn't agree to any changes this late in the piece."

"Right. So do we have to do these changes? The designs were sent to me twenty minutes ago, yeah?"

I can feel my blood boiling.

"What designs? I still don't know what you're talking about! Wait here, I'm going to get the account manager. Is it Julie?"

"Yeah, her."

I find Julie at her desk and ask her to join us and to bring the new designs. She claims she does not have time for this now, but I simply stand purposely at her desk until she gets up. As she follows me, she lets out an almighty huff to emphasise her displeasure.

"We are all busy, so I'll get straight into it. Julie, Tod, Tod, Julie. I've just found out through Tod that some designs have changed and need to be incorporated into the current build. Tell me this isn't true. If it is, who approved this work?" I do not mess around with pleasantries.

"The client rang me explaining he needed more information on the site, and the public relations company wanted videos with a rating function. Really good ideas, don't you think? They'll add to the overall website appeal." Julie sounds pleased, implying we should be pleased too.

"And you decided to go ahead and brief the designers directly without running it past me or anyone else? When did all this happen?"

"I spoke with the designer last week and as she wasn't busy, she fitted it in." She is clearly missing the point. Tod remains silent but is fidgeting like a madman, retying his ponytail twice.

"Are you kidding me? Why didn't you tell me about this so we could do a proper evaluation? At the very least to check everything still fits together. Tod's team are already at capacity delivering the in-scope work."

"The client is expecting it. He's really excited about it." She is still quite jovial, still missing the point, but she seems to think she is on solid ground so continues to stand firm.

"What about the cost and time to do this extra work? Has that at least been considered?" I am now trying to assess how much damage has been done.

"Well, the designs are already done. I checked the finances, and we are travelling well against the original estimates, so I thought we could absorb the costs. If we offer overtime, we can still get them built in time. Tod's team is awesome, and they'll get it done." She flashes a flirtatious grin his way. Tod has frozen, mid-fidget.

"I assume the designer has charged to this project. The costs you looked at are for the original scope. Of course the finances are looking good. We haven't finished the project and I can guarantee you, not everyone will have filled in their timesheets. There are still weeks of costs to hit this project. We'll need to use every last penny and then some. You do know that overtime is another expense that will need to be covered by the original budget?"

Tod is looking appreciative that someone is speaking up for his team. I am dumbfounded that someone with so little understanding of projects and financial management has been allowed to make these decisions to the detriment of both the project and the agency.

"Well, I estimated only about £4000 to £5000. We always have contingency so should be able to cover it."

"Are you kidding? Maybe it would cost this much if we were building from scratch, but we need to re-evaluate the entire site. When you add everything up, the actual estimate is at least double what you guessed. New functionality is not what contingency is used for! More importantly, it's not your decision when to use it."

"I don't agree. I know you're new to the agency and all, but we do this sort of thing all the time and it always works out in the end. We have to be flexible and accommodate the client, isn't that right, Tod?" She stupidly thinks he will be on her side. I pause to give Tod a chance to respond.

"You're right. This does happen all the time, right? And it's the reason we don't always deliver everything we originally scoped and why we need to phase it, yeah? Working long hours, getting pissed off, and chewing through the cash. It's also why we have project managers on the project, yeah? Everything's meant to go through them first. I'm not looking at this new functionality until we've got time to do it, which won't be until we finish what we are working on now. Even then I don't know if we can do it, we're already booked to start the next project." He stamps his foot to emphasise this mini explosion. Go Tod! I am trying hard to hold back my smirk.

"We need to look after the client first! Tod, your team has built the same functionality already, we can just use that." Realising now that Tod is not on her side, Julie's tone has shifted to desperation.

I interject. "The client rang me already asking for changes to be implemented free of charge within the existing timescale. You know what I said, I said no. He obviously found an easier target. Why didn't you say we'd look into it before committing? Don't you realise how tight this project is and there are penalties if we deliver late? We'll look stupid going back to the client now telling him we can't do it, but that's something you need to handle. Tod's team cannot be distracted by new requirements. If public relations want new functionality, they have to pay for it." I also stamp my foot. Tod nods in agreement and does not hide his smirk.

"No Cari, we have to do it. I've already told him we will and they're having the videos re-edited into the format we need. Tod, surely we can do this! You have a talented team. Can we offer weekend work, get someone else in?"

"We already have additional developers that are reducing our margin and they are already working weekends. Sorry Julie, if you'd run this by me first you would have known this. I should never have to hear about changes from the development team." My tone softens as Julie is realising, she has lost the battle.

"I had it under control, so I didn't think I needed to

bother you. The client even signed off the designs."

"What! He's seen them? This is getting worse! Nothing should go out the door before it comes by me. What a mess, and now I have to sort this out."

"Well yes, but it's not a mess, we just need to find someone to do it. You're over-reacting." Then she tries to convince Tod again, before I interrupt.

"Let me make something perfectly clear. Everything to do with delivery must, with no exceptions, come through me, even something as simple as changing a line of text. I don't care if client services believe differently. It's not their job and you've proven that you can't do the job."

"Cari, I don't like your tone, you don't have the client relationship, I do. You're just being difficult because I didn't go through you first."

"This is getting us nowhere. I am going to bring this up with Jake and he can sort it out with Bill. Thanks Tod, don't do anything with the new designs other than send them to me please." I leave the meeting room with Tod close on my heels.

Back at my desk, I call Mr Blue Eyes and leave a voicemail, apologising about another whinge and suggesting a joint session with Client Services and Project Management to resolve the building tension. Right now, it is time for FitUs.

Poh is dressed in trendy FitUs gear, flanked by two other FitUs representatives who could also be Caitem people. She looks so normal in this setting.

"Hi, I'm Cari."

"Pleased to meet you, Cari. I'm Poh and I'm a personal

trainer at FitUs. Have you heard of us?" She asks.

"Not until I saw the email, I am still quite new to London."

"Oh, how long have you been in London for?"

"About five months, I think, time flies so could be a bit longer."

"FitUs is a fully equipped gym that offers weights and machine equipment to suit your style. If you prefer classes, we have an excellent schedule accommodating mornings, lunchtimes or after work. But to super-charge your training, we have highly qualified personal trainers like myself."

"I've sometimes toyed with the idea of a personal trainer, one of my friends is one too, but I don't really know if it would be right for me."

"A personal trainer will customise a training plan for the results you want to achieve."

"I have a very busy work schedule. How flexible are the trainers?"

"We work around your schedule. What has stopped you in the past?"

"I don't like being scrutinised and I think that is what a trainer would do. And I am not sure that I would cope. And then there might be the yelling, I don't think I would respond well to the yelling."

"That couldn't be further from the truth. We do an initial assessment, no scrutinising, and then it's all about redevelopment. I think you have been watching too many military based boot-camp shows. Personal trainers don't yell, they encourage."

"What if my body can't handle it?"

"That's the beauty of a training schedule. We push you to your limits, starting exactly where your body is at now, and build it up. Anyone can benefit from a trainer."

"Okay, how do I know I have the right trainer?"

"You will know within one or two sessions. If the trainer isn't suitable, we find one that is."

"How much does it cost? It sounds expensive."

"The most economical way is to purchase in bundles of three, five or ten sessions. Once the bundle is used, you can purchase a second bundle or book ongoing sessions. The higher the bundle, the cheaper the individual session. Your trainer will develop a plan around what best suits you."

"Okay, sign me up! I'll take a gym membership and a five bundle."

"Excellent." Poh completes the paperwork and hands it to me to sign. I notice she has ignored my five-session bundle request and entered 'ongoing'.

"What happens now?"

"Once the paperwork has been entered into our system, a gym administrator will contact you to arrange a time for a gym orientation and book you in for your first session with me."

"Thank you, I look forward to it."

Caitem should be happy. Due to my questions, someone else decided to join, although Poh handed her over to a colleague.

Already feeling fitter, on my way back to my desk, I bump into Mr Blue Eyes.

"Where have you been?" He asks.

"I've just joined FitUs," I beam.

He asks to discuss the latest incident with project Toadstool, and I follow him to a meeting room.

"I have heard from Bill that you had an altercation with Julie. She described you as antsy and unreasonable. These are her words, not mine."

"Of course she did." I respond throwing my head back and looking up at the ceiling and then out the window.

"Are you okay?" I choose to ignore him.

"Cari, looking out the window is not going to resolve anything. I'm not saying I agree with what I heard, but I need to hear what happened from you."

"Before coming to Tyn-T I thought I fully understood the role of a project manager, but here, everything I thought I knew is challenged all the time and sometimes it gets to me. There seems to be a lack of respect for my role, or maybe it's just me. So go on, tell me what you were told, this should be good. And for the record, I wasn't unreasonable, you could say that I was a bit antsy, but for good reason." My response draws a dark expression from him mixed with a bit of surprise, as I know my tone is not pleasant and far from professional.

"Apparently you were over-stepping the client services boundaries and you were rude to Julie who is now helping Sheree. Even though client services can be difficult at times, they do play a role here and we need to try and work harmoniously together. In Bill's words you were uncooperative, disruptive and a blocker to the project, but I let him know I was not accepting any of it until I had spoken to you, so I would like to hear what you have to say." He sounds calm but authoritative, and as if he might actually believe this rubbish.

"So do you think I would be rude for no reason?" I ask.

"I believe something happened to provoke you, but I would like to hear from you."

I tell him my version of events, accidentally referring to Julie as 'Sparkles'.

"I'm really sorry Cari. Bill only mentioned the behaviour, not what caused it. This happens much more than it should, and has seen great project managers, designers and others resign or be pushed out. I'll talk with Tod and then management to get a stop to this once and for all."

"I haven't been here long, and I'm constantly fighting against them to do my job, and then running to you when it all goes wrong, as if I can't handle it on my own."

"Cari, the reason you find yourself in these situations is because you know your craft, you protect your projects and the agency. Unfortunately, sometimes to do that means you need to stand your ground and lock horns. Client services' lack of knowledge threatens them, and they fear they will lose their power. You won't be pushed out, I will personally see to that."

"So do I keep challenging them? Noddy has already made her feelings clear about Lita, and I'm supposedly uncooperative, unreasonable, disrespectful and...what was the other one? Oh yeah, a blocker."

"Noddy, Sparkles? Cari, really, do you have to refer to them by these names?"

"When they annoy me, yes, but I'll be careful not to do it in front of them." I grin.

"I'm glad it amuses you. Dare I ask if you always give people nicknames?"

"There might be others, but it's not relevant for this conversation." Wow, that sounded like something from the Caitem handbook.

"I don't think I want to know. Anyway, don't change the way you approach projects, but please watch your alternative names, we don't want to fuel this fire. We need more people like you to push this agency in the right direction. The CEO claims he wants a strong digital presence, but that won't happen if they insist on running it like a direct marketing agency."

I throw my head back again, close my eyes and say nothing. I open my eyes and see he has moved closer and is looking searchingly at me. It has the right effect and I start to smile.

"That's better. I don't want to lose you. I'm not letting you leave this agency."

"It's crossed my mind a few times but it's good to know it's not just me and that I have your support." I know leaving this place will never be my decision anyway.

"I was brought in to improve our digital

competitiveness, what you are seeing is the resistance to change." Mr Blue Eyes reveals.

"Thanks, I'll keep going. It's so stupid though, the challenges shouldn't be coming from inside the agency. It's as if the account team are the client and we work for them."

"Sometimes something has to break before it can be fixed. I'm always here to support you and the rest of the team. You don't have to fight these battles on your own. Seeing you like this tells me a lot about you and keeps my days interesting. By the way," he asks with a playful smile, "have you found out who Brett is yet?"

"Don't you start! How embarrassing. I've never done anything like that before, and no, I still don't know who he is. Do you?" I ask with a sigh, rolling my eyes.

"Actually, yes I do, but I don't want to ruin the fun for you. Anyway, I have to go and sort this out." He disappears and I stay in the room until I muster up the strength to face the team again. I cannot believe he knows who Brett is but will not tell me.

Back at my desk, I keep my head down and ignore my team. I notice there are more papers missing from my desk. Where do they go? I ask those sitting closest to me if they have moved anything from my desk and I receive a chorus of 'no' again. This agency is weird. I begin to believe it must be filled with plenty of people that Caitem would be interested in.

– CHAPTER 8 –

It is time for my first training session with Poh. FitUs is a five-minute walk from Tyn-T, literally around the corner. All entry points are guarded by card access turnstiles. The club manager takes me on a tour of the centre, which is larger than I expected. There are two studios for classes, a spin bike room, and two separate weight areas, which seem to divide the hard-core body builders from the casual weightlifters. The ladies' change room includes a steam room and sauna. The final stop on my tour is Poh's office. She thanks my tour guide and invites me to sit.

"Hi Cari, it's nice to see you again. Have you been keeping well?"

"Yes, good thanks." This is polite.

"You seem nervous, don't be. We'll all take good care of you. Each team member at FitUs has different areas of expertise. Mine is targeting dormant muscles by using strength work, but to mix things up, I incorporate outdoor sessions which my clients generally find enjoyable." This corporate spiel surprises me. I had expected less about FitUs and more about Caitem. She continues.

"As you might appreciate, training is not just about exercise, it is also ensuring you're eating a balance of nutritionally rich foods. I will develop a plan that suits your training and lifestyle." She stands up and says, "Before we get started, I need to take some measurements and calculate your BMI. This gives us the starting point and the information I need to devise the best plan." She pauses, realising I want to say something.

"I've already done a medical...." I begin, but before I can say anymore, she raises a hand to stop me, shaking her head in a no action. She writes something on a piece of paper and holds it up.

"No Caitem in FitUs". Once I acknowledge this, she spins around and feeds it into a shredder. Okay, I get it, I need to pretend this is a normal personal training introduction. Poh measures my height and weight, takes my blood pressure and does a fat pinch test.

"How often do you exercise, on average, per week?" Poh asks.

"I don't really exercise per se, but I do walk a lot as I don't have a car."

"So no weekly physical exercise?"

"I guess not."

"What is your diet like? Would you say it's generally healthy, do you snack often, do you eat out a lot?"

"Um, well, not all the time, but I do try to eat healthy." I answer opting not to tell her that I ate pizza and an entire tub of ice cream last night for dinner.

"How many standard drinks would you say you consume, on average, per week?"

"A few, but in my defence, I work in advertising, and it goes with the territory."

"Then it would be more than just a few."

"Possibly, yes, maybe more than a few a week."

"So you don't exercise, you don't eat well and you drink more than recommended." As Poh summarises, I can see that she realises getting me Caitem fit is going to be a challenge.

"Am I a going to be able to cope with this training considering what you now know about me?"

"Most clients are nervous when they start, but the sessions will be designed to build your confidence, to push within your limits, although at times it will feel like I am pushing beyond them."

"Beyond seems a bit scary, what does that mean?"

"It all comes down to trust. You need to trust me that I know what I am doing." Once it looks like the paperwork and interrogation are complete, I thank her and get up to leave. "Where are you going?" Poh asks.

"Home."

"Not so fast. We still need to do a physical evaluation."

"Now?"

"Yes, now, I need to see where you're at before I can complete the plan."

"But I haven't brought any gear with me."

"Nobody comes to a gym without their gear."

"I thought today was only a registration session, paperwork and orientation," I say truthfully.

"Apologies if you were misinformed. Please change and meet me back here." She hands me a bag, which no doubt contains everything I need, all brand-new and in my size.

Where does this stuff come from?

Back in her office, changed and sulking a little after being scolded, I remain standing as the adrenaline from what I am about to endure hits me. This feels like detention.

Poh explains we are going for a short run to a park where she will take me through a series of exercises to see what she has to work with. I do not remember the last time I went for a run. I am more of a casual jogger than a runner, who am I trying to kid? I am not even a casual jogger, maybe more of a slightly faster walker. I grew up doing court sports, particularly basketball and volleyball, which require explosive power and seems a lifetime ago.

It only takes us five minutes to run to the park, but my lungs are bursting out of my chest, and I am crouched over, hands on knees, panting. Poh is not as amused as I am, confirming the challenge she has in front of her. She lets me have a short rest, and then makes me stretch, demonstrating how to do the moves.

"You know we take confidentiality seriously. You can never discuss Caitem in any context within the FitUs walls. Nowhere is considered safe. We can talk in this park and in other locations, when I tell you we can," she says, all politeness gone. "The training and mentoring will consist of fitness, which you will greatly benefit from, along with everything you need to know about Caitem, including the rules. Unless otherwise instructed, you will receive your assignments during these sessions, and you will only ever report to me," she pauses, waiting for a response.

"An assignment is a while off though, isn't it?" Catching my breath between each word.

"Just because you're new to Caitem doesn't mean there is a grace period, you could be issued an assignment at anytime. Caitem is always working up profiles and if an assignment is classified at level zero, it could be assigned to you." I am months away from being ready, maybe years, but Poh continues relentlessly. "Initially there is a lot to absorb and adapt to, but you will. You have come this far without knowing much at all. You took the chance, and you are moving through the stages well." I realise she is trying to be reassuring, but it does nothing to make me feel better.

"So do you just train new recruits?" I ask randomly.

"No, I have my own assignments and I help with profiling potential targets. You'd be surprised how much people talk to their personal trainer and gym instructor. I become their confidant in a friendly, relaxed environment. There are three main rules at Caitem, which must be obeyed at all times. The first you already know, confidentiality. The second is, Caitem always comes first. This means before your day job, before socialising, before friends, before partners and before family. The third is that you must always follow instructions. No improvising, even if your gut is screaming to do something else; bury it and do as instructed. We've been in this business a long time and we know what we're doing. Is this clear?" she asks.

"Yes."

"Repeat what I have just said."

"Confidentiality, Caitem comes first, and no improvisation. Are you sure I can do this?" I ask again nervously. This is serious.

"The screening process is thorough. If Caitem did not think you were capable, you would not be in this park with me now. What we do, we do well."

"What is this for?" I ask as she hands me a phone.

"This is a Caitem issued phone and can only be used for Caitem. You can only call me from this phone and there are no exceptions, this phone must always be with you. If the phone rings, you must answer it, anytime of day or evening. Is this clear?"

"Yes, what happens if I don't answer it?"

"You will make every effort to return the call asap."

"What if I am in a long meeting."

"We are aware that this can happen, you will still make every effort to return the call as soon as possible, is this clear?"

"Yes. Are there people at Tyn-T you're looking into? Are there others working for Caitem at Tyn-T?"

"This is classified. You will only be given information if you need it. You may never meet any other Caitem members other than Michael and myself."

"Really? You can't even give me a hint?" I insist.

"On your feet." Poh does give me a hint, and that's to leave things alone. The training session begins.

Even though it went fast, it did not end quickly enough for me. I experienced moments of light-headedness and muscle spasms. It was excruciatingly hard. Relieved as I am to be heading home, I feel somehow refreshed.

At home, I search for a healthy option in my fridge, but realise the reality of how badly I eat is staring me in the face. Half a leftover pizza, chocolate mousse, and a packet of tortellini. My freezer holds nothing better. Fish fingers, bagels and a full tub of Ben and Jerry's Phish Food. Those frozen pieces of fish-shaped chocolates and marshmallow cannot be beaten. I opt for the leftover pizza followed by the ice cream justifying to myself that once it is gone, I'll replace with healthier options. In my food diary I write salmon and salad.

The morning after my personal training session, I wake earlier than usual with pain in every single muscle of my body. I lie flat and still, wondering how I am even going to get out of bed, let alone get dressed and get to work. Tonight is the Project Manager's dinner and I want to look better than usual. I start by moving my arms, even the smallest of movements bring a tear to my eye. I launch myself into an upright position and sob in pain. I know I am out of shape, but this is beyond ridiculous.

I grab my Caitem-issued phone and ring Poh. Poh assures me this pain is normal and that I need to push through it, then clearly states this is not an appropriate use of the phone. I explain I cannot feel like this after every session. She tells me to use the pain as an incentive to get fitter and never to let myself go again. I grit my teeth, stop sobbing and start moving.

I manage to get myself showered, dressed, onto the packed train, into my favourite coffee shop, and to the office.

I am on time, exhausted, and it has only just gone nine. I pass Mr Blue Eyes and he asks whether I had a big night last night?

"This is what my first personal training session did to me." I tell him and keep moving because his smirk says it all. At my desk, I go through my inbox and my eyes are drawn to one with the subject 'Who is Brett Ferguson?' This cannot be serious. I thought this was over. I roll my eyes and read on.

Recently there was a company wide search for an employee, someone who regularly communicates industry news and whom I would have thought was well known throughout Tyn-T. This was eloquently proven not to be the case, highlighting how little we know about those working alongside us. It should not matter whether our colleagues work in a different discipline, on a different account or even on a different floor. Therefore, we are planning a team-building program consisting of a series of events to bring together and re-connect Tyn-T, to build our team, one team! I know who Brett Ferguson is, do you?'

Look at what I have done. I thought there would have been another scandal by now to talk about, but it's back. Sure enough, people are asking me again whether I know who Brett Ferguson is. For all I know, one of these people might be Brett.

Apart from this announcement, the morning is uneventful. The conversation with Poh is on auto replay dominating my thoughts and I wonder how much Caitem must come first? I have my second session with her at lunch time, which is bad timing, as I wanted to be fresh for the Project Management outing this evening and I can barely walk, move, or function as a human being.

My life has totally changed from what it was six months ago. I moved to a different country to experience everything. I never for a second thought this is how it would play out. The stodgier food, the warmer beers, the grey clouds constantly overhead, the advertising industry, the cosmopolitan crowds, and now there is a Caitem. I look at Tyn-T through completely different lenses and wonder if anyone is currently being tracked or profiled, and if so, by whom. Could I spot a tracker or a person of interest? I swing my chair around and study each person carefully, determining what traits would make them a good guy or a bad guy. I ponder a few potentials like Noddy, Sparkles, Gregor, but decide they are not smart enough to be able to pull something off.

The first ten minutes of the training session was done through tears, but I now actually feel better. I have full control of my body. I think the twenty-minute sunbed experience also helped, the heat permeating every cell of my body, I am excited to have a glowing complexion.

When I arrive back to the office, I detour past the bathroom to review my tanned goodness. Instead of the expected sun-kissed glow, I stare at a tired and now blotchy face, this is not what I was expecting. I hope it will settle by the time the night's festivities start, which is not that far away. To make things worse I suspect I have sunburn on areas that never see nor should see the sun.

Lita decides we should start getting ready quite early, so we head to a floor that has a larger bathroom and one that is not used as often. She knows all the tricks. My face has settled a little and I can start to see a healthy glow. I delve into my makeup bag armoury to start my transformation into something irresistible.

Does it really matter? He sees me every day and if he does not like what he has seen already, then what I look like tonight is not going to make much difference.

Lita and I are exchanging war paint and regressing into sixteen year old girls, giggling, experimenting with colours, talking about boys. Then she shows me a small package that needs no introduction. The spirit of the moment takes over and I do not even consider saying no. She moves into a cubicle, lines it up, and gives me my turn. This is a nice appetiser to get us in the spirit. It is going to be a good night tonight.

The consumption makes us lose track of time, fuelling our conversation and application of eye shadow, lip stick, mascara, highlighter.

Finally, the other female project manager, Nicole, finds us and we follow her out. The rest of the project management team are waiting in the reception area. Knowing they are waiting for us makes me feel awkward, but Lita being the outgoing one, gives a heartfelt but jovial apology.

The team consists of three women, five men, plus Mr Blue Eyes and we all get along famously. Three cars are waiting to escort us through the busy London traffic. The girls pour into one car and the boys split up into the other two. I do not know where we are going, and I do not care. I just sit back and enjoy the ride.

We stop outside Shoreditch House, a place steeped in history and prestige. This is the place to be seen at and stepping out of the car reinvigorates my high. We are greeted and escorted to an immaculate dining room. Mr Blue Eyes arranges the team so we are sitting with who he thinks we should get to know better. I am seated next to Tommy and Luke, opposite Mr Blue Eyes. I would prefer to have Lita beside me for moral support with this coke-high, but it would not surprise me if others were wired too. In an advertising agency, it is an occupational hazard.

The wait staff move with stealthy precision, almost floating, filling our glasses with our choice of red, white, bubbles, or soft drink. Surprisingly, I do not feel like I need alcohol but I accept a glass of bubbles and a soft drink. The menu is exquisite and has my favourite dessert, tiramisu, probably a pimped up version.

Sitting opposite Mr Blue Eyes, I indulge in a daydream of the pair of us enjoying an intimate dinner, staring into each other's eyes. An overly animated Tommy interrupts my thoughts as he is commanding the attention of the table, becoming more exaggerated with every sip he takes. Lita, in the midst of holding the attention of her neighbours, flashes me an amazingly subtle indication that we need a top-up.

We excuse ourselves, grunting and jibing back at the comments about how females can only go to the ladies in pairs.

The usual ritual occurs, but this time, Lita wants me to line and roll, claiming I need the practice. We are faster this time, not wanting to draw attention to ourselves. We roll, cut, burn, and return to our table with that familiar teeth-numbing, metallic coating.

While we were away, everyone moved seats. This means Lita and I can now sit together. We grab our glasses and re-join the group, slotting straight back into the conversation. Unfortunately, it is about Brett Ferguson and that email.

"Have you found out who Brett is yet?" Tommy asks in a very loud voice.

"No, does anyone else know who he is? Besides you," I say, nodding in the direction of Mr Blue Eyes.

"I do, but I'm not saying anything either," Luke admits, laughing.

"Really, no one is going to help me with this?"

"Nope, way too much fun." Lita adds.

"Do you know who he is too?" I ask curiously and somewhat surprised that suddenly she knows who he is.

"Yes, we all do," she fesses up on behalf of the team.

"Fine, well at least I can entertain you all," I chuckle.

Mr Blue Eyes cuts in and announces the second part of the night is about to begin, bowling. This must be the surprise element of the evening.

"And we don't have to go far," he reassures.

"So where are we going?" Nicole asks.

"There are bowling lanes here," he replies and right on cue, our waiter appears to escort us to the games area. We are asked to leave our drinks behind, as they will be replaced by fresh ones on our arrival. Lita, Nicole and I link arms, giggling behind the boys.

"I can't do this, I'm rubbish at bowling," I admit to them.

"Who cares, it'll be fun, just don't hurt anyone," Lita says.

"Why would I hurt anyone?"

"You'll see," Lita says, making us all laugh.

We walk into a room called the Biscuit Pin, which has two wooden bowling lanes and a bar. We have the lanes exclusively for two hours. We change our shoes and divide ourselves into two teams. I manage to keep Lita and Mr Blue Eyes on my team. Being the line manager, he is wanted by both teams.

It does not take long to understand why Lita said, 'try not to hurt anyone'. Round heavy balls thrown down a lane under the influence of alcohol saw the odd one go backwards, luckily not connecting with anyone, but attracting the level of heckling it deserves. I hate to think how much this night will cost Tyn-T, but we all deserve it. This lavish evening goes a little way towards making up for the long hours we put in, and the stress we endure dealing with the various departments, especially Client Services.

As the game progresses, the true competitors are revealed. I discover I am not as bad as I thought, having managed a strike and the occasional spare. I find myself sitting snugly against Mr Blue Eyes, my leg firmly against his, chatting about nothing specific, feeling right at home, until he turns into me and places an arm behind the chair. From an outsider's perspective, this might look suspicious but as there is not much space to sit, we all look a little cosy.

"Are you enjoying the night?" He asks casually.

"Yes, I am thanks. It's great how they have all this in the one place. It keeps the spirit of the night going."

"There is something about you I find intriguing, a little mysterious," he says in a lowered tone and much closer to my ear.

"Really? I always thought I was more of a 'what you see is what you get' type of gal," I say, surprised by the change in conversation.

"I know the 'work Cari', but what is the away-from-work Cari like?"

"Well, when at work, that's what I do, I am work."

"You're not at work now."

"But it's still a work function, and I think my sub-conscious knows that."

"I want to get to know you away from work." He lets his fingers drift across my shoulder. I may have stopped breathing.

I look straight into his questioning eyes.

"Hey you two! Cari you're up," Lita interrupts with a very suspicious but knowing smirk. I want to get that missed moment back.

My bowling efforts receive a hail of 'rubbish' comments and boos, then a short time later, our two hours are up and the general public are let in. Some of our team disappear and our group is reduced to four: Lita, Tommy, Blue Eyes and me.

It's time to move on from the bowling lanes. As I stand up, so does Mr Blue Eyes, who grabs me firmly but tenderly and asks me to help him sort out the bowling bar bill. Before we make it to the bar, he pulls me into an alcove for privacy.

"I'm serious about wanting to get to know you, Cari." He places his hand at the base of my neck, gently drawing me closer. His lips connect with mine, slightly apart, teasing my top lip then the bottom with the tickle of his tongue, making the kiss deeper and more intense. His other hand slides down, to rest on my lower back, pressing me closer to him. I forget where I am, allowing myself to melt into him, a perfect fit.

We must have been gone too long for Lita to come looking for us, interrupting with an "Oi, get a room!"

She brings us back to reality. I do not know how long that kiss lasted, but it was not long enough. Even though we are no longer touching, I can feel the tension in Mr Blue Eyes, of not being long enough, or maybe that we were caught.

Luckily, it was Lita who found us, not Tommy, who joins us only seconds after Lita. Tommy and Lita both announce they need to leave, but Mr Blue Eyes wants a nightcap and invites me to join him. How could I possibly refuse? I want him badly.

We leave the Biscuit Pin and find a cosy lounge. I do not need more alcohol but as he is ordering a scotch, I opt for an Amaretto.

"Is it bad that we just got caught? Are you okay about it?" I ask.

"It's not ideal, but I'm okay, are you?"

"Sure, it was Lita and we're good friends. I'll get grilled in the morning, but she'll keep it to herself."

"Pity we got interrupted."

"Yes, it was a pity. You say you only know the work me, but I don't know anything about you at all."

"What do you want to know?"

"Lots, like what you do on your day off, whether you're single, what you like doing outside of work, how you became a line manager at Tyn-T?" I keep rambling on until he interrupts me.

"I can answer one of those questions." He takes my drink from my hand and moves into me again. His touch is amazing, intensifying the longer we are connected. He is a perfect kisser, moving through the steps as if it is a well-choreographed dance.

I pull back and kiss the palm of his hand.

"Should we be doing this here where everyone can see us? Aren't you worried we'll get caught again?"
This could get complicated.

"Do you not like it?" Is all he offers before gently kissing me on the cheek, the lips the nose. "No one here knows us, and they don't care what we are doing." He repeats the kiss.

"It's getting late and unlike you, I need to work tomorrow. So, what are you doing tomorrow?" I whisper, trying to breathe between each word, his touch making it almost impossible.

"I have things to do too." He is not really listening to me, his focus is physical.

"Like what?" I manage, while moving in perfect time with him. We engage passionately but discreetly, the sensations rippling through my body. The control almost gone. "I have appointments," he offers, but I no longer care. The need I am feeling for this man, is verging on pain and turns into frustration. I pull slightly away to allow oxygen back into my body.

"I want you," he says softly. "You are intoxicating."

He lets out a quiet moan.

"I want you too," I confess. "Please tell me you are single."

"Of course I am single, do you really think I would be doing this with you if I wasn't?"

"It has been known to happen."

"It's not my style."

I stop resisting the urge to breathe. The desire to know more about him is replaced by my desire for him. The butterflies are soothed by the scotch I can taste from his lips. We ignore the drinks being topped up. Last orders are politely offered, and we realise how late it is and how empty the lounge has become. We collect our coats and move outside. The evening air makes me want this man even more. I cannot keep my hands off him and while we wait for a taxi, I give him no choice but to wrap himself around me in an extremely passionate embrace, and one final kiss to remember the evening by.

– CHAPTER 9 –

An annoying chirping sound brings me out of my deep, drunken sleep. I do not recognise this sound but still reach for my phone, nope, not my phone. It is my Caitem phone and on the other end is Poh making sure I am up and on my way to our session, and to remind me we are meeting at the park. Poh does not usually ring me to ensure I make the session, maybe she knows I was out last night, maybe Caitem really does have eyes everywhere. The way Michael spoke about Caitem made me believe they always know what their recruits are doing.

Although my head is pounding, and I cannot remember what day it is, my body switches to autopilot. With all the excitement of last night, the alcohol, the lines, and the lack of sleep, I am surprised I responded to my phone at all. Poh will take one look at me and devise a plan to make me feel the most amount of pain in the shortest amount of time.

I draw on the magic powers of a shower, toothpaste, mouthwash, coffee, coffee, and more coffee, a banana, a second banana, and somehow miraculously make it on time. I now do not think the second banana was a good idea.

It only takes a second for Poh to release a verbal lashing, making me feel like a five-year-old caught throwing breakfast down the toilet. I try to explain, but there are no excuses. She reminds me that Caitem comes first.

The warm-up run hurts and I have lost the little

coordination I had. I might still be drunk. Every step on the pavement rattles my dehydrated brain but somehow, I manage to keep it together and keep everything in. I am not so lucky during the actual training. During the burpee set, I am sick, twice. This still has no effect on Poh, but I am determined. Through sheer stubbornness, I complete all drills with grit and attitude, not wanting her to get the better of me. My mind and body are no longer my own. I move on instruction, ignoring the clock, and am surprised when the torture ends, and I am still in one piece.

Before being dismissed, she takes the opportunity to remind me of my commitments and informs me I must see her again today, at five, at FitUs. To demand a second session must be one of those consequences, a Caitem punishment. I ask why, and she offers no explanation. How will I get through a second session of training? Only a professional sports person could go through this torture twice in one day.

As I return to FitUs to shower and change, I feel sick again. My stomach is empty and although I know my body is a temple, I need the stodgiest food possible. A bacon sandwich, maybe even two, and a very large double-shot coffee.

By the time I make it to my desk, I feel as though I have already done a full day's work. Relieved to be finally sitting down, and armed with my coffee, bacon sandwiches and no one screaming instructions at me, I get stuck in.

Lita strolls in with not a care in the world, punctuality is not her strong point. She looks at me, looks at my food and starts laughing.

"Here, I bought a spare," I say, holding up my second sandwich.

"A spare? How many did you buy?"

"Two. I inhaled one and it seems to have done the trick, so you can have it."

"Does it have cheese?"

"Cheese, no, that would make me feel worse."

"Thanks, but I need cheese. Grab your coffee and let's go." I muster all my energy to follow.

"So, missy, tell me. What's going on with you and Jake?"

Mr Blue Eyes is Jake Langley, but he's Mr Blue Eyes to me.

"Well, nothing to tell really, you saw the extent of it."

"So that was it? You were trying to wipe each other's faces off and you say that's it? You didn't hang around after we left?" She is not going to let this one go until she gets a satisfying answer.

"Fine, we had a few more drinks at Shoreditch House and when that shut, we went to a members' only lounge bar and talked until the very early hours. Well, we mostly talked. I then went home, on my own as I had a training session this morning," I say casually, hoping this is enough detail to satisfy her.

"On your own, you say?"

"Yes, definitely on my own. Even if we both wanted more, it didn't move that way. God, I hope it does soon though."

"Jake's hot and you look awesome together. So, are

you two an item? Will there be more? Have you made plans?" The barrage of questions is making me dizzy.

"He's really hot and it starts with those eyes. I hope it goes somewhere but he's our line manager, which makes it awkward, and I don't really know anything about him. He doesn't give much away. Do you know much about him?"

"Nah, he does keep to himself but he's a good manager. You sure you went home alone?" She persists. I laugh, rolling my eyes but not answering her question. "Fine, how did you manage to do training this morning?"

"Look at me! I threw up twice, I'm struggling, and I'm glad Jake isn't in today to see this. Speaking of men, are you seeing anyone at the moment, or is there anyone you're interested in?"

"Hahaha, nice try."

"So, is that a no, or I'm not going to tell you?"

"We have to organise something so you and Jake can be in the same place again." A typical Lita I'm-not-answering-your-question response.

"Fine, don't tell me. You know you can tell me anything and it won't go anywhere. Look what you know about Jake and me. If that got out, there could be trouble for both of us. It has surprised me that as a line manager he would go there, has he done this sort of thing before?" I ask.

"Not that I know or have heard of."

"If you do hear anything please let me know. By the way, did you know I have an annual leave day the same day as the Toadstool launch?"

"That's convenient," Lita laughs.

"It wasn't planned that way, but with all the changes we had recently, the dates ended up lining up that way."

"That's what they all say. Can you change your day off?"

"Usually I would, but this time I have tickets to Wimbledon, Centre Court, men's semi-finals."

"Do you have a spare ticket?"

"Ha ha, could you imagine what they would say if we both said we wouldn't be here, Sparkles would be elated."

"I could be conveniently sick."

"Do you really think it would launch if neither of us were there?"

"No chance. Anyway, I have a holiday coming up. I'm going to Ibiza, to p-a-r-t-y." She rattles off the names of nightclubs, and DJs I have never heard of. "Jake and Cari sitting in a tree, k-i-s-s-i-n-g."

"How old are you, twelve?" I respond, as we head back to the office. I love the fact that she does not take everything seriously. I could take a leaf out of her book.

Throughout the day, I see the other project managers looking as I feel. The dinner had the desired outcome, and the project managers are even getting along better. Before the dinner, most of our conversations were about work. Now that we know a little more about one another, we talk about families, hobbies and common interests, sometimes forgetting the projects altogether.

The client services team comment throughout the day,

'hard night last night', 'wow, you look rubbish' and 'do you think you should be here?' but it does not stop their stupid questions about things they should already know, Noddy is still the worst offender.

The day becomes a haze of answering emails, constructing status reports and luckily, only one formal meeting with Tod and Lita. The meeting to start planning for Lita to be the go-to girl for this project and launch day.

It is almost five and most people leave for the weekend. The ones remaining are those who have just returned from an extended pub lunch. These are usually the creatives who believe it is their right to blow off the afternoon and charge this time to a project under a 'conceptual idea generation' code.

Lita wants me to go to the pub, but I refuse, offering a personal training session as my excuse.

"On a Friday afternoon? You already had a training session this morning!" Then I catch the flicker in her eye, and she starts to grill me. "You're seeing Jake, aren't you!"

I cannot be bothered arguing and give her a teenager response of 'whatever'.

Once left in peace, I reluctantly change into my gym gear, and head over to FitUs. I meet Poh in the reception area and she instructs me to follow her. We are not running and have passed the park. We stop at a swanky, fresh juice bar close to the park. The air is filled with citric aromas enticing you to order a juice. Poh orders two, mine is much greener than hers, we take a seat.

"This is a safe area, and we can speak freely. But always

be aware of your surroundings. How did you pull up from this morning?"

"Okay," I answer, still annoyed for pushing me so hard, even if it was my own fault.

"You need to treat your training seriously. You should not be partying the evening before. You should know better than that."

"How do you know I was out partying?"

"Really?"

"Okay, but it was a work function, and this is still new to me. Believe me, I now know what it means, and I don't want to go through a session like that, ever again."

"I have brought you here today because we have an assignment for you."

"A what?"

"We have completed a profile on a person of interest occupying a role at Tyn-T and we need more information." Poh pauses.

"What?" The world has stopped, the walls of the juice bar are gone, the other people are gone, there is no noise, and it is only Poh and me sitting at a table.

"Caitem has an assignment for you, and this is a briefing session."

"You can't be serious. I can't have an assignment so soon, no way."

"I am serious. This is a briefing session and Caitem has an assignment for you."

"I'm not ready for this. I've only just started my

training! As you saw this morning, it isn't going that great."
She holds up her hand and tells me to take a drink of my juice.

"It's a tailing exercise. We need to know who this person connects with in the agency. Who he speaks with, corridor conversations, lunch dates, sporting engagements, meetings, anything. We have a profile for you and instructions on how to infiltrate, but remember, no improvising. You will report to me daily and if you need to speak to me by phone, only use the Caitem phone. You can contact me anytime, day or night." She is business-like, and this is obviously quite normal for her. For me on the other hand, this is the complete opposite of normal.

"I'm not ready for this, it's too soon. I don't know how to tail someone or infiltrate, especially if I don't know them, or even if I do."

"You are ready for this and it's not too soon. Caitem knows best and would not give you an assignment if they did not believe you could carry it out."

"Caitem cannot know how I feel right now, how unready I am. I don't agree. I can't do this, I need more time, can I have more time? Surely there's someone else who can do this assignment?"

"No, you are ready, and this is your assignment, and you will do it. I need to run you through the profile. Keep drinking the juice. It'll help with the shock."

"Why, what's in it?"

"Vegetables."

"And?"

"Wheatgrass."

"And?"

"Apple juice."

"And?"

"And nothing."

"How are vegetables, wheatgrass and apple juice going to help? The only way it will, is if you add a shot of vodka."

"Cari, drink it, you need the vitamins, I am not convinced you even know what a vegetable is. This is a serious matter. I need you to be calm so I can brief you."

"I'm as calm as I will ever be, what is my assignment?"

"As I said, we need information about a person of interest who occupies a role at Tyn-T."

"What sort of information?"

"Who he communicates with in the office, corridors, online, meetings, anything."

"Okay, but how do I do that?"

"We have worked up a profile and have instructions to get you started."

"Okay, then who is this person of interest?"

"A Mr Brett Ferguson."

"You are kidding now! This has got to be a joke." I start to laugh, a roaring laughter that catches even me by surprise.

"So, you know who he is already?"

"Actually, no. I made an accidental corporate announcement trying to find out who he is and what he does."

"Why?"

"Because he sends about ten emails a day on industry

news and no one around me knew who he was. I replied to one of his emails and asked him direct, but instead of sending a reply only to him, I sent it to the entire company."

"And?" Poh replies with a smirk. Was that an attempt at a smile or does she already know about the email?

"Now, even if I ask someone who knows him, they won't tell me. They think it's fun for me to find out for myself. If I really do need to find him it's going to get weird."

"This scenario works to your advantage."

"I haven't been able to find out who he is, and I sent the email weeks ago. What makes you think it'll be easier now that I have to find information about him? I can't believe it's him of all people. What on earth has he done to be in this position?"

She does not answer the last part of my question but explains this is what Caitem does. They provide the background information and how to initiate and continue communications with the person of interest. In this case, Brett is part of the events team, and my first task is to join this group. The only information Caitem is interested in, is information directly from Brett.

"One of my friends knows who he is, but she won't tell me either."

"Who?" She asks.

"Lita, why?" I reply curiously and somewhat reluctantly. "Do you think she's part of this?"

"Don't worry about Lita, your assignment is Brett. Join the events team and start learning who his connections are, and report to me daily."

"What has he done that made him a person of interest?"

"An ongoing investigation has identified Brett as a possible connection, and as such he needs to be investigated. As it's an investigation piece it's suitable for a level zero. This is serious and I expect you to take it seriously. If it turns out he is involved, it may be reallocated. We won't know until we understand the circles he moves in."

"Does this mean we're not doing a training session now?" I change the subject, realising we have been sitting here for a while and it is getting late.

"No, we need to go through the profile to make sure you understand it." She hands me a folder with a FitUs Training Plan cover.

Inside are two pages starting with the confidentiality blurb. The second page is Brett Ferguson's profile, including his birth date, physical characteristics and a photo. He is not bad looking and he looks familiar. I may have crossed paths with him in the office, although I do not think so. I pick up the photo and look at it closer, trying to work out why I feel I have seen him.

Oh no, it cannot be. I freeze, look at Poh, look back at the photo, and start to feel sweat break out all over my body.

"I am glad you have recognised him," Poh says.

"Recognise him? Oh My God!"
I cannot breathe.

"I can see by your reaction you recognise him from

Thailand."

"What do you know exactly?" I ask, blushing.

"This is why you came onto our radar in Thailand. Mr Ferguson is a person of interest we have been monitoring for a while. We believe he is connected to something, but we are having difficulties finding the links. When you had intimate relations, we had to profile you and you were cleared. We continued to monitor Mr Ferguson, but there was nothing of interest, until recently, at which point the process to recruit you began."

"Really, and there was no one else who could have done it?"

"You were put through the process, and now we are here."

"So, the person I made the company-wide announcement about, is the same person I had a holiday fling with, in Thailand, and now you're saying I have to reconnect with him?"

"I suspect he already knows you are at Tyn-T, and that is why he has kept his cover. It will be as uncomfortable for him as it is for you, but it will play out in your favour."

"So, what am I going to do?"

"We will go through the rest of his profile to make sure you are prepared."

"Seriously, knowing all this you still think I'm the right person for this assignment?"

"Yes, it's because of all of this. I need you to memorise his profile and stop questioning the process."

Brett Ferguson is the Tyn-T Communications Officer. He is interested in cars, Thai cooking and he reads Stephen King. He is a low-risk person of interest, and my instructions are to join the events team and identify any connections he has, no matter how insignificant. That is not for me to decide.

"The only thing I know about him are the emails he sends out. Do you want a copy when he sends them?"

"No, we already have his emails tagged. Now, if you don't have any more questions, this briefing session is over. See you Sunday."

The weekend has not come soon enough. I am only capable of collapsing on my couch to clear the craziness of recent events out of my head. It has been an incredible twenty-four hours. I have been launched into this parallel world of persons of interest, tracking, rules, training and Mr Blue Eyes, who despite it all, is still very much occupying my mind. I want, need, to see him again. He has cast a spell on me, and I yearn for him, a sensation I have not felt for quite some time, and that was a lifetime ago.

Sure, there have been other men, there are always other men, but until you feel this sort of connection you do not realise the others were superficial. Does he feel the same? Is he as beautiful and as strong on the inside as he is on the outside? Are his kisses and touches reflective of who he has made me believe he is? I need to know everything about him. Does he play sports, watch sports, have a hobby, have a pet, what are his quirky habits, is there a food forbidden from his fridge?

The couch is my friend, just me, my duvet and pillow, the perfect party. My eyes close and I drift in and out of sleep, but my mind continues to tick over as I imagine the intensity of next week. I wrap myself deeper into my surroundings looking for comfort, but my stomach still churns. I cannot opt out of Caitem, and I cannot run back to Australia. How can I balance delivering my projects for Tyn-T with my commitments to Caitem? My head races with thoughts of Tyn-T, Jake, Caitem, and Brett, and then I am out.

– CHAPTER 10 –

Apart from my Sunday training session with Poh, I spent the weekend in hibernation to give myself time to work through recent events. I came to London to experience different things, to inject some adventure into my life, and so far, I have not been disappointed.

It is Monday morning. I am energised and feeling stable enough to tackle what lies ahead. To get a jump on the week, I arrive at Tyn-T earlier than usual. The office is so quiet I can hear it breathe, and the creaking of its bones as it begins to wake up and face the new day.

My weekend clarity and the new training regime have increased my energy levels and I am seeing the world through new eyes. Even the discovery of more missing papers from my desk does not worry me, as my new can-do attitude makes me determined to unravel this mystery today. Since joining Caitem, I am suspicious of everyone and everything. Part of me suspects, as ludicrous as it sounds, I might be watched and that is the reason my papers go missing.

By the time the team roll in, it feels like lunchtime. I have spent more time than usual on Brett's emails, trying to uncover any hidden messages, but as I do not know what to look for, I decide to leave it to the experts, Caitem.

When Lita arrives, I ask her about joining the events team. She is very excited and before I can say any more, she sends an email to the team coordinator. Good ol' Lita enthusiasm. I soon receive a welcoming email from the events coordinator, Charlie, as well as a meeting invite to attend their next session.

Across the room, I see Mr Blue Eyes in a serious conversation with the Managing Partner for my account, Bill. They look intense, however, this only adds to Mr Blue Eyes' appeal.

My eyes linger inappropriately, taking every inch of him in. He is wearing blue denim jeans, brown leather shoes, and a black v-neck jumper with a white t-shirt underneath. The sleeves are slightly pulled up, revealing toned arms and his watch. The conversation ends and he begins walking in my direction. Be calm, do not blush. Be calm, do not blush, act casual, composure, breathe. My pep-talk is not helping.

"Good morning. Do you have a moment, is this a good time for a chat?" He asks professionally, smiling with his eyes and acknowledging the rest of the team with a nod.

"Sure," I return casually, with an equally professional smile, realising Lita is studying every move. Lita's interest has not gone unnoticed by Mr Blue Eyes, and I will need to make sure she is less obvious. As I stand to follow him, I throw her a 'what are you doing?' glare. Knowing what she is thinking has made a silly schoolgirl grin take over my face.

"How are you?" He asks politely, once we're out of earshot.

"Good thanks, and how are you?" I reciprocate the greeting and the politeness as we find a vacant meeting room.

"I'm good too, thanks. I just wanted to let you know I met with Bill, and he was not aware of the actual behaviours of some members of his team. In fact, he thought you were not a good fit for his account and maybe even Tyn-T, basing his judgement purely on what his team have been saying. I set him straight, and by the end of the conversation Bill was quite angry and he's going to do something about it."

"Wow, this is a surprise. What's he going to do, what can he do, and if you had not intervened could I have been fired?"

"You will not be fired, he has a voice but not the power. Bill should not have purely taken the word of his team, and now he is going to do what he should have done in the first place and find out what is really going on. If the current structure isn't working, he's going to look into changing the team, swapping non-digital with digital and reducing the number of client services on this account."

"Ouch, that's not going to go down well, although it'd definitely be a good thing. Can we make sure we keep Sheree? We work really well together. Oh, and if Bill doesn't have the power, who does?"

"Firing someone is never down to a single person, but you don't not need to worry about it. It is not going to happen. Bill was unaware how digitally inept some of his team members are, and he's making this a priority. Any changes will not affect Sheree. She has a solid relationship with the client. So, hang in there, it'll be sorted quickly. Bill can't afford to let anything jeopardise this account."

"Well, I better get back to it. Thanks for letting me know. See ya," I say, heading to the door.

"I look forward to seeing you again. Let's make it soon," he says softly, inches away from my ear. I feel his breath on my cheek.

He peers out the door to make sure we are alone, before reaching for my arm, moving his hand down to my wrist and lingering on my fingers. Then he leaves. His eyes told me if we were somewhere more private, he would have taken this opportunity.

I leave the room with goose bumps until I see Lita walking away with a pile of papers, and an 'I am up to no good' expression on her face.

Like a cat, Lita is moving through the office. I follow her, a few paces behind, stopping every now and again pretending to check my phone. Even though Lita has not seen me, everyone else is watching with enthusiasm. Their faces telling it all, obviously entertained as they switch their attention from me to Lita then back to me. She reaches the shredder and starts feeding sheets into it.

"Hi," I say.

"Hi," Lita responds, startled, which turns into a nervous chuckle.

"What are you doing?" I ask, noticing some of my work on top of the pile.

"Getting rid of some old papers, best to shred them. It's company policy."

I grab my sheet of paper. "Is this from my desk?" I ask

waving it around and realising I was only working on it this morning.

"Yes, but I thought it was old and I wanted to make sure it was disposed of properly. I don't want a client to see it lying around."

"Why would a client see it lying around, and why would they care? Lita, what's going on?"

"Nothing, I just told you, it's for security reasons."

"Lita-a-a-a, people don't just pick papers up and shred them, it's not normal. I understand the security and confidentiality aspects of our work, more than you realise, but really?"

"Fine. I'll tell you but you have to promise to keep it to yourself, promise?"

"Of course, absolutely, who am I going to tell anyway?" This is either something funny, sinister, or Caitem related.

"I've seen random people pick things up from desks and read them, so I thought I would start shredding any papers left around." She repeats.

"You have already said that. What is the real reason? I promised not to tell anyone, c'mon. I need to know now."

'Fin-n-n-e. I just bought a shredder for home and shredding is so therapeutic, I do it as soon as I get home from work, that's what gave me the idea in the first place," she explains convincingly.

"I was not expecting that. So let me get this right. Instead of having a glass of wine to unwind, you have taken to shredding, and now you thought you would start at work, for no reason other than you like it? Are you the one who's been taking the papers off my desk?"

"Yes, as I said people just walk around and pick things up and I can't just shred nothing, it has to be something worth shredding, something that needs to be disposed of securely. I don't have anything left to shred in my flat and I have been missing it. And by the way I usually shred while having a glass of wine." She says chuckling.

"You're bonkers! How can anyone get addicted to shredding, you loon?" I say, now laughing hysterically, attracting plenty of attention, which makes us laugh to the point of tears. I grab my papers from her pile, promise to give her all my shred-worthy papers, and leave her to it.

As Mr Blue Eyes promised, a review of the client services team must already be on its way as Noddy, Gonzo and Sparkles are whispering amongst themselves, and one by one, meeting with Bill.

I overhear a conversation that the argumentative Sparkles, will be moving to a print account once project Toadstool is implemented, and she is not happy about it. I would not be happy either if I was her, but as I am me, I am ecstatic. I will get more work done as I will not have to answer her endless questions, and if there are fewer of them doing the same amount of work, they will be busier and less likely to nosey into what I am doing.

My computer pings to remind me it is time for my inaugural events meeting and I am nervous about Brett. If I recognised him from a photo, he is sure to recognise me. Even though quite some time has passed since Thailand, not all our encounters were under the influence. Surely, I left some level of impression on him, in a good way.

But do I want him to recognise me? Yikes, double edged sword. I think my ego can take a hit. Please do not recognise me. Or maybe it is the opposite, he has already recognised me, and has been going out of his way to avoid me, which means this could be as uncomfortable for him, as it will be for me. On the other hand, I am intrigued to see what this man is about, how he behaves and maybe an insight as to why he is a person of interest.

I cautiously enter the room scanning for his face, but I am pretty sure he is not here. I introduce myself to those closest to me. Lita arrives fashionably late as usual, probably caused by not reaching her shredding quota. Once everyone is seated, I scan the room again. He is definitely not here, and his name is not mentioned as an attendee. Has Caitem got this wrong?

"This is a small team for an agency of this size." I comment to the room.

"If this was all we had, we would not achieve much. Not everyone attends the meetings but still help with events. We have another seven regulars, and there are others we can call on if needed," The coordinator, Charlie explains.

This meeting is focused on the next big event, the ten-year anniversary of Tyn-T, being referred to as 'Versary', a play on the words 'very important anniversary'.

Due to the importance of the anniversary, the event is

to match it stature. It could well be the biggest event Tyn-T has hosted for quite some time. Everyone on the team is needed to participate in the organisation in order to pull it off.

I suggest the absent members should get additional tasks. Everyone agrees, and another Versary meeting, this time mandatory for all, is scheduled for the following day. This means, if Caitem has got it right, I will finally meet Brett.

The next day, I am late for the Versary meeting and interrupt what seems to be a serious conversation. Looking around the room, my eyes lock with the man who slightly resembles the man in the photo.

"Ah, here's the person who's been keen to meet me. I'm Brett Ferguson, pleased to meet you." Brett reaches out to shake my hand. "Cari wasn't shy in the way she went about trying to find out who I was. I hope I don't disappoint." He pauses, allowing the synchronised laughs to have their moment, and now everyone's eyes are fixed on me.

"I hope you don't disappoint either," I reply wittily, which causes a new round of laughs, and turns everyone's attention back to Brett. He acknowledges with a slight squint and a smirk.

His photo does not do him justice as he is hotter than I remember, but not in a Mr Blue Eyes kind of way. Brett has more of a mysterious, bad boy vibe.

I apologise for the interruption, sit in the closest empty seat and the conversation continues. I find it hard to concentrate and even harder not to look at Brett. Each time I sneak a peek, he catches me, giving me an annoyingly confident grin in return. I cannot tell whether he remembers me, or if this is due to the unfortunate email.

I am intrigued by him, and by the fact I am the only one at Tyn-T who knows his potential secret. Actually, if you include Thailand, then there are two secrets. How hard can this assignment be?

The last item on the agenda is to form task squads, and from out of left field, Lita nominates to team up with Brett and me. I can only assume this is her way of continuing the email debacle. We stay behind to discuss our task and Brett volunteers to start looking at client information, past and present.

Lita and Brett are getting along very well, considering she first denied knowing who he was. The good thing is that I can finally report something back to Poh, even if it seems unimportant. But as I was told, it is not up to me to decide what is important and what is not.

The next morning begins with another training session, following the same routine. Meet Poh at FitUs reception, jog to the park, stretch, exercise, and talk. She tells me more about Caitem and my responsibilities and I provide her my daily update.

"Joining the events teams is working out. As luck would have it, I am in a sub task group of three with Brett."

"Who is the third?"

"Lita, it was her doing that this happened, a good coincidence which has made it easier for me."

"Is that all?"

"I will be meeting up with Brett and Lita later today to discuss our teams' progress."

"Where will the meeting be?"

"Not sure, maybe just around a desk or in a meeting room."

"Do you have anything else other than Lita?"

"No."

"You need to move faster, we need to know who he is connected to and he needs to be sharing information with you."

"Why does he have to share information with me?"

"When he is relaxed, he may mention names, places he has been to, and you might overhear phone calls."

"Okay. I have only just met him, but I will see what I can do. So far, the only other person I can report on is Lita. You don't think she is involved with this do you?"

"Lita is not a concern for you, your focus is Brett, understood."

"Yes, understood."

This is not going to be easy. We have a relationship, a weird one, and I cannot see that changing to an information sharing level, any time soon. What if we do appear friendly and people start speculating, especially if they find out about Thailand. What about Mr Blue Eyes? If a rumour starts about Brett, how will he react, and how will it affect what we have, whatever we have? I cannot tell him the truth or even allude to it. Caitem comes first and I would be breaking the confidentiality agreement.

"Shelley, hi, it's Cari, is this a good time for you?"

"Sure, how's it going?"

"You will never guess what happened to me today."

"What?" She asks, intrigued.

"Remember the guy I hooked up with in Thailand?"

"Yeah, how can I not? You two were pretty full on."

"Well, he works at the same place as I do."

"He does not? Of all the places." She says laughing out loud.

"I know, right."

"Does he recognise you?"

"I don't know."

"He must! You two were at it for days."

"I know, it's bad if he does and bad if he doesn't."

"Maybe you can pick up from where you left of." Her laughter not subsiding.

"Erm, I don't think so, and you know I am into someone else!"

"Erm, when in London!"

"You are terrible, I am not doing something with one when I have my eyes on someone else, especially when they are both at the same place."

"Live a little."

"I think I have lived a lot since leaving the sunny shores of Australia."

"Then dating two men at the same time can't hurt."

"It's not going to happen, I'm going now, seeya."

As soon as I see Lita, I remind her we need to check

in with Brett, to make sure he has started collating the client information. She accuses me of being keen. I remind her there is not much time to get everything done and besides, it is a nice distraction from project Toadstool.

Brett sits one floor below us, which holds the boardrooms, the CEO's office, his executive assistant, and the rest of the Communications team. His desk is nicely nestled by a window allowing in natural light, but also means no one can see his screen. He also has a perfect view of the floor and can see everyone approaching. My healthy paranoia kicking in again.

"Hi girls," he says.

"Hi," we echo.

"How's the archive trawling coming along, anything we can do?" Lita asks.

"I've been making a spreadsheet of all the major accounts past and present, and I think we could do some interesting things with them."

"Great, can we look at the spreadsheet?" I ask, so I can get a look at his screen and desk.

I only temporarily glance at the spreadsheet, as I notice he has an active instant messenger session that is flashing the name 'Topsy'. Who on earth is Topsy?

Brett, clearly not comfortable with us invading his space, closes his laptop and claims he will put the file somewhere we can all access. For normal people, this would be their cue to leave. Not for us.

Lita riffles through papers on his desk and comments

on the next newsletter draft. I ask if he writes all the newsletters, even the ones sent by the CEO. I want to find out if he was behind the snippet 'Who is Brett Ferguson?'

He just smiles. It is a simple question, and most would provide a simple answer like 'yes' or 'no', but not Brett.

We soon run out of reasons to hang around and recommend a working lunch to start brainstorming ideas.

"Have I lived up to your expectations?" Brett asks confidently, leaning back in his chair. This time, there is something in his eyes that makes me think he may remember Thailand.

"You haven't done anything yet."

"Haven't I?"

"Digging into archives isn't anything special." I respond keeping the conversation safe.

"I wasn't referring to the archives."

"We have to go, seeya." Was all I could answer, as that statement implied, he may actually remember, and I was not keen on finding out in front of Lita.

"Okay then. See you ladies later."

My gut is screaming he knows. Equally as odd, during my exchange with Brett, Lita seemed quieter than usual, not like her at all.

"Are you okay?" I ask as we head into the lift.

"Yeah, fine."

"You sure? You seem quieter than usual, you have lost your pep."

"Yeah, I'm cool, just tired."

"Have you been out?"

"A bit, but work is also nuts. I am still trying to handover my other work, which is more of me doing and less handover."

"That's crap, is there anything I can do, give you some papers to shred?" I ask chuckling, this brings back the Lita I know and love.

Back at our desks, we see Noddy packing up her belongings which gives me mixed feelings. Very happy to be seeing the back of her, but part of me, only a small part feels sorry for her as this move cannot be good for her.

"Are you going somewhere?" I ask jovially.

"Actually I am. Another account needs my help, and we don't need two account directors on this account. It makes sense for me to join the other team and it's a good opportunity for me."

I wonder how much choice she really had. "What sort of account are you moving to?" I enquire.

"It's a print account, but they want to try and go after some of the digital work."

I do a mental victory dance but try not to show it. "Well, it's a shame you're leaving us, you'll be missed. The other account must be really pleased you're joining them." Sometimes, you just have to play the game.

"Ah thanks, I'm sad to be moving from this account too."

So now, we are down to one digital-savvy Account Director, Sheree, and the Account Manager Sparkles, who will leave at the end of project Toadstool. This is certainly a good day.

Armed with a folder, Brett collects Lita and me from our floor and we head out to lunch. I do not introduce him to my neighbours and avoid all eye contact. Letting people know this is Brett Ferguson would only be asking for trouble. We follow Brett to a café.

"So do you come here often?" I jokingly ask Brett.

"Yes."

"Wow, man of many words. How long have you been working at Tyn-T for?"

"Long enough," he replies matter of fact.

"How did you get into Communications? Are you a copywriter?"

"Fell into it," he replies, not offering any additional information.

"For someone in the field of communications you certainly have a grasp on the English language," I retort sarcastically but playfully.

"Hey kids, enough of the chit-chat, we're meant to be discussing Versary," Lita interjects.

Throughout lunch, I continue to try and spark up non-Versary conversation with Brett, but get nothing from him and the occasional annoyed look from Lita. We do however come up with a brilliant idea, and a very excited Lita immediately rings Charlie. She loves it too. We are super excited.

Brett just smiles and finishes eating his lunch. I wonder what is going with him, and why he is a person of interest. I wonder what his secret is, and most importantly, I still do not know if he remembers me.

As we casually stroll back to the office, I try again to get more information out of him, but again, I hit a brick wall. Throughout lunch, Lita has been acting like a jealous girlfriend, or as if she is protecting him. Surely, she is not tangled up in whatever he could be tangled up in. She cannot be romantically involved with him because it was not that long ago, she claimed not to know him.

Maybe this crush is recent and she is embarrassed to say, although she knows all about about Mr blue eyes and me. Maybe this is her way of letting me know.

- CHAPTER 11 -

Today's training grind is replaced by a biometric review to see how far I have progressed since starting the 'getting me into shape' regime, and I am ecstatic with the results.

I have lost fifteen pounds and many inches across my entire body and the changes are noticeable. More importantly, I can feel the difference. It is the little things I have noticed, like being able to dodge people easier on crowded streets, better focus, and a sharper memory. My lungs no longer feel as if they are going to pop out of my chest whenever I run. I can get through a morning session without being sick, even if I have been out the night before, I have become much better at hiding my sins. In real terms, I have dropped two dress sizes. I am still a long way from matching Gillian's size zero, but it is not a goal of mine.

At the end of the evaluation, we leave FitUs with a moderate jog and I assume we are heading for the park. However, we continue straight past and into the juice bar. Poh orders our standard drinks.

"How is the assignment progressing?" Poh asks not wasting any time.

"I haven't found out much about Brett, or who he talks to, other than Lita, and I saw a conversation on his computer with someone called Topsy."

"Do you know who Topsy is?"

"No, do you?"

"Is that all?" She asks ignoring my question but I am never surprised anymore. I am more surprised when a question is answered.

"Brett doesn't really talk about himself. Do you want me to find out who Topsy is?"

"No, Caitem has already started profiling him."

"So, you know who he is?"

"Yes."

"Who?"

"It is not important. Is there anything else?"

"No, that's all so far."

"This isn't enough progress," Poh claims not hiding her irritation.

"You need to step it up. To have only one contact is not enough," Poh says in her usual serious tone.

"There are two if you include Lita," I correct her.

"It's not good enough, you need to step this up," she reiterates.

"How do I do that? I've joined the events team and I'm working directly with him. He doesn't share much. Maybe he doesn't speak to many people, and he isn't involved in whatever this might be after all," I offer, thinking I have all the answers.

"This is the problem we have with Brett. We can't find his connections, yet we know they are there. The longer this takes, the more important it becomes. We must know the circles he moves in. You need to get closer to him. Caitem is blocked and Caitem does not like being blocked."

"You make it sound serious. Is it still a level zero assignment? And what do you mean exactly, by getting closer to him?" I enquire, picking up her sense of urgency.

"It is always serious and no, the classification has not changed. Being on the events team is not getting the results we need. You need to get him away from the office, develop stronger ties, personal ties. If he's involved with something he may not make his connections at work. You need to see if he has contact with anyone outside."

"That could be tricky. What if he remembers Thailand and thinks I'm interested in that again and then pulls back because of it?" I'm hoping to convince Poh to change this assignment or give it to someone else.

"You need to get him away from the office. He won't turn you down. We have profiled him and can anticipate his response. Thailand works in your favour. Remember, this is a job, and you need to get into an environment where he relaxes his guard. See who contacts him away from the office, try to get into his flat, see if there are any papers lying around, listen to phone calls. He's more likely to be less vigilant in his own surroundings."

"How can you anticipate his response? Maybe he doesn't remember Thailand, nothing he has said or done makes me think otherwise. Besides, I'm also sort of seeing someone. What happens if he finds out I'm interested in someone else?" I ask slightly raising my voice.

"And your point is?"

"And it could get messy. Brett might find out and then he could back off. Or worse, Jake might suspect something is going on and end it with me. I don't want that to happen. I really like him."

"Caitem comes first, before partners. You know this and you should not need to be reminded. Brett is the only priority."

"But what happens if Brett has a girlfriend and causes a problem and compromises everything?" I continue to look for reasons to convince Poh.

"If he has a girlfriend, we should know this already. You should have already confirmed this by now. Can you see why we need to step this up?"

"Does he have a girlfriend?" I ask curiously, ignoring the fact that it is actually my job to find out.

"We don't believe so, nothing serious."

"But what if he doesn't go for it, and he's not interested?"

"Our profiling leads us to believe he would be interested, so make it work. He was interested once, and the interest will still be there. We are done here," Poh says, getting up to leave.

"Goodbye." I say and remain seated, thinking she is right. If I was doing a better job, I would know if he had a girlfriend. Any little interest I show Brett, he is going to think I want to pick up where we left of in Thailand, how do I balance this? How do I get closer to Brett without jeopardising what I am building with Mr Blue Eyes? I cannot cheat and I cannot explain it to him. He will know something is not right, he is too observant not to.

If something more does happen with Brett, maybe I should end it with Mr Blue Eyes. Oh no, I cannot end it with him, I cannot pretend I prefer Brett, I do not want to end it. My heart sinks and I am on my own to deal with this. There is no one I can talk to. I have to get to work but that is the last place I want to be.

"Hi Shelley, can you talk?"

"Sure, what's up?"

"You know, life, it seems to be getting complicated." I say despondently.

"Really, I thought you were loving the adventures of London."

"I am, mostly, but sometimes it just gets hard."

"You having trouble with Jake?"

"No, well, not that I am aware of."

"Then what's up?"

"Another guy, maybe, well not really."

"What do you mean another guy, I thought you were really into Jake?"

"I am but this other one could come between us," I confide, strolling reluctantly towards the office.

"But how? He can only come between you if you let him. Is this other guy the one from Thailand?"

"Yes."

"I am not sure I am seeing the problem; do you now want both of them?

"No, I only want Jake."

"Still not seeing the problem, you know you are a big girl and can make your own choices."

"Ha ha, very funny, but yes I am hearing what you are saying," I agree. Except that I can't, in fact, make my own choice in regards to this. I remember the confidentiality agreement and whether this is in some way crossing that line. "Of course I have a choice. Thanks Shelley, I feel better already."

I hang up feeling deflated, and trudge the last few streets to the office. Heading towards my desk, I see Mr Blue Eyes sitting in Lita's chair, which is empty because it is still too early for her. His gaze is fixed on me, and I casually approach my chair, sit, turn on my computer, take off my coat, and drink my coffee. He looks even more beautiful than usual and all I want to do is hold him tight, but I cannot help feeling he is going to slip away.

"How was your weekend?" He asks.

"You're in early. To what do I owe the pleasure?" I respond, keeping it strictly business.

"I'm usually in early. Are you okay, you seem a little flat?"

"I have a lot on my mind, but I'm fine." I beam, forcing the biggest smile so he drops this line of questioning before he sees my secret anguish. I did not realise how much I felt for him until the conversation about getting closer to Brett, and what it might mean for my budding relationship with Jake.

The realisation of this being more than an office crush has hit hard. I am truly besotted with this man and do not want to give him up. I never thought for one moment that Caitem would be so intrusive. I assumed it would be like any other project, and Caitem like any other client. Now I see why they make you sign up to Caitem comes first.

"Alright, but you know you can talk to me about anything?"

"Thanks Jake, I know, but truly I'm okay, although that might change after you tell me why you're at my desk first thing in the morning."

"Maybe I just wanted to start my day by seeing you. You are a good distraction. If I am being truthful, my thoughts aren't always pure," he claims, looking around ensuring no one can hear our conversation.

"Jake, you can't say those things in the middle of the office!"

"I like it when you blush, but look around, there's no one here and it's perfectly natural to be speaking to one of my project managers."

"I hope you don't speak to all your project managers this way."

"Only Tommy," he jokes.

"Funny. I like to see you too, but what's the real reason you're here?"

"I told you, I wanted to see you. How are you, really?"

"I am fine, really. So why are you really here?"

"Okay, okay, but I really do like seeing you, so never hesitate to find me to discuss even the smallest of issues."

"Yes, Jake."

"How is everything on the account? Are you and Lita coping with the workload? I want to make sure you have the support you need."

"Yes, we're doing okay. Toadstool is stable but will get busier the closer we get to the launch. Lita looks after the day-to-day while I deal with issues and Alex, sometimes they are the same. Oh also, Sheree called me on my way in this morning, we have approval to commence a new project which we are calling Frogmen, to keep the amphibian theme going."

"Which piece of work is that?"

"The piece where Sheree and I went to Alex's office, and he got up and left the building halfway through our briefing session."

"Oh, that's excellent for Tyn-T. But what about you and Lita, can you handle another project right now?"

"It is not the best timing to be starting a new piece of work. As you know, the start of any project is hectic, and remember how eccentric Alex is? That alone will add more time."

"Actually, that was the answer I was hoping for."

"Really?"

"Really. That's why I'm here."

"See I knew there was a work related something you wanted to talk about," I slightly gloat. Happy that I was right.

"Shall I continue, or do you want to bathe in your own sunshine some more?" He replies. I make a gesture which indicates I am back to being professional and he should continue. "We have a new project manager who has just joined us, but I have my reservations about him. I'll give him a chance to get through probation, but I need you to keep an eye on him. I want to split him across yours and Tommy's account. It will give me the opportunity to see if he is useful. What do you think?"

"I guess I could give him a go. It could work. If he's good, then he could be an asset and help with the long list of other tasks we have."

"Good morning, good morning," Lita greets, nodding at us. Mr Blue Eyes stands, vacating her chair.

"So when shall I expect him?" I ask Mr Blue Eyes, ignoring Lita.

"I'll set up a meeting as soon as we're ready. Thanks for your help, it's much appreciated."

"Anytime, bye." I watch him leave and turn to Lita, knowing full well what she is about to say. "Before you start, he was here on business," I tell her as her grin grows wider.

"Ah ha, if you say so. Early morning visits, huh? Things must be going well."

"We have a new project, Frogman, and we're getting another project manager to run it. So there, told you it was business."

"Cool and cool, is it a he? I hope so, and I hope he is cute, we need some eye candy around here."

"You are funny, it is a he, and I hope he is good so they can actually help."

"Boring."

Mr Blue Eyes has arranged a meeting to introduce me to the new Project Manager, Corey. Corey is about twenty-five. He is attractive in an obvious pretty boy way. He dresses well and has a confident smile. If I had to label him on first impressions, I would say he is a player wannabe. He has the assets but is probably a bit too arrogant to know how to use them effectively.

Corey has had previous experience working in smaller agencies, but there is something about him that does not sit well with me. I give an overview of the account and the client and explain that he needs to be aware of Alex's habit of soliciting freebies by approaching various people on the team. He assures me he has had experience with this sort of client behaviour before. Finally, I stress the importance of giving the client an updated project plan as soon as possible.

Corey makes himself comfortable at Noddy's vacated desk. I direct him to the project folders and expect him to get stuck in, but a short while later, he is laughing loudly, dragging Sparkles and Lita into his entertainment. He is watching an online video.

Being only his second day at Tyn-T, I would have thought he would want to make a good impression.

"Everything okay, Corey?" I ask, giving him a subtle hint to get back to work.

"Yeah man, come and look at this, it's really cool, one of my friends sent it to me, it's gone viral," he chuckles.

"Sorry, can't at the moment, are you okay with

Frogman?"

"Yeah man, when do we brief the creative team?"

"As soon as Sheree writes the creative brief but she can't do that until she knows when this needs to be delivered. You need to recalculate the dates and let her know." I am sure we just discussed this.

"Cool man," he says, completely ignoring me to turn his attention back to the video.

I can see how he would have gotten away with this behaviour previously, as he has some childlike, playful, quite endearing qualities. Sparkles is taken in by him already. He is probably good at talking himself out of sticky situations due to his vast amount of practice. He seems to be one of those project managers who leads you to believe everything is going well until the very last moment, when it is revealed that the project is way behind, and you are left with one almighty mess. I hope he surprises me in a good way.

Our Versary mini squad has made good progress, mainly through Brett's research into past and present clients. We have good ideas on how these clients can be showcased and the Hilton International ballroom has been booked. The bonus of holding a party in a hotel is the option to stay the night, which allows those who usually cannot attend events, the option to stay the night and really enjoy the evening. Lita, Sheree, Kelly and I take advantage and book a suite.

Upon booking the Hilton we asked, if possible, to see an event in action. To our surprise, they found a way to make it happen, and we were invited to attend another organisation's anniversary bonanza held in the same ballroom.

Lita, Brett, the event coordinator, Charlie and I will be attending, and it is tonight. I had assumed Lita and I would go together, maybe have some dinner and pre-drinks, but she has a prior engagement and will meet me in the Hilton reception at eight.

I decide to use the opportunity to get some one-on-one time with Brett and hide behind email while doing it.

Message: Pre-party drinks

Hi Brett, As the party starts at 8, how about we get a quick drink before? Cheers, Cari.

Re: Pre-party drinks

Hi Cari, Is this your way of asking me out on a date?

I snort at his arrogance and tap out my reply: 'Drinks, not date. Is that a no?'

His response is almost immediate. ' Is it just you and me?'

I take a moment before my next reply. 'Yes, Lita is busy and I haven't asked Charlie.'

'So, I'm a second choice?'

'Forget it, I'll see you at the Hilton at 8.'

'I'll meet you at Joe's, around the corner from the Hilton at 7. I'm looking forward to our date.'

I roll my eyes and close my emails, now that I'm expected to be ready an hour earlier, I have to leave work in a hurry, bumping straight into Mr Blue Eyes.

"Where are you off to in such a hurry?"

"A few of us are going to suss out the Versary event

location. I have to be ready for seven."

"An events location, and what do you need to get ready for?" He asks with squinty eyes.

"Sorry, have to go, need to get home to change, talk to you later." And with that, I scurry out of the building. This was my best option to avoid a situation where I might have needed to lie. I am not ready for that. I need to keep telling myself that this is a job.

Due to a delay on the tube, I am going to be late and as there is no mobile reception in the tunnels, I cannot let Brett know. I finally emerge from the underground and find Joe's, which is not an easy task as it is tucked away from the main streets.

"I'm so sorry, someone took sick on a tube in front of mine and we were held up. Can I get you another drink?" I ask Brett.

"I thought I was being stood up. I'll have a Star, thanks."

I order his pint and decide on a vodka soda for myself. It could be a long evening. "Have you been waiting long? Again, I'm really sorry, I hate being late."

"Half a pint's worth."

Why does he have to answer like this? As if I know how long it takes him to drink half a pint?

"Just for the record, this is not a date. I thought we all could meet up beforehand, but Lita said she had stuff to do."

"Sure you did, you don't have to hide it. I know you wanted a date."

"Wow, you do think highly of yourself. This is just a quick drink before the party."

"What are you going to do now that you have me all to yourself?"

"Really? Well that's easy. I'm going to have this drink and talk about the party tonight."

"That's boring, you could be wasting an opportunity."

"Wasting an opportunity for what?"

"You could ply me with alcohol and have your wicked way with me."

"If I wanted to have my wicked way with you, I am sure I wouldn't need to ply you with alcohol first."

"What are you waiting for then?"

"You're so full of yourself, how does your ego fit into a room?"

"Don't tell me you've forgotten?" He asks.

"Forgotten what?" I ask, tummy starting to knot.

"Thailand. Have you lost your sense of adventure?" He notices I have drained my glass. "You must be thirsty," he says mockingly, and heads to the bar to retrieve another for me. Seeing him dressed in smart trousers and a shirt revealing that tuft of chest hair piques my interest.

"So, you do remember?" I say as he resumes his position on the opposite side of the table. "I wasn't sure. You didn't seem to recognise me when we met at the office."

"Would you have preferred me to have mentioned it when we met?"

"Very funny, no, but what about all the other times?" I

ask, downing half of my fresh drink in one mouthful.

"There was never a good time. Anyway, I wasn't sure you remembered me, especially after that email you sent around. It dented my ego."

"To be fair, I didn't know your last name, and let's not talk about that email. I can't believe of all the people I entangle myself with in Thailand you turn up in the same place that I work at. What are the chances of that?"

"I think it means there's unfinished business," he smirks.

"You already knew who I was, didn't you?"

"I did."

"Why didn't you introduce yourself like a normal person?"

"I was going to, and then that email came out."

"That's even more of a reason, I got so much crap about that."

"I thought I could have some fun."

"As soon as I walked into the events meeting you knew who I was, you prat. You should have introduced yourself way before that session."

"I introduced myself, politely, if I remember correctly."

"Fine, I am changing the subject," I say rolling my eyes again. "How do you think the evening will go?"

"I think it's started well, but you still haven't answered my question."

"What question?"

"Have I lived up to your expectations?"

"I know now that you're probably asking about Thailand."

"And?"

"And as if I am going to answer," I laugh.

"You have definitely lost your sense of adventure. But that smirk tells me you haven't forgotten."

"What are you like? You know that was just a holiday fling. You know what happens on holiday, stays on holiday?"

"I haven't forgotten either, the beach, the cabin, the outdoor shower, the moonlight," he says with an incredibly cheeky, sexy, inviting expression.

"It's almost eight, we should get going."

Lita and Charlie are waiting in the reception area, and I can see by Lita's expression she has already seen us arrive together, her eyes are fixed, moving from Brett to me. We do not offer an explanation. Lita is clearly bugged about something, but I put it down to moodiness.

We are escorted to the ballroom area, where the guests are welcomed by big banners and dancers who bend like a Cirque du Soleil troop, moving in sync with the music, instantly getting their guests in a party mood.

At the top of the staircase that leads into the ballroom, is a group of pseudo-paparazzi snapping and yelling at us to pose. I can't help myself. I strike a pose, giving an over the shoulder, hand on hip, hands on my head, and all with a big grin. This is mad but so much fun, and a complete surprise. Our party-goers will enjoy this experience.

Walking down the staircase into the ballroom,

makes for a grand entrance. You can see the entire room which has been transformed into a big movie theatre with popcorn machines, dark purple velvet draped everywhere and hundreds of guests, all dressed as their favourite character. It is easy to spot Freddy from A Nightmare on Elm Street, Audrey Hepburn from Breakfast at Tiffany's, Edward Scissorhands, Fred Flintstone with Wilma, and the entire cast of Shrek. Three huge screens play movie trailers with their famous one-liners being overlaid.

We head to the bar for a drink, and stay together most of the time, only separating when we want to participate in the entertainment. I have fun being videoed on a green screen performing acts such as surfing, riding a horse and having a sword fight. At the back of my mind is a nagging reminder that this evening is the perfect opportunity to get closer to Brett. I head back to where I left him.

"Where are the other two?" I ask.

"Ladies, then dancing," he answers.

"And you don't want to join them?"

"A man in the ladies room doesn't go down well."

"Very funny. You don't like to give a straight answer, do you?"

"Am I meeting your expectations?"

"Can you give that question a rest? I'm never going to answer it. Actually, I will answer it. No, you're not. You haven't done anything yet and Thailand does not count."

"You haven't been watching closely enough," he responds.

"I'm pretty sure I haven't missed anything."

"Let's get a drink." He leads me away from this bar towards one of the other bars. On the way, he directs me to a side area, pulls me in close, and kisses me passionately, with real wanting.

He pulls away momentarily, reacting to my surprise, then pulls me in even tighter. There is no denying his strength. It is not roughness, it is manly, and this time I respond with an intensity, that takes me right back to Thailand.

"Now I've done something," he says proudly, still holding me close. "Let's get that drink."

I take a big step back and can see he is pleased with himself, as if he just gave himself a ten out of ten. I follow him to the bar, I really need that drink.

Lita and Charlie join us straight from the dance floor, still moving with the music. Lita grabs Brett and they disappear. Charlie and I chat and walk around the party, taking it all in.

It doesn't take us long to realise how drunk we are, and decide to join the many party-goers on the dance floor. We spot Brett and Lita, who are dancing rather close. I am drunk and I do have a wild imagination, but she knows about Mr Blue Eyes, so why wouldn't she tell me if she is into Brett? Surely she is not connected with Caitem or involved with whatever Brett is involved with?

I do what any drunk person would do. I bounce over to them and hang an arm around both, until all four of us are jumping up and down and around in a little circle. Instantly we are surrounded by the cast from an array of Warner Bros movies acting out their characters, no one has a thought of tomorrow, ourselves included. No one can stop laughing, it is infectious, and my cheeks are aching.

As the party continues, we share our time between the dance floor, the entertainment and even though we ran out of drink coupons a long time ago, the bar.

On my way to the ladies' room, I spot Brett and Lita in close proximity, oblivious to their surroundings. There is something going on. Their conversation looks serious for a bit of party fun, and I look for an alternative route.

Oh, what a tangled web we weave. In the one night I have deceived Mr Blue Eyes and possibly Lita, and all for what? How could I so easily transform into this person, ignoring everything I believe in, for something I cannot even pretend to understand?

I need to speak to Lita and find out what is going on between them, and whether she knows he is a player. I know there is no easy answer to this question, but I have started down this path and it is up to me to control it as best I can.

- CHAPTER 12 -

After another drunken Thursday evening, I wake with my familiar pattern of trying to piece together how I got home, relieved that I am on my own. Next, is how I am going to get myself to the office. My only saving grace is that I do not have a training session scheduled for this morning, but sadly I do not have a fish finger bagel either.

Oh no, that kiss - kisses - Brett, Lita. I pull the duvet over my head and sob. At least I will not have to worry about seeing Mr Blue Eyes today. My current state is making me much more emotional and my thoughts much more irrational. Mr Blue Eyes may not be in the office today, but Brett and Lita will be.

My mind wanders to Poh and how fast this has happened. 'Get closer' she says, 'Caitem comes first' she says, and instantly I obey like a well-trained puppy. This is just a job and I have not cheated, I did not want to do it anyway.

I am late to work but my head hurts too much to care. I do however, care that Corey is nowhere to be seen, and neither is Lita, but that is just Lita. Corey should be trying to make a good impression and when he does stroll in, it's with not a care in the world.

"Good afternoon, Corey," I state letting him know that I have noticed his tardiness and I am not impressed.

"Good afternoon, I had a sesh last night and it turned

out bigger than planned," he chuckles as if it is perfectly normal. His behaviour resembles someone who has earned the right to take those little perks you get after proving yourself. Nothing he has done has impressed me and I do not hold out much hope that my opinion will change.

"Corey, have you reviewed the Frogman project plan yet? You need to let Sheree know the due date for the creative brief, and the client needs to know when we can deliver." I am expecting a 'yes'.

"Well, not really, I've been quite busy on Tommy's account. There were some emergencies he needed me to help with."

"Okay, that's good, did they get sorted?"

"Sure."

"Can you fix the plan this morning? It's really important and it shouldn't take you long."

"I don't really believe in doing project plans. They're always changing, and it seems such a waste of time."

He what? I must remember I am meant to be giving him a chance to prove himself, and I breathe. "A project plan is a living document, which means it needs to be constantly revised and updated to reflect any changes. Otherwise, how do you know when things are required to be done and delivered?"

"Well, that's easy, I just know, I do the calculations myself, it's not rocket science." His 'I know better' attitude is making my already pulsing head pulse harder.

"I'd like the project plan updated by lunchtime, thanks." I leave no room for negotiation.

"Okay, we'll do it your way," he responds with a cockiness that I just cannot deal with today.

Lita arrives in time to save Corey from the verbal lashing I was about to unleash, and we leave the building for our morning coffee.

"Corey is doing my head in! Anyway, how did you pull up after last night?" I ask, curious to get to the truth about Brett.

"I need something stronger than coffee and a decent amount of food. I think I'm still drunk," she responds light heartedly. I can only assume things have gone well with her and Brett. "What happened to you last night? You just disappeared," she says.

"Yeah, I got to that really drunk self-preservation stage where I needed to go home. Sorry I didn't say goodbye to any of you."

"No probs, I was munted, I think we all were." Lita responds with a groan.

We make small talk about the event and then I test the waters.

"Can I ask you something?"

"Sure."

"Is there something going on between you and Brett?"

"Why do you ask?"

"You seemed quite close on the dance floor, and I saw you later in deep conversation, too deep for a party."

"Sort of," she offers coyly.

"Sort of? Come on Lita, you know all about Jake and me, so spill it."

"All right, all right, I really like him, and I know there's something there, but he blows hot and cold and it's pissing me off, that's what we were talking about. I was trying to figure out where I stood with him."

"What do you mean hot and cold?" I query.

"One day he's into me and then he isn't."

"Like what?"

"I wanted to meet up with him before the party last night, but at the last moment, he blew me off. Then I see you two walking in together, which made me think he was with you, but I hoped it was just me being paranoid."

My feelings of guilt re-emerge.

"Ah, so that's why you said you had plans before the party, why didn't you just tell me? Did you ask him what he was doing?" I stop breathing momentarily.

"Yeah, he said he had to help a mate out with something and that you two met on the way in."

And, breathe. I am glad I found this out, or I could have dropped us both in it. Still, if he did not have anything to hide, he would have told her the truth. This is good for Caitem but bad for Lita.

"So how long has this been going on? Do you see him regularly?"

"It's been going on for a while and I really like him. How I feel makes me do strange things because he makes me nervous."

"Strange things?" I ask.

"Yeah, I wave to him like the queen, or curtsy, or pinch

him to get his attention, you know, like what we used to do in primary school. It's so embarrassing, and don't you dare repeat that to anyone."

"So, when I asked if anyone knew Brett, you knew who he was? You cheeky monkey?"

"Yeah, but I had to keep it quiet. You know how it is being in the office." I still wonder if she is involved in whatever Brett is involved in.

"The queen, oh dear, you do have it bad." We both start laughing and I give her my best Queen's wave. "What do you think of Corey? I am not really sure about him at all."

"I think he's a right royal twat, and he has to go," she blurts out, and we both resume laughing. I am relieved she sees it too, as it will make the case against him stronger for Mr Blue Eyes, who also has his doubts.

Later, when Lita leaves for a meeting, I take the opportunity to see Brett. I am not nervous. It is the opposite to how I felt the morning after I first kissed Mr Blue Eyes. I feel nothing for Brett other than the rumblings of anger, blaming him for putting me in this situation to cheat on Jake and deceive Lita. It does not matter that I signed up for this, my irrational mind is blaming him, it is his fault. If I did not have this assignment, I would never have met up with him or reciprocated that kiss.

The elevator doors open, and I can see Brett is not at his desk. I ask some of his colleagues whether he is in today.

"Yes, I am. To what do I owe this pleasure?" Brett says from behind me. Nothing has changed.

"Just seeing how you pulled up from last night. I think Lita and I are still a bit tipsy." I say at a whisper.

"You should be careful standing that close to someone. You don't want to give the wrong impression." Brett smirks.

"Would you prefer me to announce out loud that we might still be drunk? What impression would that be?" I ask, holding his gaze.

"You didn't need to come down here to ask me how I am. You could have sent an email."

"Yes, I could have, but you know what I'm like when sending emails. Anything could happen. Anyway, you still haven't answered why you didn't reply to my company-wide email?"

"Yes, I did, I said I would have some fun with it."

"I got so much stick from sending that email, you could have said something."

"I did."

"I mean to me personally, not in front of everyone. Whatever." He can be so frustrating. It is like playing mental ping-pong. I change the subject. "It was good we went last night, we got lots of useful information."

"Yes, it was, some information was more useful than others."

"Do you have time to jot down some ideas while they're still fresh in our minds?" I ask, ignoring his insinuation, but trying to make the most of this opportunity to do my job.

"Yep."

I follow him to his desk, and he wheels over a second

chair for me. Brett opens a design tool on his laptop and together we start laying out the ballroom. The entrance, the stairs, the stage, where the showcase pieces can attract the maximum attention and then how everything else could fit. While engaging with this exercise I am scanning my surroundings for information on his laptop, his desk and even himself. I start ruffling through papers on his desk until he brings my attention back to the screen. I am bored watching him work and begin to discretely draw on his hand. He lets me continue for a while before he pulls his hand away and gives me an 'are you a child' look. I need to get back to my work and leave him to it.

On my way to the lifts, I glance back, and he is looking at what I drew on his hand, rolling his eyes with a very obvious grin.

I return my attention to Corey who again is not working. He is surfing the web and watching online videos.

"I take it you've finished the project plan if you're surfing the web?" I ask directly.

"I was waiting for you to come back. I have some questions." He responds with yet another delaying tactic.

"Do you know how to use a project plan? If not, then I can show you enough to get you started."

"Sure I do."

"Then why are you surfing the web when I need you to be looking at the project plan? You know how important it is."

"I'm keeping up to date with what's going on in the

industry. That's important, Cari."

"Absolutely, but not when you have work to do. Let's do it now. Open up the file." I wheel a spare chair to his desk.

"Where is it again?"

"So, you haven't even looked at it?"

"No, I said I was waiting for you as I had some questions."

"How can you have questions about something you haven't even looked at? Was the question where is the file?"

"You know what I think about project plans, they're useless."

"Okay, if you don't want to use the project plan, forget about it, and tell me what the key dates are? When do we need Sheree to have the creative brief ready? When do we need to book all the resources for the project? When can I tell Alex, it will be completed by?" Lita is smiling at her screen, avoiding eye contact with me. Corey opens the proposal, scrolls down to the milestone table, writes them down, and starts calculating a new timescale using pen and paper. Unbeknown to Corey, I have already recalculated the milestone dates. Twenty minutes go by, and I leave him to it, reminding him lunchtime is in half an hour and that is when I expect the revised dates.

Corey is stubborn. If he knew anything about project plans, he would have realised he only needed to update one date to come up with the new timeline. Schoolboy error!

Brett has appeared, hovering between Lita's desk and mine, armed with an A3 printout of the ballroom based on our morning's session. It has moved on considerably since I left him, and it is easy to visualise how it would look dressed up. We contact Charlie, she too is impressed.

"When did you get the time to do this layout?" Lita asks Brett.

"Cari and I threw it together this morning." He is as casual as ever. Lita does not like this at all. She makes an excuse and walks off. Brett leaves too, but in a different direction.

At least now I understand the trigger for Lita's moods, but she knows that I am into Mr Blue Eyes, so why is she being such a brat? Is she jealous? Just as well she does not know anything about the kiss, or worse still, Thailand.

This does not help my current mood, and this latest episode shortens my fuse which I am about to direct towards Corey.

"It is midday and I need to know what date Sheree needs to have the creative brief ready by?" I fire at Corey.

"Tuesday next week." He replies promptly.

"Tuesday next week?"

"Yes, Tuesday next week, definitely."

"So, if it needs to be ready next Tuesday, when does she actually need to start writing it?" Hoping he will catch on and see the problem.

"If she starts today, she'll have it ready in time."

"Okay, so have you seen Sheree today and asked her whether this is possible?"

"No, not yet."

"And half the day has gone, which means Tuesday looks unlikely, don't you think?"

"Do you know where she is, I can send her an email and ask her?"

"This is ridiculous! Open the project plan and go to line five. Tell me what it says."

"Project kick-off."

"What happens if you change this date to, say, Tuesday next week?"

"It says the creative brief will be ready Wednesday the following week."

"And when does Sheree need to start the creative brief?"

"It says next Thursday at the latest." Corey replies, reading the plan correctly.

"So, there you go. Project plans are useful after all."

"Okay, cool."

"Please update the proposal with the new dates."

"Sure."

My search for Lita finds her in our kitchen chatting to someone I do not know, so instead of interrupting, I give her a signal that I need to see her. She ends her conversation and moves my way.

"Are you alright? You seemed peeved when Brett came over."

"Yeah, I'm fine, I just needed a drink."

"That exit was not one driven by thirst, you looked annoyed."

"I felt excluded, we're meant to be a team."

"It's just that I had a spare ten minutes, and I went to

see how he pulled up last night. Then I said we should jot down some thoughts about the event while they were still fresh in our minds. He had time there and then so we spent a whole five minutes doing a brain dump. The rest he did himself."

"He was obviously keen to show you."

"Erm, he came to both of us. He stood between our desks. I reckon if we wanted to be pedantic, he was more towards yours than mine."

"It didn't seem that way to me. He never comes to my desk."

"I think in your situation he would want to be discrete, like you said you were keeping it quiet. Jake rarely comes to my desk, and if he does, it is completely work related. You know I'm into Jake, right? Not Brett? He was just showing us what he did, both of us. You really do like him, don't you?" I need to allay her insecurities. Even though they are warranted, this is nothing but a job for me, and something I could never explain.

"Yeah, I do, I just don't think he feels the same. It's as if he's keen on someone else and isn't sure which way to go."

"What on earth makes you think that? Has he mentioned anyone else?"

"I thought it might be you."

"Me? Why me?"

"There was the email thing which, knowing him, he would have loved, then the way he introduced himself at the meeting, then when I saw you walk in together..."

"Hang on, wait a minute, remember it was Jake, tall dark and handsome Jake, who you caught me kissing, and I told you all about the rest of the evening? With all that, why would I jump to Brett?" This is torture.

"I know about you and Jake, but Brett doesn't, and I'm not even sure it would stop him if he did."

"Well, I'm not into Brett." This is the truth. I cannot tell her about Thailand now that I know how she feels about him, and Brett cannot either.

"Yeah, probably just my paranoia and too many hangovers, you know what it's like when you first realise you're into someone."

"So do you have plans to see him soon?"

"Working on it."

"Good luck, but one question, do you think he's a bit of a player? There's something about him, or maybe it's just that ego of his."

"I always fall for the players. Don't worry, I know how to handle them, but I'm not sure if he is anyway," she laughs.

"Okay, just be careful."

Caitem comes first is going to screw with us all. I never thought for a moment when I signed up that it would affect anyone else.

My Saturday morning training begins with the normal park session.

"What is your update on Brett?" Poh demands.

"I went out with Lita, Brett and Charlie on Thursday night, and Lita and Brett are sort of seeing each other."

"What does 'sort of' mean?"

"That she really likes him, but I am not sure that he is

into her as much."

"Why do you think that?"

"Um, Brett kissed me at the party and, he does remember me from Thailand."

"And."

"And that is why I don't think he is into Lita that much."

"We have done a low level profile on Lita. She's been cleared, but we'll do a deeper dig."

This does not freak me out as much as it should, as her behaviour is quite odd at times although, odd seems to be who Tyn-T employs.

"I doubt she is involved. I think she has a crush and that's it."

"Who is Charlie, and did you see conversations between Brett and Charlie?"

"Not other than party talk."

"Are you sure?"

"Yes."

"We will profile Charlie too."

"Did Brett have conversations with anyone else at this party?"

"Not that I saw, we did a lot of dancing with people dressed up in costumes."

"And how is that relevant?"

"It was hard to talk to some of them as they had head pieces and all sorts of stuff attached to themselves."

"Is there anything else to report."

"No, other than this isn't just affecting me anymore, it is going to impact four people."

"Caitem comes first." Poh responds, unmoved.

"Yes, I know. Now that I am closer to Brett, what do I do? How do I manoeuvre between Brett, Lita and Jake" I ask, not really wanting to know the answer.

"Your assignment has not changed. Find Brett's connections."

I do not respond, I put my head down and put all my efforts into completing the session so I can start my weekend.

This is going to get messy. I wish I knew if there were other Caitem people at Tyn-T, as just knowing would bring me comfort. Ideally, I wish there was someone I could talk to about all of this.

– CHAPTER 13 –

A brand-new week ahead and I can see all the different aspects of my life moving towards each other. It is like a wheel which I am in the middle of, balancing the spokes. Project Toadstool, project Frogman, babysitting Corey, Versary event planning, training with Caitem, getting more intel on Brett, craving Mr Blue Eyes' company but finding excuses to avoid him because of the guilt. If one spoke breaks, I fear the wheel will no longer turn.

I arrive early as usual and on my way through the doors, I can see the ever-animated Tommy trying to get my attention. As we draw closer, I can see frustration all over his face.

"Hi Tommy, how are you, is everything alright?"

"Hi Cari, I am okay thanks. How are you?"

"I'm good thanks, what's up?"

"I know you have a lot going on in your account, but is there a chance I can have Corey soon? I have tasks I need him to do, and if he can't do them soon, I am going to have to find someone else. We are swamped too."

"Hang on a minute, this doesn't make sense, Corey has been missing deadlines in my team saying he's working on emergencies in your team."

"What!" Tommy roars, arms flapping in the air. "Corey's been saying the same to me about your project!"

"Surely not? Can he really be that stupid? If he hasn't been with you, and he hasn't been with me, where has he been spending his time?"

"I haven't seen him at all," Tommy informs me.

"He goes missing for half day chunks at a time." I am gobsmacked.

We have both been around long enough to know the game Corey is playing, but did not think he would be so brazen to think he would not get caught. Fired up, we march in search of Mr Blue Eyes.

"Good morning Jake, sorry to bother you, we really need to speak to you. If this isn't a good time we can come back later." Tommy asks, a lot more polite than I have ever been.

"Sure, let's go into a meeting room," Mr Blue Eyes says. "Have you two just arrived? You're still wearing your coats."

"Cari and I bumped into each other on the way in and started discussing Corey's availability. I have allocated tasks for Corey and as he isn't doing them, they are not progressing, sorry boss." Tommy explains.

"Perfect question to be asked, as you know the arrangement was to share him to see where his skills are, Cari, has he been caught up in your team?" Mr Blue Eyes questions.

"If only that was the case. He has been disappearing from my team saying he has been working on emergencies in Tommy's team."

"Really?"

"Yes, really, and he has been disappearing in half day

blocks of time, actually, that is the excuse he uses whenever I notice he hasn't been around."

"And Tommy, he has not been with you at all?"

"I have not seen him beyond the introduction meeting we had."

"Why are you laughing?" I ask Mr Blue Eyes.

"It's at Corey's stupidity, thinking he was smart enough to play this game."

"Well, I don't think it's funny. He's been lying to us and thinking we are stupid. You had concerns about him, and they are warranted. Why did you hire him?" I ask.

"He had good references and relevant experience, and remember, it's a panel process, I am just one vote, for the record, I voted no, or if it was a yes, to put him in a lower ranked role."

"When he is at his desk, he spends his time surfing the web. He's such a waste of space," I add.

"I agree, we should get rid of him. It is going to take more energy to get anything out of him than it's worth. He is like Thor without his hammer, useless." Tommy advises.

"You just insulted Thor and compared Corey to Chris Hemsworth, which is a huge insult to Mr Hemsworth, huge." I retort laughing out loud which triggers a chuckle from Tommy and Mr Blue Eyes.

"Thanks for letting me know. I'll take it from here and I'll let you know what the next steps are."
We both thank him and leave the meeting room.

"What was with the Thor reference?" I ask Tommy as

we head to our floors.

"I watched Avengers last night with my little ones, it just popped into my head."

"Which one?"

"Both."

"Not which child, which movie?"

"The last one, Endgame."

"Wasn't he fat and the opposite of Thor?"

"Yes, but he is still Thor." We both laugh and part ways.

Back at my desk, I find a very confident Brett sitting in my chair going over Versary plans with Lita. I drop my bag off and tell him to stay seated while I get another coffee. Returning, I am disappointed to see him still sitting in my seat.

"Are you on the afternoon shift?" Brett asks sarcastically.

"I've just come from a meeting, thank you very much," I reply. Seconds later, Mr Blue Eyes passes our huddle of three, nods in our direction and stops at Corey's desk.

I am trying to concentrate on what Brett and Lita are saying, but I am more interested listening to Mr Blue Eyes. The fact that this is the first time Brett, Mr Blue Eyes and I have been in the same space is not lost on me, and I do not like it.

"Would you like to take a seat?" Brett asks.

"Yes, my seat, are you going to get up first?"

"I'm happy to share if you are."

"There are plenty of spare chairs around," Lita directs Brett.

"Yeah Brett, get off your ass, and get your own chair," I tease, hoping to avoid a Lita tanty.

"Where's the fun in that?" He retorts with a grin. Brett is not subtle, and his playfulness is heard by those around us including Mr Blue Eyes, who flashes me a smile before leaving with Corey. Brett finally surrenders my chair and leaves.

Even though Lita is sitting next to me, I send her an email. I think our neighbours have heard enough.

Subject: That's progress.
Morning visits, that's encouraging!
xx

After waiting a while for a reply, I ask Lita if she got my email. She asks, "What email?"

Oh no! Have I done it again? I look in sent items and to my horror, see that I sent it to Brett. Crap! What is wrong with me and email? It is too late to recall it as I have a reply.

RE: That's progress
Then my job here is done. Dinner?
xx – promises, promises.

My heart is racing but I need to keep my cool. I nervously chuckle.

"What's so funny? Share." Lita demands.

"Nothing worth sharing."

The email banter continues until I accept the dinner

invite. I suggest in two days' time, when Lita will be in Ibiza. I will feel less guilty knowing she is not in the country, and won't see her the morning after.

Corey has returned and is not looking his normal jovial self, then shortly after, Tommy and I receive an email from Mr Blue Eyes asking us to join him for a quick update, now if possible.

"Hi Cari, Tommy. Thanks for meeting with me at such short notice. I have just spoken with Corey."

"That's good, what did he say?" Tommy asks.

"Corey feels he isn't getting the right support from you," Mr Blue Eyes says directing this comment to me, "and that he hasn't been given the opportunity to show what he can do. He mentioned his creative interest, and that since being here he hasn't done much in that area."

Tommy and I look at each other, dumbfounded.

"I have to take his concerns seriously," Mr Blue Eyes continues.

"But what about the emergencies he was fixing in my team?" Tommy reiterates.

"He claims he never said that."

"Oh my god, so he is calling me a liar?" I respond with heat. "Why would I make something like this up? Did you ask where he disappears to for big chunks of time?"

"Yes, he says he was doing work on your project, talking to designers, developers, creatives."

"He did not?"

"Yes, he did, he was confused as to why you thought

he was working with Tommy."

"Wow, he is good. Are you going to investigate further? Speak to these people? He can't get away with this?"

"No, I want you to. It will be better for you to do it subtly. If I do it, it will draw attention to the problem."

"Wow, as if I didn't already have enough to do, but don't worry I will be thorough. Also, since when do you start at a new place, in a mid-range position and make demands on what you want to work on, then use that as an excuse to not do what you are supposed to do? Is that acceptable now? If so, then I don't want to work with him!" I stomp.

"I don't want to work with him either," Tommy supports.

"Cari, you know the answer to that. I understand you are frustrated, but for now, Corey will continue in your team on project Frogman, and I have agreed with Corey that you will mentor him. Treat him as if he has no project management experience."

"I can't believe this, can't he go to Tommy now? Sorry Tommy."

"No Cari, he is staying with you."

I have no more words. All I can do is put my elbows on the table and cradle my face in my hands. This is crazy, he has clearly been caught out, and yet there are no consequences. He has inferred I lied and now, I have to give him my time. It is clear there is nothing I can do about this, so without acknowledgment I get up, leave the room and return to my desk.

– CHAPTER 14 –

As the restaurants closest to Tyn-T will likely be serving co-workers and clients, Brett has chosen a Japanese restaurant further away. This feels like a real date, but without the excitement or nerves. He is not Mr Blue Eyes, he is a job.

As this 'meeting' was arranged ahead of time, it meant I could plan my work attire to be suitable for evening. There is no reason to make an effort for him by going home and dolling up.

I arrive at the restaurant a few minutes early and to my surprise, once again he is already seated.

"Hi Mr Ferguson, have you been here long?"

"Half a pint worth," he grins. Not this again.

"You know that doesn't answer the question."

"Ten minutes," he says, gesturing at the seat opposite him.

"This place is nice, have you been here before?"

"A few times."

"What do you recommend?" I ask as I start looking through the amazing array of sushi and sashimi choices presented impecably with pictures on the menu.

"Saki is good a place to start."

"I actually meant food wise."

"I recommend sharing a selection of pieces and some side dishes. Is there anything you don't like?"

"Besides your ego?"

"Funny. Shall I order then?"

"I don't like baby octopus."

"Allergic?"

"No. They look like spiders with their crumpled-up legs, and the big one's suckers creep me out. I think a sucker might suck onto something on its way down."

"Seriously?"

"Yes, seriously."

"Okay. No octopus of any size," he chuckles.

I could eat sushi every day. There is something refreshing about the mix of wasabi, soy sauce and raw fish that always makes me feel healthy. Brett recommends sake again, but I order wine.

The food and drink keep flowing and the conversation becomes freer. Our only interruption is when Brett gets a phone call. He frowns, obviously recognising the number, but rejects the call. If this were a real date, he would have gained brownie points, but the fact that he did not answer is bad for Caitem as it could have been a contact. After many more glasses of wine I give in to the sake.

"So, Lita?" My conversation now unfiltered.

"Lita?"

"Yes, Lita, anything going on I should know about?"

"No."

"Really?"

"Yes, really?"

"If I asked her the same question, what do you think she would say?"

"The same."

"Well, I think you're wrong. I think she's quite into you."

"And?"

"And are you into her too?" I ask, knowing this is a weird conversation to be having on what is meant to be a date.

"We go out sometimes," he says, showing no discomfort at all.

"So, it's nothing then? If she knew I was having this conversation with you, she'd kill me." I am not able to stop the words from flowing out.

"She's cool, we have fun," he says.

"Well, don't you think it's a bit odd that you're out with me?"

"Nope, Lita knows we're not really dating or exclusive. We hang out."

"Are you sure she shares the same sentiment?"

"We're not here to talk about her," he says firmly.

"I doubt Lita would be happy knowing you are dating other people."

"We're not here to talk about her," he repeats with a little more emphasis.

"Oooh, who's a bit touchy," is all I can come back with, but it is the end of that conversation.

The conversation continues to be light, a little annoying, playful at times but has a consistent flow, mostly due to the Caitem profile insights. We eat a healthy portion of Japanese delicacies and once the second bottle is emptied, it signifies the end of the dinner.

"Thanks for the dinner, it wasn't as bad as I thought it was going to be."

"You thought it was going to be bad?"

"I wasn't sure which Brett I was going to get, pleasant or egotistical. I got a bit of both which balanced out. It is getting late, and I need to work tomorrow, where is the best place to get a cab from around here?"

"It's not that late, why don't you come back to mine for a nightcap, I live around the corner?"

"Hmmm, really, a nightcap? Sure, why not? You can then call me a cab."

"Sure."

Brett does not live far from the restaurant, in a nice tree-lined street. His flat looks nice too, in fact everything looks nice in my alcoholic haze. His apartment has generously sized rooms for London, which makes me think his job in communications pays well.

He asks what I would like to drink, and I ask for Amaretto. He pours two glasses and plays some music, and that was all I needed to start dancing. Another weird thing when confronted with a weird situation. To make matters worse, I get him to join me. This is the last thing I remember until I peep through squinted eyes to reveal daylight. My head is pounding, and as soon as I realise where I am - still am - my heart follows. Flashes of the evening return, flicking in front of my eyes like a slideshow.

I have crossed the line, betrayed a friendship, and

possibly thrown away any chances of a real future with Mr Blue Eyes.

My heart shatters. Every muscle is paralysed. I do not dare move in case I wake Brett. A small teardrop forms and rolls down my nose, dropping silently onto his pillow. I need to pull myself together and get out of here. I need to be on my own where no one can get to me. But it is too late. He is awake and he rolls over to check on me.

"Good morning," I offer with a forced smile. My mouth is as dry as the Sahara Desert and my tongue is sticking to the roof of my mouth. "How much did we drink last night? I am dying."

"It is a good morning and yes, we put a few away," he replies, jumping up and heading to the bathroom.

When he returns, he stands at the end of his bed, cocks his head to the left and keeps looking at me as if it is the first time he has really seen me, or he is having a flashback to Thailand.

Nothing can take away this crushing feeling. I feel dirty. I am now involved with two men at the same time, from the same workplace, and one of them only because I have practically been told to get involved with him. I have sold my soul to the devil! I need to get away from here.

"There is a pot of coffee brewing," he claims.

"How did that happen?"

"Pixies." He disappears and, two minutes later, a hot mug of perfectly filtered black coffee appears. I take a moment to enjoy it.

"Unexpected turn of events," he states.

"Yes, quite." I cuddle my coffee mug trying to extract every ounce of comfort from it.

"Plans for today?"

"Yes, actually there's that thing called work. Speaking of which, I really need to get moving as I need to go home and get changed."

"I'm not going in today. Working from home."

"Nice for some. Do you mind if I have a shower before I go?" I need to wash the night and Brett off me.

"Sure. Can I join you?"

"Erm, no," I say, and take the towel on offer to wrap around my naked body.

I turn on the shower and start snooping around his bathroom. Really, what do I expect to find in here? I hear his voice, sounding serious, and move my ear closer to the door, but I can only make out a few words. Craig, Thursday, and some sort of reassurance that it will be okay. Brett hangs up and starts shuffling around, so I dive into the shower worried he might actually join me. I have the quickest shower in history.

"Sorry, I couldn't hear you in the bathroom, were you talking to me?" I ask, trying to catch him off guard.

"It was work," he replies, grabbing then kissing me. In the cold sober light of day, I cannot keep this up and pull back teasingly, claiming I am going to be even later than I already am.

"I'm jumping in the shower."

I am left on my own in his flat. At superwoman speed,

I dress and start quietly opening drawers and looking at items on benchtops. Then I spot his phone and scroll through the menu until I find recent calls and the number. I find some paper and write it down. My heart is racing, and I start perspiring. This is not helping my hangover.

"What are you doing?" Brett asks making my internals jump to the ceiling and scrunch the piece of paper into my hand.

"Don't scare me like that, I'm fragile. I noticed your phone wasn't docked so I was putting it back, so it won't go flat." I try to control my facial muscles, so I do not look guilty. "Is everything all right?" I ask, drawing on all my strength to work out whether I have been caught.

"Yeah, I'm a bit fragile too, just need to get a razor," he responds. Once he returns to the shower, I do not move for a good minute to level out my breathing. I check the piece of paper to make sure the number is still legible and place it in my bag. I top up my coffee mug and continue to snoop. He does not leave much lying around. I softly thumb through some papers, but find nothing unusual, so I sit down and enjoy the rest of my coffee.

Brett wanders through the kitchen with a towel around his waist, his body glistening with water droplets. If this were any other man, I would dry him myself, but in this situation, it repulses me.

"Thanks for the coffee, but I really need to get moving. Thanks for last night, it was, um, fun." I jump up from the table.

"Aren't you forgetting something?" He asks, grabbing my arm. I freeze, thinking he knows what I did, but instead, he draws me tightly into him and kisses me, giving me no choice other than to respond. I can feel his enjoyment through the towel.

By the time I get home, shower again, board my train and grab another coffee I arrive to work late, for me. As I get to my floor and head to my desk, I am startled and mortified to see Mr Blue Eyes in the office today. It is Friday, and he is on my floor speaking to Bill.

This I did not contemplate, and therefore I am so far from prepared I panic. If I had a choice, I would choose to see Lita instead. I hope he is not hanging around to speak to me. I cannot possibly speak to him, so I evaluate my exit strategies. I could bolt and take everything with me, or drop my bag and coat and make it appear like I am late for a meeting. I choose to bolt and attempt to exit by stealth, but he is near the only exit, and I feel his eyes follow me out the door. I do not stop to wait for the elevators and head for the stairs. I find myself at FitUs and go straight to Poh's office to find it empty. I ask another instructor where she is, and I am directed to the gym. I do not care that she is with a client, I need to get her attention and make it obvious I am waiting for her.

I stand my ground until she gives in. After all, Caitem comes first, and I do not know who that client is.

"I need to see you," I desperately demand, holding back the tears.

"I am with a client," Poh states.

"I need to speak with you, it can't wait," my eyes are welling up.

"I will be done in fifteen minutes, meet me at the juice bar," she offers and returns to her client. I stroll aimlessly around the streets, sit in the park, and then head to the juice bar. Poh follows me in, and I wait for her to order the usual two drinks and select a table.

"I can't do this," I blurt out.

"What can't you do?"

"This whole getting closer to Brett. I really like someone else and I feel so dirty and riddled with guilt, and its making me feel sick."

"Take a deep breath and tell me what's brought this on."

"I have got closer to Brett, too close. We slept together last night, and my heart feels like it's going to explode. How do people do this? Nobody told me this was something I might have to do," I continue, spluttering.

"Where did this happen?" Poh asks, ignoring my emotions.

"At his flat."

"And did you find out anything?"

"Besides how shallow I am?"

"Yes, did he make phone calls, leave papers lying around, anything?"

"Yes, well no, but I have something." I retrieve the number from my bag and tell her what I overheard.

"Then it was worth it. This might be the breakthrough

we need."

"So can I stop now? Can I back off from Brett?"

"No, this is just the start, we will find out who this number belongs to and work up a profile. You need to keep monitoring until we tell you otherwise. This is what it means to put Caitem first. We don't discourage relationships, but separating life from this job is a skill, and not something everyone can do." Poh is cold as ever in her delivery, but there is some warmth in her words.

"This is ruining my life. Maybe I don't want to put Caitem first anymore," I say dramatically.

"You still have choices, but Caitem does come first. You knew what you were signing up for. Relationships, work, family are secondary to Caitem and there is no exception."

"I know, but you're meant to be my mentor. I need help to work out how I deal with all of this."

"Working for Caitem is a unique job that really makes a difference. You need to find the balance that works for you, what you can live with. If we could get the information any other way, we would."

"Have you ever been in this situation, trying to have a relationship with someone? Can it actually work?"

"Everyone is different. I do have my own challenges, but I make it work. This has been a useful early experience for you to realise what it means for Caitem to come first. You will learn and find your balance."

"Are you saying I should end it with Jake? That relationships never work?"

"I am not saying that. I am saying this is the job you have signed up for and it is entirely up to you how you coordinate your life, as long as Caitem comes first."

"I have to get back to work now. Thanks for seeing me. For the record, I don't feel any better."

I wander the streets for a bit longer and treat myself to a custard filled croissant from a French patisserie. It has given me a sugar filled hug and I feel I can face being in the office, as long as Mr Blue Eyes has left the building.

No such luck, I walk straight into him. Why does he always seem to be roaming around rather than at his desk doing whatever he does? Is he stalking me, or is this karma? The universe punishing me perhaps?

"Is everything all right? I saw you steam out of here," he asks with his puppy-dog eyes.

"Yes, I'm fine, just needed some food and a coffee," I lie, and feel my eyes welling up again. Please do not cry, please stop, I beg myself silently. I look away to try to stop the tears, hoping he does not notice.

"Follow me," he says. Of all the people who work at Tyn-T, he is the one person I do not want to see right now. We enter yet another empty meeting room and he closes the door behind me.

"Out with it," he says, crossing his arms.

"It's nothing, I think I'm just tired, we've been working long hours on Toadstool and I'm covering for Lita while she's on leave. Then there's the mentoring of Corey, all the gym training I've been doing, and I had a few drinks last night."

"Cari, I know you a little better than that, and I'm not buying it. What really has got you in this state?"

"That's the real reason. I'm tired. It's been hectic for months and it hasn't slowed down once. There were all those problems with the account team, I was questioning my abilities and whether I belonged here. At one time I thought I was going to get fired from my first job in London."

"Cari, I know you can handle the pressure of project work. You got through the fiasco with the account team weeks ago. Tell me what's wrong. I hate seeing you like this. Maybe I can help. Is it your family, is it me, is it London, do you need some time off?" He pleads.

He genuinely cares. His eyes are deep and questioning and I feel the longing radiating from him. He ignores where we are and pulls me into him. His body is warm and strong. His arms enclose me, comforting me as only he can. He wipes my cheek and kisses me gently on the lips. He makes me forget everything and I melt into him.

"That's better," he says, as he sees the smile return. My whole body is smiling. But it does not last and the tears come back. Stop it, you stupid woman, I tell myself. Mr Blue Eyes is shaking his head from side to side. He is desperate to know what has caused this.

"Are you okay to work today?" he asks.

"Yes, definitely, it will keep my mind occupied."

"Just tell me that it isn't anything I've done, personally or professionally?"

"Jake, you are perfect, it most definitely is not you."

"I'm not perfect, but I'm slightly relieved. You know you can tell me anything, any time? If you do decide to go home, let me know and I'll cover your projects for you."

"I'll be fine, seriously, it's nothing. I just need sleep and loads more coffee. I only have to get through today and then it's the weekend. Anyway, why are you in the office today?"

"I had to swap my day off as there is an important management meeting today. It happens sometimes."

"Is everything alright?"

"Sure, everything is fine, nothing to worry about. It's hard to get everyone in a room at the same time, and the first time they could, just happened to be today."

"Thanks Jake, you mean everything to me. I promise this won't happen again. I don't make a habit of being emotional at work. Everything's just caught up with me. See I am human." I am not sure whether I am trying to convince him or myself.

"That's what worried me. It's not like you at all."

This is my cue to leave, and I head to the ladies' room to tidy myself up. With the aid of cold water, a hand dyer with a rotating nozzle, and the isolation of a cubicle, I manage to get rid of my blotchy eyes and pull myself together. It is back to business as usual.

– CHAPTER 15 –

The weeks are disappearing, and the launch of project Toadstool is drawing closer. The team have put in a mammoth effort, collectively rolling up their sleeves, rallying together, and are at the brink of delivering a fine piece of digitally crafted art.

Lita returns from Ibiza a lesser version of the person who left, evident by her inability to talk. I am impressed that she is still vertical. We pretend to have a progress meeting and leave the building. Once away from prying ears, she tells me she has come straight from a club, onto a flight, home to change and now she is here. Lita could not take an extra day to recover as she has used all her annual leave and did not want me running the project on my own. To ensure she does not blow her remaining brain cells or mess anything up, we agree to only allow Lita to do mind-numbing work for the day. The upside is she may not be focused on Brett.

The ferociousness of this project's schedule to ensure everything gets done to the quality acceptable by Tyn-T and the client, has borne a routine the team has become accustomed to. At the end of the ten-hour workday, we head to the same restaurant, are greeted by the same waiters, and drink more than we eat. Most times I miss my last train to get home and need to find Lita on her platform so I can borrow her couch.

Even though this industry is fuelled by alcohol, it is

best not to flaunt it. I cannot arrive to work wearing the same clothes I left in, so on our way into work I detour past the shops. I now have a fabulous Reiss collection. Even the shop assistant knows this routine, and is ready for us, making for a very swift shopping experience. I keep essential toiletries in my top drawer in the office, which means the morning after the night before, we are always dressed up, cleaned up and ready for the day ahead, except when confronted by Sparkles.

"Good morning Cari, is that a new top, it looks good on you?"

"Thanks, yes it is."

"It looks like Reiss, is it?"

"Yes, it is. Is there something I can do for you Spark-Julie?" Almost.

"Can we have a quick chat? Do you have some time now?"

"Sure, I'd love to." No attempt to hide my sarcasm. We move to a quiet part of the office.

"I don't agree Lita should take control of the launch," she announces.

"Why do you say that, and why now, only days before the launch? This arrangement is not something new." I am only functioning on adrenalin, caffeine and have at least two pickled organs. What I am hearing is baffling me. Why has she decided to bring this up so late in the game?

"After seeing her over the last few days I don't think she can do it, and besides, we need a suit to look after the client and reassure him things are going well."

"You know Lita was away for a few days and despite this, she caught up and is on top of everything?"

"If she hasn't been here, then it's all the more reason she should not be taking the lead."

"You haven't been involved for the last few weeks, I haven't seen you at all! And why do you keep referring to yourself as a suit? It's stupid." I can feel my temples pulse.

"I've been around, maybe you haven't seen me. Suit is a common term."

"You haven't seen all the issues that Lita's resolved. She knows this project intimately and she gets along with all the developers and the client. The client doesn't have a problem with this, Sheree doesn't have a problem with it, I don't have a problem with it, and you shouldn't have a problem with it either. Besides, it's not your decision to make."

"I should have a say in who runs the launch. If I'm not comfortable with it, it should be addressed."

"So what do you suggest, that you run the launch?"

"Yes, and I don't know why you're laughing."

"Really? You don't know why I'm laughing? Because it's ridiculous. There's no way you can run the launch. Lita is doing it and that's that."

"I know what to do. You can give me the list and the order we need to do things in, and I'll make sure they happen when they're supposed to. I've managed things into production before."

"Yes, and I bet things needed to be fixed after. Look, Julie, a system launch is like no other, completely different to adding enhancements. Things always go wrong, and you won't know what to do. You'll panic and slow things down. You haven't been working closely with the team and you don't know the technical side, which means you'll constantly bug the team, disrupt the flow and waste time. I don't have time to argue with you anymore. Let's see what Bill and Jake think about the arrangement."

We find Bill and Jake chatting in the kitchen and when they see us heading towards them with purpose, they stop mid-sentence.

"Hi, sorry to interrupt, but can we please talk to you? I assure you it won't take long."

"Both of us?" Bill questions.

"Yes please," I respond.

"Sure," Mr Blue Eyes says with an almost please-don't-let-this-be-another-clash-of-disciplines in his eyes.

"As you know, I won't be here on Friday to cover the launch of project Toadstool, but Lita has been running development while I've been looking after everything else. She and the team, including the client, have known this for a long time and we've been planning towards it," I say rapidly.

"Where will you be?" Bill asks.

"Tennis, men's semi-finals. When I bought the tickets, the original plan had project Toadstool already live. Everyone has known about this since the date moved back."

"Bill, I'm aware of this and there are no concerns from my perspective," Mr Blue Eyes acknowledges.

"So, what's the problem?" Bill asks, looking at Sparkles

and then me.

"Well, I don't think Lita can handle the delivery," says Sparkles, "no offence to her, but I think she can be too erratic and I'm not confident she can handle the pressure of the day."

"That's rubbish. Firstly, you knew this was the plan for weeks like everyone else, so why wait until now to dispute it? Secondly, she can handle it and if you were closer to the project, you would have seen the various pressure situations we hit, that she handled perfectly," I snap back. I just want to hit her.

"So, there were problems, and you didn't let me know?" Sparkles says cockily, thinking she has one over me.

"I haven't seen you for weeks, which to be honest has been great. I don't need to tell you about every little issue we encounter. Everyone has agreed to Lita taking the lead on launch day. We shouldn't even be having this conversation."

"Okay, okay, you two need to settle down," says Mr Blue Eyes. "I agree with Cari. We need Lita for the launch. It's already been agreed with Sheree, the client and me. She will do an excellent job and she has my support. We will ensure Lita provides you with the same updates she provides Alex. If you have any concerns, then direct them to Sheree. Bill, do you agree?"

"Absolutely," Bill responds.

"That's what I said." I can't stop myself from getting another stab in, which is not appreciated by Mr Blue Eyes.

"Are we all okay? I don't need to remind you how important this launch is to the client and this agency do I,

Julie? Cari?" Mr Blue Eyes asks.

"I still don't agree but I accept it," Sparkles says.

"Perfectly fine by me, just as it was weeks ago. Thanks Jake, thanks Bill," I answer and immediately leave so I do not have to continue this stupid conversation.

The evening before the launch, Mr Blue Eyes, Lita, Tod, Sparkles, Sheree, and I evaluate how far the project has progressed and run through the plan. We are all excited that we have finally made it. We double-check everything.

Predicting what will happen tomorrow is futile. We can only hope we move from one task to another as smoothly as possible. I leave for the evening looking forward to my bed and to the tennis the next day. I desperately need 'me' time, away from Tyn-T, Caitem and Brett. Wimbledon tennis, centre court, men's semi-finals is a perfect way to do that.

– CHAPTER 16 –

I wake up feeling excited with a small element of guilt. Excited to be going to Wimbledon to walk the prestigious grounds of an event I have only had the luxury of watching on television. Always wanting to be there, secretly wishing I was good enough to play there. The guilt is from abandoning the project on launch day, but I have complete confidence in Lita.

For such a traditional event, I opt for sporty but classy. Even though it is sunny now, I put on layers, and grab a coat in case it rains. I feel like a little kid at Christmas waiting to open all the brightly coloured presents. The semi-finals boast a superstar of our era, one in each game. These games are the main attraction and, in my opinion, the matches of the tournament.

On my way to the tube, I ring Lita to check the launch process has kicked-off and everything is okay. I take the tube to Southfields, which is closer to the event than Wimbledon station. I disembark and walk with many others down the hill towards the main gate.

As I get closer, I see he is waiting. He looks perfect as usual, wearing Diesel jeans, a blue v-neck jumper, and a shirt revealing some chest hairs. He has a lightweight coat draped over one arm. This is one Friday I know what he will be doing.

I ordered two tickets thinking I could convince someone to come with me. Never for a moment did I think it would be with a man I have genuine feelings for. He greets me with a smile and a lingering kiss. Any guilt is replaced by a sense of playfulness. I am here on a workday, a very important workday, and here I am at Wimbledon, with Mr Blue Eyes.

Walking through the gates, I feel my eyes well up, glad they are hidden by my Ray-bans. I am making myself dizzy looking left and right, needing to take in every inch of this magnificent place. I want to take a thousand photos so I can remember every single moment of this magnificent day, but too embarrassed to do so. Mr Blue Eyes grabs my hand and asks if I am okay. As I melt into the surroundings, I check my phone. Four missed calls from Lita, uh oh. Please do not let anything interrupt this perfect day.

"Jake, I think there might be something wrong back in the office, I have a lot of missed calls from Lita."

"Do you want me to check in with her?"

"Thanks, but I'll call her now. I am the one who convinced everyone that Lita could handle it, so let me find out what's going on first."

"Hey, I saw the missed calls, what's up?" I ask Lita.

"Did you listen to my messages?"

"No, I saw I had missed calls from you so dialled your number."

"Julie is trying to take over control of the project. She's telling everyone she's the point of contact and not me."

"She is what? Why does she think that? We've been through this already and it was made clear that you are the lead. Has this been going on since kick-off?"

"No, she just got into the office and she's demanding

that everyone reports to her, and not me."

"But it's after ten and this process started at seven thirty, right?"

"Yes, I know. She has the project plan in her hand and she's asking all the developers where they're up to and if they're not doing what the plan says, making them explain why. You have to do something! This is crazy."

"Has everything been moving well, are we on track?"

"It's been going as well as it can. We've had to swap a few things around, as expected, but we're mostly where we're supposed to be. It's the swapping around of tasks that Julie is freaking out over. She wasn't here and doesn't know why or what's going on."

"Lita breathe, I'll see what I can do from here."

"I'm so sorry to interrupt your day. If we can get her to stop doing this, everything will be okay, I promise."

"I know it will be, leave it with me, I'll get back to you."

I hang up and bury my face in my hands. Mr Blue Eyes directs us to a drinks tent, orders two glasses of champagne and encourages me to take a few sips. Then demands an update, a little reminder that he has skin in this game too.

I explain everything, ending with, "It's a mess and you're my line manager and you're here with me." I take another sip of the nectar with the magic bubbles. Mr Blue Eyes has his hand on my arm offering comfort, but it is not helping. I have professional pride and a stupid need to impress my colleagues, even more my line manager, and not just because he is Mr Blue Eyes.

"At least escalating is instantaneous. I'll ring Bill and remind him about the agreement we had," he reassures me.

An hour later, I check my phone for messages and to my surprise there is one from Julie demanding I call her. I tell Mr Blue Eyes I am not doing it, and even though I can see he is not impressed, he lets it go.

We take a stroll around the grounds. At this time, only junior and doubles matches are being played. There is a big crowd watching my fellow Australian, Pat Cash. He still moves well for someone his age and is still sporting his traditional black and white chequered headband. I am eager to get to centre court as I do not want to miss a moment, and allow Mr Blue Eyes to lead the way. Centre court has a feeling of grandeur, and a chill goes through my body. It is smaller and more intimate than it appears on television.

We have excellent seats and even Mr Blue Eyes is impressed. We are sitting on a lower level, in the sun, and almost in the middle of the court. Please do not rain. Even though there is a roof, there is something special, and more traditional about playing in the natural elements.

The players are not due yet and the stadium is only half-full, luckily for me, as my phone rings again.

"Hi Lita, what's up?"

"Nothing has changed, that idiot is still around and it's getting worse. We, and the project is in trouble." A frantic Lita spews down the phone.

"Really, Jake rang Bill to get her to back off."

"Well, guess what, she hasn't, and she looks like she is

going to blow a gasket."

"Well, that could be a good thing," I joke.

"Not funny."

"Okay, I get it, bad timing. Seriously, how bad is it?"

"We are officially behind, and not everyone is working as they don't know what to do."

"Can you see Bill, if not can you find him and pass your phone to him? I need to speak to him."

"Okay, hang on. How's the tennis?"

"Great, but it hasn't started yet. I can't believe Sparkles, what is she thinking?"

"How's Jake?"

"Fine."

"He's next to you, isn't he?"

"Yes," feeling the colour of my cheeks start to turn pink.

"I can see Bill, hang on, I will hand the phone over."

"Hi Bill, It's Cari. How are you?"

"I am good thanks, are you at the tennis?"

"Yes, I am, but Lita has just called to let me know that Julie seems to believe she has control of the launch today. She's taking over. Can you please tell her to leave it to Lita?"

"Julie tells me everything is under control and it's going well."

"Well that's not true at all. Have you spoken to Lita? The team is frantic. Nothing's getting done. We were ahead of schedule before she arrived and now, we're behind. Can she be given something else to do today? If this continues, I guarantee you it won't go live today, and we will be hit with the first of the penalties."

"Cari, Julie says differently, she said some of the developers are behind, but she has it covered."

"Bill, it's not true. Lita says the developers are all over the place and Julie keeps running to her because she doesn't know what to do. She isn't technical. She thinks it's just a matter of following a list without knowing the implications. Please don't take her word for it. This isn't personal," I plead, while watching Mr Blue Eyes' expression turn dark.

"Cari, enjoy the day, we have it under control," Bill says confidently.

"Bill, it's not the first time Julie has told you an untruth. If everything was okay, why would Lita be telling me differently? She knows far more about the project than Julie. Even Jake was concerned when I spoke to him. I need Julie off the project. Please make this happen." I hang up.

"Crap, crap, crap I can't do anything, and Julie has convinced Bill everything is going well. Is there anything you can do, Jake? If we let this one go, we definitely won't go live, we won't get any more work from Alex, we will be hit with the penalties, and we'll look like idiots. Game set and match to Sparkles."

Mr Blue Eyes has gone quiet and is perfectly still until he reaches for his phone and makes a call.

"I need a distraction for Julie Kiraky, project Toadstool, she's being destructive. Can I leave it with you?" He asks and hangs up.

"Who was that?"

"No one you need to worry about. Give Lita a call in fifteen minutes. The situation should be resolved."

I see from his expression that I should not push it, but I cannot help myself.

"C'mon, tell me who you called! It's got to be someone higher up than Bill. Was it the CEO, CTO, COO?" I inquire with a laugh, giving him a playful nudge.

"Cari, it's not important. We're at the tennis so let's enjoy it. The problem will be sorted."

"But it has to be someone higher up than Bill. Surely you can tell me? I won't tell anyone, I promise."

Mr Blue Eyes ignores my efforts and places a finger on my lips. Stubbornly, I continue but he just keeps shaking his head. Then he leans in, kisses me and tells me to drop it. Fine, point taken, I will leave it and ring Lita. As he predicted, Lita has control. Sparkles has left to attend an emergency. Even though I would love to know who orchestrated it, this occasion in this beautiful stadium is more important. To celebrate, we have another glass of champagne along with a serve of strawberries with cream, another fabulous Wimbledon tradition.

The first of the semi-finals is about to start and we nestle into our seats. I have my camera at the ready to start taking those one thousand shots. The players are introduced to their adoring audience and again my eyes well up. Opponent number one, and then the first of the two eighteen grand-slam title superheroes are met by an almighty roar as they wave to their fans. Out of the corner of my eye, I see Mr Blue Eyes quizzically looking at me and not at the court. He lifts my glasses and smiles.

"I didn't realise how much this meant to you," he says, placing a hand on my knee and then turning his attention to the game.

The match is won in four sets, intimidating his opponent of the court. I am in awe at the speed they move, how much court they cover making millimeter perfect shots. The players are much taller than I expected. The second match goes according to plan, another win in four sets. It is going to be an almighty Wimbledon grand finale, a game not to be missed on Sunday afternoon.

Now that the euphoria has subsided, I call Lita and I am assured, that since Julie left everything is going smoothly.

It is only five o'clock and a bit too early to head to dinner, so we roam the grounds one final time. As I would not take money for the ticket, no matter how insistent he was, Mr Blue Eyes organised dinner. The restaurant is small and cosy, but due to all the Wimbledon snacks we consumed during the day, neither of us are overly hungry for food. I do not want this evening to end, but there is only so long we can occupy this table and Mr Blue Eyes finally settles the bill. He hails a cab, provides an address and I find myself at his place. He unlocks his door and we enter. I do not notice a thing around me, as all of my attention is fixed on him.

This is it, the moment where so many moments promised to go. Never in the right place, never in the right moment. We are here, I hope we are here, we have to be here. There is no fear, just desire. There is no hesitation, just want. I do not see anything other than him. I yearn for him completely, without walls and without doubt. He is talking to me, I can see his lips move, but I am lost in my desire, I cannot hear him.

I do not respond with words. I move to him, and he senses my meaning. We stand an inch apart, my heart pounding. I do not look up as I know it well. I want what I do not know. In one fluid movement, he locks me against him, and I feel his strength and then his intentions. The ferocity, the tenderness, the dance.

With a passionate kiss, his tongue weakens me. My knees are trembling, and I do not know if I can stand for much longer. My tongue laps at his now naked chest, not stopping until I reach his groin, and his groan tells me he cannot stand for much longer either.

We are locked together, fighting to take what we want. His hands explore first, and his lips follow their path, I want to feel this man inside of me and I make my intentions clear. We fit perfectly, we move together effortlessly, we surrender explosively.

Waking up seeing those smiling eyes is everything I dreamt it could be. To kiss so freely, not looking over our shoulders, but best of all, knowing we are not leaving this bed anytime soon. He has exceeded my already high expectations. Now, he has me completely.

I cannot stop grinning. It is Saturday afternoon, and we head to one of Mr Blues Eye's favourite local jaunts. In the light of day, I can see we are in a trendy part of London, reasonably central with a buzzing high-street boasting lots of laneways. I feel a strange level of comfort walking his streets as if we had done this hundreds of times.

After several more hours of conversation and food he tries his best to encourage me to stay, and move straight into our Saturday night date, which this time, is in my neighbourhood. As hard as it is to resist, I need clean clothes, and I must make sure my place is ready for him. I have planned a similar night of dinner and drinks, and during conversations we agreed to watch the Wimbledon final together. I am going to use my womanly charms to ensure this date extends into the tennis. All is right with the world.

Saturday night continues from where brunch left off. Italian cuisine and Chianti fuel us for the activities to follow behind closed doors, which already started during dinner. The growing familiarity intensifies with every touch, and I learn something new about this perfect body. I have touched, kissed, licked every millimetre of this man.

Waking up next to Mr Blue Eyes is as perfect as the previous morning and I know I am exactly where I am meant to be, in his arms. The Wimbledon final is not going to wait for anyone, and we reluctantly peel ourselves apart and make our way to the sports bar.

One of Londoners' favourite past times is watching sports in pubs, usually football, which seems to last all year long. Luckily, Wimbledon is prestigious enough to take priority today, and we are surrounded by dedicated tennis fans. It is very clear who is supporting who.

The match is ferocious. Deep into the fifth set and it feels like one of the longest finals on record. When a break occurs, his supporters know it is his for the taking. The now nineteenth grand slam winner is crowned champion. The runner up apologises for his outburst of emotion, wiping back the tears. Many of us join him. The match is heralded as one of the best, surpassing the battles between Borg and McEnroe, Sampras and Agassi or Federer and Nadal.

I am exhausted from watching, the adrenaline leaving my body. Or is it the realisation that duty calls early in the morning, and this epic date must come to an end? The parting kiss matches the passion and longing we developed for each other. I miss him already.

- CHAPTER 17 -

With the demands of the project launch, babysitting Corey and Wimbledon, I have not been able to put Caitem first, which was not missed by Poh, however during that one week I was allowed a reprieve, something I never expected. Apparently, Caitem considered it more important for me to deliver the project successfully and maintain a good reputation at Tyn-T. This meant someone covered for me, the details of how this happened was like most other things, not information I needed to know, but now Caitem business is expected to resume as usual and so is the training.

It is early Monday morning and I meet Poh at the usual place to jog to our park. I fear this session is going to hurt as during the reprieve, all the rules were thrown out the window. This body was not my temple, but it was Jakes.

"You have been privileged a break from Caitem duties, but this is over, do you understand?"

"Sure, and thank you, it was a tough week. Did anything happen I should know about?" We only just started, and I feel wobbly.

"You need to step it up, we need you back in his apartment as we believe the majority of business, if any, is conducted there and not at Tyn-T."

"So, you think he is involved in something?"

"More so than we did before, but still not certain, and

not sure to what extent."

"And I am still the right person to be doing this?"

"Yes, you have a relationship, and it is crucial it continues."

"You are making me nervous. What do you think I might find in his apartment?"

"We are not sure, anything you find must be reported back. Do not make a judgement call."

"Is there any other way of doing this besides going to his apartment, look what happened last time?"

"Last time you obtained a phone number and a name."

"That's not what I meant. But was the number useful?"

"That is not important," and that was the end of the conversation and the training, what a difference a week makes.

The team that worked the weekend take their time arriving to work. Well deserved. They are mellow, and we all quietly congratulate ourselves. We still do not know what happened to Sparkles, but no one cares. Who did he call?

Next on the work agenda is Versary, which is only a week away. A mandatory Versary meeting is set in one of the two boardrooms, with lunch supplied to ensure everyone's attendance.

A lot of information is shared, the most significant being the venue has no bookings the evening before, so we can start setting up earlier than we planned. Once the meeting formalities are complete, Lita leaves for another meeting and I linger to resume Caitem business.

"Hey," I casually say to Brett.

"Hey," he mimics.

"What are you doing tonight?"

"Sounds promising."

"It might be." With no response other than a cheeky grin I continue. "How about I bring some food and drinks around to yours tonight?"

"You don't need to bring food or drinks."

"Er, yes I do."

"Okay, I'll play it your way."

"I am not playing; it's meant to be a nice gesture."

"It is certainly a gesture."

"See you at seven?" I ask.

"See you at seven," he agrees, and I leave the room. I feel sick and try to convince myself this evening does not need to go the same as our last encounter.

Armed with Mexican takeaway and two bottles of wine, I buzz Brett's number and he lets me in. Entering his flat feels familiar and I am more or less comfortable being here. There is still no sense of romance, only an overwhelming feeling of guilt.

He has arranged plates, cutlery and glasses on the counter. I open the packages to mouth-watering aromas while he pours the wine. We pick our way through the buffet, down a bottle of wine and flirt.

"How long have you been at Tyn-T?"

"Too long," he replies, offering no more information than when I first asked him that question. Caitem probably already knows.

"What's too long?"

"You don't give up, do you?"

"It's a simple question and it's called conversation. We could just sit here and stare at each other if you prefer?"

"I can think of something else we could be doing."

"I bet you can."

"Let me show you." In one fluid movement, he puts both glasses down, grabs me and we are kissing, deep and animalistic. The wanting is evident and this time there is nothing to stop him. We move into the lounge and onto the floor. Then Brett is spooked by something.

"What's wrong?" I ask, not the reaction I was expecting while rolling around on his floor, maybe he could sense the guilt oozing out of my body.

"It's my buzzer, someone's at the door downstairs."

"Your buzzer? What buzzer? I didn't hear anything. Are you expecting someone?"

"As if," he says, looking at our half-dressed bodies.

"Hello?" He asks through the intercom.

"Hellloooo," a female voice replies, sounding muffled but familiar.

"Hi, what's up?" I can see from his face that whoever it is, it is not good, so I scramble to straighten myself up.

"Surprise. Can you let me in?" The female voice asks. It is Lita!

"Sure, give me a few minutes." Brett puts the intercom down and now I am panicked.

"What's she doing here? She can't find me here! Can I

get out? What am I going to do, Brett? Do something!" I am freaking out looking at the windows as an escape route.

"No, there's only one entry and exit. Go into my spare room, take the wine and both glasses, I'll get rid of her."

"One entry and exit is a fire hazard, shit, shit, shit."

While I scurry to the spare room, Brett clears away the dishes, straightens himself up, does a quick look around, and buzzes her in. I cannot believe this is happening. I am stuck in Brett's spare room, and he is out there with Lita. I make sure the door is firmly shut and pour myself a glass of wine.

What am I supposed to do with myself in here? Then I realise this looks like Brett's study. Using my phone for light, I quickly but quietly go through his drawers and papers. I do not have time to read what I am finding, so take pictures of everything, praying the flash goes undetected. Once I have opened every drawer and looked in every file, I check my watch and realise I have been in here for over an hour and Brett is still entertaining Lita. I have nothing to do other than recheck all the drawers and shelves, finish the wine, grab a blanket and lie on the mini couch.

I am startled by the sound of a door opening and Brett walking towards me. It takes a few seconds to register where I am.

"Has she left?" I ask, disoriented.

"Yes."

"When?"

"Just now."

"What time is it?"

"Ten past eight."

"In the morning?"

"Yes, in the morning, look, daylight," he points to the window.

"Crap, I can't believe I spent the night in here. Did she spend the night?"

"Yes."

"Oh no, I don't want to know. This is so wrong, I have to go," I say, squirming.

"It's not what you think."

"You don't know what I am thinking. This is so wrong, I have to go."

"There's no hurry, it's still early and we have to finish what we started."

"Are you insane? I'm not doing that after you just spent the night with Lita while I was in here. There are some lines I just won't cross."

"Nothing happened, we only kissed. All I could think about was you in here."

"But she spent the night, are you saying you have a conscience?"

"Yes, she spent the night. It was late and I didn't want her to go home on her own, so she crashed here."

"I can't believe this happened. Did she suspect anything?"

"Nothing."

"So where did she sleep?"

"In my bed."

"Oh no, something did happen."

"Nothing happened, we slept."

"There's no way you had her in your bed and just slept. She must have tried. You must have been tempted?"

"She did, but I could only think of you in here and it was driving me crazy."

"Why didn't you call her a cab?"

"I told you, I wasn't thinking. We drank wine, and I drank even more wine with Lita. Knowing you were in here and that I couldn't have you drove me insane. Now stop talking." He moves towards me, pulls me tightly into him, the intensity heighted from last night, and this time there will not be any interruptions. We move from the couch to the floor, another item being removed in every move. We knock over the wine glasses and the bottle, but neither of us care.

We remain on the floor, covered mostly by the blanket, trying desperately to catch our breath. He devoured every inch of me, only stopping due to exhaustion.

"I've been at Tyn-T for two years," Brett admits.

"So that's how I get you to talk?"

"I've never experienced that level of desire while another woman was in my bed."

"It was knowing you couldn't have something that was within your reach," I respond playfully.

"Never again."

"I can assure you I will never be locked in your spare room again, for any reason."

"Just the thought of that does something to me." Brett

replaces the blanket, covering me with himself and a passionate wanting. There is no denying his lust, but this time I grab the blanket and head to his bathroom. He does not let me get that far and we crash onto his bed.

"Stay here."

"I can't, I have to go home, get changed and get to work. I'm already late."

"So, take the morning off, the day off, stay here with me. What's a few more hours? I'll make it worth your while," he says as he attempts to unwrap the blanket.

"Stop. Fine. I'll stay the morning, but I really need a shower, food and lots of coffee."

Brett smiles and kisses me with the same desire as always. He hands me a towel, throws on some shorts and leaves me to it. I shower, get dressed and join him in the kitchen.

"You've been busy," I say, accepting the coffee mug. "Don't you need to go to work today?"

"No, I'm working from home."

"You do that often, can you do that whenever you want?"

"Not really, but I'm waiting for a package."

"A package. Is it anything interesting?"

"No."

Now that I know a package is expected, I need to stay and find out what it is. It could have something to do with what he is mixed up in. If I am not going into work, I need to ring Mr Blue Eyes, crap! And Caitem, and I do not have their phone on me. I left it home charging, truly believing I would be home last night. I decide to start with Caitem, as they come first. The only way I can get in touch with Poh is to ring her at FitUs and hope she is there.

"Hi Poh, its Cari, I won't be able to make our training session today."

"And why is that?"

"I'm not going into work today."

"Oh, are you not well?"

"Not exactly. I'm on my mobile."

"One moment please." Poh pauses, the line goes silent and then clicks. "Are you in a secure location?"

"As much as I can be. I'm standing outside in the open but there's no one around."

"Where are you?"

"Outside Brett's place. He just told me he's working from home today waiting for a package. He wants me to stay with him and I said yes, thinking the package might be of importance. Also, I took some photos of papers in his study, but they're on this phone."

"Why didn't you call me direct on your issued phone?"

"I don't have it on me. I accidentally ended up spending the night at his place and left my phone at my place charging."

"Do not send me the photos directly from your phone. You will need to download and print. Stay with Brett and see if you can get any information on the package. If the address is handwritten, get a photo. If you can determine the courier, take note. Ring me on your issued phone when you're back at home." Poh hangs up.

One phone call down, and one bad one to go. I feel sick through and through. As morally wrong as it is being with two men at the same time, I look at Brett as a job. I have no feelings for him, and I never will. My insides get twisted between his overwhelming passion and the fear of doing something that will affect the relationship and this assignment. I am in love with Jake. If he ever found out what I have done, it would be over. Even if he knew the real reason, he is not the sort of man who would accept this behaviour from someone he is involved with. I bend over with my hands on my knees and feel as if I am about to vomit, this time I do.

"Hi Jake, it's Cari, how are you?" My voice is shaking, surprised words can even pass the lump in my throat.

"I'm good thanks, how are you?"

"I know this is short notice, but I need the day off. I just don't feel well."

"Are you okay, you sound shaky?"

"I am. I just woke up and went back to sleep and now I just woke up again and I'm already really late. I just need more sleep."

"Wish I could join you."

"I don't think we would get much sleep," I respond with a chuckle. Tears fill my eyes knowing what I am doing to this man.

"I think it's much better for you to sleep then. I can feel your kisses."

"Oh, how I wish, I can feel you and can't wait to see you again."

"Me too, I'll let you get back to sleep. I'll be thinking of you alone in that bed and what I could be doing to you."

"Jake, stop it or I won't be able to sleep."

"Let me know and I'll be there in a flash."

"Right, I'm going. Miss you, see you tomorrow."

I hang up and burst into uncontrollable silent tears. How can I do this to this man? How can I do this to me? I want him so badly. I pull myself together and buzz Brett's apartment so he can let me back in.

"Everything sorted?" Brett asks, as I return to his lounge room.

"Everything's sorted but I could do with another coffee. And what does this bachelor have in his cupboards to eat?"

"Croissants, bread, ham, cheese, bacon, eggs, Weeta-Bix, muesli, take your pick," he responds.

"That's quite the selection, how about a bacon and egg croissant?"

"Coming right up."

"Thanks."

I take my second mug of coffee and my phone and sit at the kitchen bench to observe this man in action. I send a text to Lita letting her know I will not be coming in today, as I have hit the wall and need to catch up on sleep. She instantly calls me back.

"Hi, that was fast," I respond, gesturing to Brett that this is Lita. He smiles and wickedness enters his eyes.

"Are you taking the full day or just the morning?" Lita

asks.

"Full day, I need sleep so I'm having a duvet day. I've let Jake know."

"Cool," Lita acknowledges.

"You sound chirpy," I say.

"I am."

"What's brought this on?"

"Hang on a minute, I need some privacy. Guess where I spent last night?" Lita asks. Yikes.

"Where?" I ask eagerly, playing along and moving into Brett's bedroom for privacy.

"I surprised Brett last night with wine and beer and ended up staying the night with him."

"Wow, you go, girl. How was it?" I respond with the right level of excitement, shaking my head as I stare at his bed.

"He seemed a bit distracted at times, but it was just what we needed."

"So did things go well, or do I not want to know?" I ask, laughing.

"We didn't, you know, but I reckon he wanted to. We kissed a bit, but it was just nice spending that time with him away from work."

I'm not sure what I am more surprised at, Lita telling me this or Brett telling the truth. Maybe he is not as bad as I think, and he does have some morals.

"I'm so happy for you, I'm glad it's finally moving in the right direction, but just be careful that you don't get hurt, you don't know that much about him, do you?"

"It's cool. If he's a player, I can handle him. If things progress, we could go on a double date. That could be fun, don't you think?"

"Erm, I don't think so. Jake and I need to keep this exceptionally quiet, so please don't mention anything to Brett. Our situation is different from yours." Holy crap, I never thought Lita might tell Brett about Jake and me. What if it just slips out?

"Yeah true, I won't, besides, we aren't that close yet."

"Thanks. Anyway, I better go, my duvet is calling me, I'll see you tomorrow."

"Coolio."

I hang up and drop onto Brett's bed to clear my head. This situation is crazy. Brett knocks on the door and enters. I do not move from my position, feeling heavy and floppy. He takes this as an invitation to join me. His desire is no less evident but now the faint aroma of bacon is making me hungry, not for him but for the delight that must be waiting for me in the kitchen.

"Is everything okay? Why did you go into the bedroom?" Brett asks.

"Yeah, it was Lita. I didn't feel comfortable with her telling me about you while I was sitting here watching you make me breakfast."

"What did she say?"

"That she spent the night here and that you're making progress. I'm telling you, she is really into you."

"I told you, we aren't exclusive."

"Are you sure about that? Nothing she says indicates that she's seeing other men, or even open to the idea. The only man she talks about is you."

"Yes, I'm sure."

"How can you be so sure?"

"We had the talk about exclusivity."

"You did? When?"

"Last night."

"Really?"

"Yes, really."

"And what happened?"

"We agreed that what she and I are doing is casual, we're not exclusive."

"Of course you did," I respond with a deep sigh and a roll of the eyes. "You're not planning on telling her about this, are you?"

"No, are you?"

"Not in a million years, I never want her to know this happened, or what happened in Thailand, ever."

"Good, we agree."

"What are you going to do if she puts the heavy word on you?"

"She won't. She knows where she stands."

"What if she develops feelings and wants to be exclusive with you? Females are different from males you know."

"It won't happen. I won't let it happen."

"You can't control someone's feelings. So, you really

don't want anything serious with her? We should really stop this. Lita is an awesome chick and if you gave her a chance, you'd see that."

"I think it's clear what I want. I can stop seeing her," he says matter-of-factly.

"No! Why would you do that? She would be devastated. We should stop and you should give her a chance."

He drops the utensils and moves to my side of the bench, grabs me and kisses me with authority. He kisses my neck and runs his hand up the back of my shirt. "If you hadn't noticed, this is what I want. Why are you okay with me doing this with you, and meeting up with Lita?"

"Not sure really, maybe I believe the non-exclusivity, we are casual right?" I reply.

"Right, but we don't have to be."

"As if you would want to give up your wicked ways."

"When I am having this much fun, why not."

"I'm hungry." I change the subject.

"Me too."

"I actually meant for food."

"Boring."

Breakfast is perfect, but now that I have finished, I watch the clock wondering when the package will arrive. I need to get away from here, to stop this pretence and stop Brett.

I shake off Brett's continuous advances claiming I need to check my emails and make myself comfortable on his lounge. I flick through my emails and then the photos I took last night. Some were taken at odd angles, but I am happy at the clarity and hope there is something worthwhile.

The buzzer sounds and Brett lets the courier in. I peek through the lounge room window to see if I can catch a glimpse of the truck, but no such luck. The courier hands over a package and Brett returns to the kitchen clutching an A4-size parcel, which looks soft. It is probably bubble wrapped. To my surprise, he places it on the breakfast counter. How am I going to maneuver myself to see what it is without looking suspicious?

"Can I grab a glass of water? I'm a bit dehydrated from all that wine I drank on my own last night," I say jokingly.

"Sure. I have water in the fridge or juice."

"Thanks, where are your glasses?"

He grabs two glasses; I pour some water and place them by the package. Between sips, I do my best to check the label and look for any other markings. I really want to take a photo but cannot think of a way to make this happen, so after I feel I have exhausted all possibilities, I move into the lounge, grab my phone and continue to look busy.

"I really need to go."

"Really? I thought you had the day off."

"I do but I need to get home. I've been in these clothes since yesterday. Is that your buzzer again?"

"Sounds like it. I'll get rid of them. Back in a minute." I sprint to the package with my phone and take a few snaps before sprinting back to the lounge. My breathing has shot through the roof, and I concentrate hard to level it out. Brett returns and I start to arrange my things so I can leave.

"Right, I'm out of here, thanks for breakfast, I really needed it."

"You sure you need to leave?"

"Yes, definitely, and besides, aren't you meant to be working?"

"Yes, and I will."

I grab my bag and head for the door, but Brett blocks my pathway expecting a farewell gesture. He pulls me into him and shows me his appreciation for staying this morning and finishing what we started last night. I do not share his appreciation but play along, happy to know that I will be gone in a few seconds.

- CHAPTER 18 -

Brett, Lita and I arrive at the Hilton International to start the enormous task of transforming the ballroom into something worthy of a ten-year anniversary. Being alone with the two of them is uncomfortable and awkward. Lita openly flirts with Brett, and it is obvious she still has no clue about his extracurricular activities. I keep myself busy to limit interaction with them. The sooner we get this done, the sooner I can get out of here. I actively seek tasks as far away from them as possible and I am relieved when more helpers arrive, which include Hilton staff members. It is time to get busy.

Working on something different, being creative is therapeutic and it allows my brain to unclog and wander aimlessly. It is not long before I am thinking about Caitem. I printed all the photos I took at Brett's, including the parcel, but I have not called Poh as she requested, and she has not called me either. I need to see her in person to give her the pictures and I am questioning whether waiting until my training session in the morning is too long.

After five solid hours grafting, we complete every task scheduled for today. We stay on to hail our success with some well-deserved drinks. The Hilton's staff members who stayed and helped, now honorary events team members, are automatically included in this mini celebration of twelve.

Lita is sitting with Brett, and I am sitting several people away. I can hear her telling him about her Ibiza trip, even though she has been back for some time now. Maybe they have nothing else to talk about, although Brett is not a great conversationalist. Knowing the next day is going to be huge, the celebrations taper off and we go our separate ways.

The following morning, armed with my overnight bag and supplies, I leave home earlier than usual. While most only have work and the party today, I have a session with Poh.

London is just waking up, and I feel refreshed and ready for the day. As other early risers arrive at the office, suitcases in tow, the excitement grows.

I am pumped about the evening, the first event I have officially helped organise and one of the biggest for Tyn-T. It has taken an army of people, buckets of time, and a flexible wallet, but it is going to be worth it.

I am looking forward to some serious girly time with Sheree, Kelly and Lita in the privacy of our suite. We are bringing supplies including cheese, biscuits, crisps, pretzels, nuts, vodka, gin, wine, soda, water, diet cola, orange juice, lemons, limes, Berocca, and headache tablets.

Sheree and Kelly are going to take full advantage of the spa. Unfortunately, Lita and I will not be able to join them until our event duties are complete.

As I leave the office to meet Poh at the juice bar, I feel a bit aggressive and sulky as this is putting a dampener on my day. Even though I have learnt this is the emotion associated with Caitem, I will never get used to it. Poh is already seated.

"I have ordered you a vegetable smoothie. Do you have the photos?"

"Yes, and I also managed to get a photo of the package." I hand over a raft of papers concealed in a FitUs folder.

"You called me over a day ago. What took you so long to get the papers to me?"

"I knew I was seeing you today and I've been spending all my time at the Hilton getting ready for the event. Brett was there too," I explain innocently.

"You know the rules. It is not acceptable to sit on this sort of evidence. Nothing is more important than Caitem. These might be crucial, and the delay could have evaporated any benefit, especially regarding the package. You have obviously interpreted our recent leniency as licence to make your own decisions. This is never the case. You always do as we say. Caitem always comes first, do you understand?"

"Yes, but I was with Brett and so I was still doing my job. What happens now?"

"I need to get these papers back for analysis. Meet me back here in thirty minutes for your training."

"But I need to get to the Hilton to continue the setup for the event!"

"Thirty minutes, here, don't be late."

Damn Caitem.

When I am finally done with Poh and arrive back at the office, there are no events people, including Lita. I shut down my computer, grab my bags and head to the Hilton. My body feels energised after the training session and I can feel a party buzz growing.

"Hi, how are things going?" I ask Lita when I find her

in the ballroom.

"Where have you been?"

"I had to get a few things done and they took longer than expected."

"Have you checked in?"

"No, I thought I'd come and find you first, have you?"

"Yes, c'mon, I'll go with you to our room, it's awesome."

"Are the girls up there?"

"They should be, if not they will be in the spa. Guess what?" Lita asks in the privacy of the elevator.

"What?"

"Brett's booked a room," she beams.

"Ha-ha, so I don't expect you'll be sleeping in our room."

"I don't expect you'll be sleeping in our room either?"

"That is my plan," I confirm with a sly smile.

"So, Jake has booked a room?"

"Yes, he has," I beam. The doors ping open and we giggle like schoolgirls.

Spending the night in Mr Blues Eyes' room will be the highlight of my evening. The thought of waking up wrapped in those manly arms, seeing those glistening eyes and perfect jaw makes all my woes disappear and my whole-body smile.

When we enter our suite, we find Sheree and Kelly wrapped head to toe in terry towels, drinks in hand, with a vast array of snacks and beverages meticulously arranged on the side table. They waste no time filling two more glasses, and turn up the music. I have barely taken a sip when Lita says she can hear a phone ringing from a bag. It takes me a few moments to realise it is my Caitem phone.

"It's Poh, do you have company?"

"Yes, that is correct. One moment please." I tell the girls I am going into the corridor to take the call. "Okay, I'm free to talk," I tell Poh.

"Where are you?"

"I'm at the Hilton hotel, outside my room. There's no one around."

"Okay, just listen. The papers were of value. It means Brett is no longer a low-level risk and we need to look closer into his associations."

"What? Okay, does that mean Brett will be moved to someone else higher up than me?" I allow myself to get a little excited that this nightmare might be over, tonight.

"In normal circumstances, yes, the person of interest would be transferred."

"In normal circumstances? These aren't normal circumstances?"

"No, these are not normal circumstances. You will continue with this assignment."

"Why does it have to stay with me? Surely this now needs someone more experienced."

"If we move you, he may become suspicious and change his behaviour. But you will need to be more vigilant."

"Do I have to do something else now? Could I be in danger?"

"Nothing changes. Continue to track Brett and see

who he communicates with. Do not change your behaviour. The trust must remain intact. Do you understand?"

"Yes, I understand. But could I be in danger?" My party buzz is beginning to disappear.

"No. So unless there is anything new to report during the evening, call me in the morning."

"Okay." I hang up.

I knock on the door and Lita lets me in. After the shock of Poh's phone call, I am forced to have a shot from Lita's well-stocked fridge, which is void of hotel stock and filled with ours. The shot returns my buzz, and I can now truly appreciate our amazing suite.

There are two super-king-sized beds made up with crisp white linen. A lounge area complete with an L-shaped sofa, floor lamps, tall lush-green plants, a television, coffee table, desk, chair, and mirror. One full-length mirror outside the wardrobe and another in the bathroom. Floor to ceiling drapes gives the room a sophisticated yet cosy feel.

Lita and I head back to the ballroom, leaving Sheree and Kelly to enjoy the room and facilities. It is approximately two hours until show time and the ballroom is a hive of activity. Tables are being repositioned due to some occupational health and safety regulation about how far you can carry hot food. The bar tables are in place but empty. The carpet needs to be vacuumed and the dance floor swept and mopped. The events army roll up their sleeves and we get stuck in.

The two hours fly by, and the ballroom is dressed, and the events staff are in position ready to welcome arrivals. Lita and I re-join the girls in the room to get ourselves ready. The shots have been replaced by man-sized cocktails and we forget we have a party to prepare for. We are interrupted by a knock at the door to reveal Kelly's friends, who gave up waiting for her downstairs. We quickly apply the finishing touches, gulp down the last of our drinks, have one shot for the road, and we are on our way.

We make our fashionably late entrance through the grand doors at the top of the stairwell, and pause to take it all in. It looks remarkable. Hundreds of people mill about dressed appropriately for the James Bond theme. It is easy to spot the many different Bonds, villains, Bond women, and strangely enough, a few cars and cats. There is a lot of entertainment loosely representing our past and present clients, black jack, roulette, a miniature car racing track, skittles, basketball rings, a duck hoisting game, a scientific experiment section, and a miniature horse racing track.

Even though we helped organise it, the staged paparazzi still catch us by surprise, and we pose and play along. On my way down the stairs, I scan the room and spot Mr Blue Eyes, and I cannot take my eyes off him. He does the same. I want to go to him, but I must keep my distance for now, and follow the girls to the bar, all this excitement is making us thirsty.

Brett appears and Lita latches to his side. I wave him a hello and he discreetly returns a mischievous grin. My strategy is simple, avoid Lita and Brett, get to Mr Blue Eyes as quickly as possible, and make sure I do not sober up.

With our drinks in hand, we start doing the rounds. The roulette table is the most popular as the chips can be traded in for drinks or even a bottle of Champagne. Sheree is an instant winner, and the bottle of chilled Champagne takes us only five minutes to drain. We are very, very drunk and none of us care. Between the four of us, we accumulate enough chips to trade for a second bottle of Champagne, this time taking a bit longer to consume. Our next stop is the dance floor. Sheree and Kelly are our real entertainment and my cheeks hurt from laughing.

After hours of dancing, Sheree and I opt for a change of scenery and head to our suite. We pour two enormous vodkas, collapse on a bed and start talking. Kelly and Lita soon join us.

"I hope you have left us some goods?" Lita inquires.

"I actually forgot about the little bags of powder, this is perfect timing, let's go." I respond. We start to indulge with no concerns of being interrupted or picking up a toilet cubicle disease.

When we decide to re-join the actual party, I let the others go ahead of me so I can find my balance, freshen up and drink a large glass of water.

Sauntering down the corridor towards the elevator, I meet Mr Blue Eyes. He is a vision, dressed as a casual Bond but still wearing a tie, which I decide to hang from while announcing how sexy I find him. Insisting he should join me in my room, I lead him back down the hall. He neither accepts nor declines, he just follows. I hang the 'do not disturb' sign and fasten the safety latch. He is impatient, tender yet strong. I feel drunk but no longer from the alcohol, it is he who intoxicates me. There are no barriers, he knows he has the freedom and takes it. His hands have learnt my curves and I have learnt his. We are naked, we are intense, we battle to dominate. I cannot find a way to get close enough, I want to be in him, I want him to be in me.

After we're done, I fasten his tie and tell him to go ahead of me while I make myself presentable. The look in his eyes tells me if he had his way, we would not leave this room. I kiss him deeply and see him out the door, reminding him this will continue later.

When I make it back to the party, the girls quiz me on my whereabouts. I imply I was distracted, aware only Lita knows what that might mean.

The party continues to rock on the dance floor. Tonight is an endurance sport and if it was not for the time-outs, I would be done. I need another one right now, a quiet moment with no music, no booze, and no people. The alcohol, the substances and the ferocious pace of the last few months are finally catching up to me, so I sneak away unannounced, heading to the sanctuary of our suite.

In my intoxicated state, with my ears ringing from the constant dance music, I exit the elevator at the wrong floor, but I do not realise until I get to the room and see the wrong number. As I turn and head back towards the elevators, I see Brett coming out of another room.

"Cari, what a lovely surprise. Are you looking for me?"

He asks confidently, yet a little stunned.

"No, I actually got lost looking for my room. This is the wrong floor. They all look the same to me." I keep moving towards the elevators.

"Come on, you can admit it, we're both adults."

"Were you taking a break from the party too?" I ask, ignoring his comment, I keep walking. In some bizarre superman move, Brett manages to get in front of me and stops me in my tracks.

"Why are you in such a hurry? You're here now, so…" I remember that look in his eyes and what happens next.

"I'm not in a hurry, just need to find my room, I need some time out."

"Is that an invitation? If so, I accept."

"Hahaha, no it's not, and besides, why would we go to my room when yours is right here?" I point to the room he just came out of.

"It's not my room."

"Well, we're still not going to my room. I need to put my head down for five minutes, alone."

"I promise to let you have your five minutes, then you're mine."

"What am I going to do with you, Mr Ferguson? You don't know when to give up."

"I can think of many, many things you could be doing with me, and many we have done before. And for the record, I don't give up on the things I want." He takes this as his signal to press me hard up against the wall. He has one of his hands on the wall behind me, the other around my waist, and I respond, unwillingly. It is a passionate, strong, familiar kiss and his intentions are clear. I come to my senses and push him away, he gets the hint.

I wait until Brett is out of sight, then look to the left towards the elevators and see Mr Blue Eyes leaning against the wall, his eyes fixed on me. I can tell by his expression he saw and probably heard everything. He does not say a word or move a muscle. I try to take a step towards him, but I cannot move, and my heart is pounding at a frightening rate. I can feel my eyes start to fill with tears and I try hard to fight it, looking away in shame. I cannot take the elevator, as it would mean walking right past him. I cannot go down the corridor, as that is where Brett went. I am trapped.

"Jake, it's not what you think, really it's not." I need to say something, and this is the best I can do. I can barely stand straight from the wave of emotion that has hit me, the shock has paralysed me, and I am fighting the urge to blink. The ache in my chest is unbearable. I know what this means. He says nothing. His face is dark.

"Jake, say something, please."

"How long has this been going on for?" He demands, with no change of expression or stance. "How long?" He repeats.

"It... It's... not what you think."

"Cari, it's not what I think, I am asking how long has this been going on?"

"It's nothing, a kiss."

He looks disgusted in me, and rightly so. It must only be two hours since we made love in my suite. I respond by shaking my head and start to splutter as the pain overwhelms me. I lean against the wall and slide down to the floor. I clutch my knees and bury my head in them. I can hardly breathe.

"Go away," I demand. I do not want him to see me like this. I am ashamed, and I would rather save what dignity I have left. My senses are on high beam, fuelled by vast amounts of alcohol and cocaine, leaving me in an uncontrollable mess.

"Go," I demand louder.

"Cari, get up," he says, offering his hand.

"No, go away, please."

"I'm not going anywhere until you stand up and pull yourself together."

I reject his extended hand and wobble to my feet on my own, sobbing.

"Jake, if you don't believe anything please believe I never planned this, and I would never want to hurt you. It was just a kiss, a stupid ugly kiss, and I pushed him away, you must have seen that." I risk a quick glance up at his face. His expression is still dark. His eyes are his windows and I see something new, hurt. Caitem has infected my world and now his.

"You should go and get yourself cleaned up," he advises, and leaves me standing against the wall.

Locked in the privacy of my room, I hang the 'do not disturb' sign again and let out all the emotion.

"Shelley, I ruined everything," I sob uncontrollably

down the phone.

"Cari what's going on, why are you so upset are you okay?"

"Can you come to the Hilton? I really need you."

"That's where your party is tonight, isn't it? Why do you want me to come over?"

"Please come, I really need you."

"Tell me what happened."

"You are going to think I am horrible, because I am."

"I won't think that, you are scaring me now, tell me what happened."

"Jake saw me kiss another guy."

"Why were you kissing another guy?"

"See, I am horrible, he hates me now and I have ruined everything." Tears keep pouring out.

"Take a deep breath, I bet it's not as bad as you think."

"Can you come to the Hilton, I'm in room 506? Can you come now, please?"

"I'm in the area so I will see you shortly."

"Thank you."

While I wait for Shelley, I do the best I can to pull myself together. This is my world and my mess. I pour a strong vodka, have a line, turn on the music, grab a flannel, fill it with ice, and rest it on my eyes to reduce the swelling. I shower and wash my hair, letting the hot water play over me. I look almost normal. The remaining redness in my eyes can be explained by alcohol, but I try reducing that by blowing cold air from the blow-dryer directly into my eyes.

My charade is complete and just in time as Shelley is at the door. I tell her all the gory details and she does not think I am horrible which makes me feel only slightly better. I convince Shelley to stay with me for the rest of the night.

I scan for Mr Blue Eyes, Brett, Lita, Kelly, or Sheree but see none of them, so we head towards the bar, and get a large vodka for Shelley and something soft for me. Then I spot Sheree dancing with Julie and some other account directors. Kelly is deep in conversation with Craig. I dismiss any thoughts of how Craig might be involved in Brett's mess, or even if the Craig I heard Brett mention on the phone, is this Craig. I catch Sheree's attention and she immediately bounces over to us and I introduce her to Shelley.

"Where have you been?" She asks.

"Being drunk around the place and had to meet Shelley, where's Lita?" I respond, keeping it light and forcing a smile.

"I haven't seen her for ages. I thought she was with you. Come and dance," she says, dragging us both by our arms behind her. We accept, as there is nothing else we can do. The Hilton is my prison for the rest of the evening, and I need to do my time.

I lost Shelley somewhere between the dance-floor and bar, and decide to head back to my room for the final time. I need to get out of these clothes and unwind. The closer I get to my room the louder the party noises get. I open the door to the after party and there are people everywhere. On one bed, Kelly is painting Craig's fingernails ruby red. He'll regret that in the morning. On the other bed, random bodies are sprawled. Some I recognise, others I do not. In the lounge area among others are Lita, Brett, Mr Blue Eyes and Shelley, all enjoying more drinks, snacks and a stupid drunken conversation. Lita runs up to me and gives me a big hug, saying she has not seen me all night and wants to know what I have been up to.

I look at Mr Blue Eyes, at Brett and then at Shelley and decide to sit on the bed next to Kelly and marvel at her paint work, doing my best to ignore Brett and Mr Blue Eyes behind me.

When Brett joins us on the bed and openly flirts with me by trying to paint my nails, Mr Blue Eyes says his goodbyes and makes his exit. I follow him.

"Jake, wait!"

"Yes, Cari?"

"Jake, I'm sorry, I'm really sorry, I pushed him away. You must have seen that."

"I know what I saw, and I know what I heard. That was not an accidental party kiss. It looked a lot more to me, there was a familiarity."

"I don't want Brett, I want you. Can I still come to your room later or even now? We can talk and sort this out and you'll see it was nothing."

"I think your night looks full already."

"I don't want to be in that room, I want to be with you, I love you Jake, please, let's just go to your room and sort this out." I try to grab his arm, but he moves away from me.

"I think it's best if we stay in our own rooms."

"Best for who? It's not best for me. I want to be with you. Don't you want to be with me?"

"Cari, we made love and then I saw you kissing another man. Do I want you right now? No. Go back to your room. Brett will be wondering where you are," he says, angry and hurt. The elevator doors open, and he disappears. I ruined our perfect evening together. I hate Caitem!

- CHAPTER 19 -

Six AM and the last of the party goers leave our suite. Finally, we hit the beds. Lita disappeared hours ago but I am too tired to question her whereabouts. I fall asleep immediately.

Our alarms start chirping at seven-thirty and I notice Lita has not returned. The room looks like a party bus has driven through it. My head is pounding, my stomach is gurgling, and when my heart remembers the evening's events, it rips in two all over again. I am thankful to be with Shelley, Sheree and Kelly, who will be a good distraction. I think about Mr Blue Eyes in his big empty bed and about how our night should have been. He was genuinely hurt and disappointed in me. He no longer looks at me the way he used to. I am tainted. Caitem comes first should be rebranded, first comes Caitem, then comes hell.

Breakfast is served until ten and there is no way we are leaving without it. Lita returns and in one fluid movement, she slithers in-between Shelley and me. Our silent exchanges reveal she spent the night with Brett, and she is beaming. She deserves the happiness, I just wish it was with someone else. I wonder if Mr Blue Eyes invited someone back to his room out of spite. I do not believe he is that type of man, but he probably did not think I was the type of woman to kiss another man only hours after being together. The ache demands tears, but I must hold them back. If I start now, I will not be able to stop.

One by one, we muster the courage to get up, shower, take Berocca, have coffee, clean the room up a bit, pack our suitcases, consume the last of the cocaine, and crawl back into bed for a sixty-second break. This cycle continues until we are done and then somehow make it to breakfast in time.

Waiting in line to check-out, I am completely in my own hungover world until I am pulled out by a neighbouring conversation.

"Hi, I was in room 607 and I'd like to check out." I look at the man. That was the room Brett was leaving when I accidentally landed on the wrong floor. When Brett said it was not his room, I assumed it belonged to another Tyn-T person. I pretend to look for my card so I can concentrate on this conversation.

"Certainly, Mr Stratford, how was your stay?" The receptionist inquires.

"Sounds like there was a good party here last night," he responds. That confirms he is not a Tyn-T person or a client.

"I apologise, Mr Stratford, if it disturbed your stay. There was a very special anniversary celebration held in our ballroom." Her response is well rehearsed.

"I was not disturbed, thank you," he reassures her.

"Will the rest of your party be checking out this morning too?"

"Mr Fuller will be leaving in about an hour. Can you book a car for him please?"

"Certainly. I have attached your receipt to your account and placed it in this envelope. Hope to see you again,

Mr Stratford."

When I make it to the front of the queue, I ask for a pen and paper to write this information down: 'Room 607, Mr Stratford, Mr Fuller, saw Brett come out of room during the evening.'

While we are waiting for our taxis to take us to the office, unsure why we are even trying to work today, I grab my Caitem phone, the piece of paper with the information and move away from our group.

"Are you in a secure location?" Poh asks.

"Yes. Outside the hotel. I've information for you."

"You don't sound well."

"I don't feel well. Party last night."

"Do I need to remind you?"

"No, I know, but you told me to call you first thing in the morning."

"We have different perspectives on first thing."

"Well, it's the first time I could get free and call you. Anyway, I have some information."

"What is it?"

"Room 607, Mr Stratford, Mr Fuller. Brett was in their room last night."

"At the Hilton? Are you sure?"

"Positive."

"How?"

"I saw Brett come out of 607 and then Stratford checked out next to me from 607 this morning. He said Fuller would be leaving in an hour and wanted a car called for him."

"Do you know where the car was going?"

"No, he didn't say."

"Is there anything else?"

"No, that's everything."

"This sounds useful and they may have been careless. This could be the break we need."

"What do I do now?"

"You need to pull yourself together. You know the rules of Caitem. All of them apply, all of the time."

"I wasn't asking about that. Believe me, I know the Caitem rules. I mean, what do I do about Brett? Can I stop?"

"Nothing has changed, Brett is still your assignment, and I will see you this afternoon for our session." Poh hangs up the phone.

I do not know how I will get myself into a state where I can train. However, if there is one thing I have learnt so far, it is to trust my body and hide any discomfort. I know I can push through no matter what state I am in: hungover, lack of sleep, muscle strain, a cold, a flu, she stops for nothing and expects me to perform every time. Today though, I do not have the mental strength to push through the barriers that she will make me strive for. I am too tired, too hungover, too emotional, and way too scared to face up to what I have lost. I fear this session may be the one that kills me. I want to hide under my duvet and only come out when the world is right again. The only small consolation is that Mr Blue Eyes will not be in the office today. Seeing him look at me like he did last night would be too much to handle.

Everyone in the office is feeling the effects of the party, which has been hailed an incredible success. It seems that Tyn-T has been awarded more work based on the party alone, proving that no matter what, there is always business to be done. Craig is amusing us in his attempt to find nail polish remover. Sheree is sent home due to her obvious disfunctioning and some other party-goers leave too. I do not have that luxury.

Corey is still plodding along with no sense of urgency, but he has managed to get the Frogman designs ready for Sparkles to review. I do not understand why Corey had to arrange a review for today. I am sure it is a conspiracy to torment me, although he must also be feeling the effects of the evening.

"Corey, the designs look okay, but how was the budget?" I ask.

"I have gone over but don't you think it was worth it?"

"Not if it's going to cost Tyn-T to complete the project."

Corey and Sparkles continue the conversation and all I hear is blah, blah, blah as all I can think about is last night's events, until Sparkles snaps.

"I can't believe you think this is good. It makes me want to vomit! It's a mess. I can't bear to look at it any more. Get it out of my sight," she says.

"Excuse me, did I hear right?" I ask.

"Yes, you heard right, it makes me want to vomit. Look at it. There's so much on the page it makes me dizzy."

"That's a bit strong, don't you think? And not at all constructive. Are you hungover from last night?" I reply sarcastically.

Corey is shocked into silence, a first for him.

"I'm not hungover. If I was, it might look better. It's all over the place, it's not balanced, and it's too busy." She flicks it towards Corey and something inside me snaps.

"There is no excuse for your response. It's rude and unprofessional. But seeing as we are being completely honest, you make me want to vomit. I have tolerated your imbecilic behaviour for long enough. If you can't provide constructive criticism, get off my account. I've had enough of your attitude, your lack of digital knowledge, you're steaming through my projects like a freight train, adding no value whatsoever. This is your last project and to be frank, as there is no future for you on this account you might as well leave now. I'll get Sheree to review these designs." Even though I am being unprofessional, rude and disrespectful, today I do not give a crap.

When this meeting is relayed to Bill, I will gladly take the rap as this time it is deserved. Hopefully, they will fire me, and I can leave all this.

Sparkles has lost her sparkle and sits in stunned silence. Corey too is stunned, but he turns the designs face down just in case they really do make Julie vomit.

"Okay, we're done here, this review is over. I'll get in touch with Sheree and let her know what's happened. Corey, I think you've done a good job except for managing the budget. We'll deal with that separately." I grab the designs and leave the room. Corey does not want to be left alone with Sparkles and follows closely behind me.

"Corey, don't think what I just did was acceptable. I was out of line and unprofessional and I will be pulled up for it," I explain.

"That was awesome. I've never seen a project manager take down an account manager like that. She deserved it, what a bitch."

"Yes, she did deserve something, but not what I gave her. I'm a senior member of Tyn-T and there is never an occasion where that behaviour is acceptable."

"So, what do I do now?"

"After I talk with Sheree, we'll try this again with her."

"Okay, thanks."

"Oh, and we will discuss the budget next week."

I text Mr Blue Eyes. Lita is bouncing around oblivious to everything. She is floating on residual fumes and the euphoria of Brett. I do not want to know the details, but I know I will not be spared. Blissfully unaware of the damage caused last night, all she wants is coffee. Ironically, I would have found some respect for Brett if he had not spent the night with her.

"So, last night, good night was it?" I ask, forcing a joyful tone.

"Awesome night. Second night I've stayed with Brett and he keeps getting better," she laughs.

I try to stay engaged in our conversation, but I am focused on my phone, concerned about what it means that he has not replied to my text. Surely the time spent together means something, at least a conversation, or maybe he thinks we already had it.

"I don't need details. Just be careful. Like I told you, I think he's a player."

"He's not that bad, we had a really good night together."

"And you were the only one he was with last night?"

"Do you know something I don't? Did you see something? Was he with someone else, tell me?" Lita drills me.

"No, I know nothing, I didn't see anything, nothing at all. I'm just a passenger in my own life. I can't believe we did more coke this morning. My head is mush. I just don't want you getting hurt." That much is true, but there is nothing I can do to stop the inevitable.

"Do you really think Brett is a player?"

"I would put money on it. He has player written all over him. Look at how much he flirts with people. Are you exclusive?"

"No, not yet, but I'm sure we're not that far off. I'm used to players, and if he is playing me, I know how to play back," she reassures. I believe she could handle a player, but I fear that Brett is not a normal player.

"How was Jake last night, did you stay with him?"

"No, although that was the plan. But as Shelley was with us, I thought it best I stay with her. Also, when I got to our room, he left shortly after as he was wrecked. Next minute it was six in the morning and I crashed," I reply, chuckling. Just saying his name aloud makes me want to burst into tears.

"Shelley is cool, she fit right in as if she was part of the crew and knew everyone."

"Yes, she is talented like that and lucky for her she doesn't have to work until much later today and has gone home for real sleep."

"Lucky for her, not so lucky for us, but I couldn't sleep now even if I tried."

I agree with Lita and move to a secluded part of the office to ring Mr Blue Eyes. There is no answer, and I leave a message. I do not know what to do with myself and decide to look for Brett. I find him at his desk looking fragile. Knowing about the possible significance of room 607, I expect him to be different somehow, but there is no change. Maybe it means nothing.

"Hey, how did you pull up?" I ask as normally as I can.

"Hey, to be expected," he replies in typical Brett fashion.

"Lita is beaming today. You know this is going to end badly for her." I say straight to the point. Brett tilts his head to the side as if to say 'whatever'. "Doesn't it bother you?"

"Are we doing this again, why should it bother me?"

"The fact that you're sleeping with two women at the same time, knowing full well Lita is really into you."

"I'm not, and we discussed this before, she knows where she stands. Here's a question for you, why doesn't it bother you?"

"Are you serious? Of course it bothers me, why do you

think I keep bringing it up?"

"Not Lita, why does it not bother you that I might be sleeping with someone else?"

"Why should it bother me?"

"I think it does and that's why you keep bringing up Lita. You really want me to stop seeing her because it bothers you that you don't have me to yourself," he claims arrogantly.

"I can assure you that is not the case."

"So this is just some fun?"

"I'm not concerned about me, I'm concerned about Lita."

"I'm not."

"You're not what?"

"I'm not sleeping with two women."

"Erm, I am one, Lita is two, or are you saying there are more?"

"You are one, there is no two."

"What about last night? Lita spent the night in your room."

"Again, nothing happened."

"Bullshit, she was beaming this morning and said you have progressed as a couple."

"Not to that, we didn't," he answers, laughing.

"This isn't funny. I don't know why I came up here in the first place."

"I do, but you just won't admit it. Stop trying to make out I'm the bad guy. It takes two to tango and she's your friend."

This is my cue to leave. I cannot deal with him

anymore and I bolt out of the elevator and straight out the front doors. I need air. I ring Mr Blue Eyes again and leave another message, this time a bit stroppy. I am so angry. My emotions are all over the place.

I keep walking and end up at the training park, sitting on the bench I normally use for my warm-up stretches or as a torture device. I watch mothers with their prams, office workers on breaks, students lounging about with their noses in textbooks, lads trying to outdo one another in football, office workers with briefcases and coats. This jolts me back to reality and I hurriedly return to the office to pack up.

I avoid the banter about going to the pub. That is for the hard-core revellers proving they have stamina. They can have it. It is time for me to face the consequences of another night of debauchery. I remind myself tomorrow is Saturday and I can sleep all day if I want to.

I meet Poh at FitUs and we jog towards the park. Poh stops when I trip over a cobblestone. No more jogging for me. When we get to the park, we do not stop. We do not stop at the juice bar either.

"Where are we going?" I ask

"This assignment has taken a turn and we've been called in."

"What does that mean, where are we going?"

We keep walking until we arrive at an office building. We enter a room, sit and wait. The furnishings are basic, which makes me believe this must be a Caitem location. Michael joins us, which is the first time I have seen him since I signed the contract.

"Cari, welcome. You don't look well. Still not looking after yourself. You know what is expected, and Caitem comes first." Michael states.

"It was a special occasion. Is that why I'm here, am I in trouble?"

"Your indulgences will be dealt with later. The reason Poh and you are here is because there has been a significant turn in your assignment."

"What does a significant turn mean?" I ask.

"The two men at the Hilton you linked to Brett, is the connection we needed to understand their operation."

"I don't understand?" My head is exploding.

"Before the sighting, we knew about the individuals and others too, but didn't know how or if they were connected. Mr Fuller, we identified as part of another operation, but we didn't know it was connected to this one. Mr Fuller and Mr Stratford are here from Russia to pick up and deliver documents relating to foreign policies and there were lists of chemicals, which could be used for biological weaponry. The fact that you saw Brett coming out of their room is a rare and lucky break. We suspect Brett is their courier and that he may be more deeply involved." Michael pauses. I have no words, reverting to how I felt when this process first began. "As a consequence, all parties involved are being marked and tracked, to be picked up this evening."

"Oh my gosh, really? Brett too?" I ask.

"All parties involved will be brought in for questioning."

"Why are you going to wait until this evening? Why not now, if you know who they are? Aren't you worried you could lose them?"

"We need to ensure we have located all those involved, and that our people are in place to pick them up at the same time so they can't tip anyone off. It's going to be a long night and all transport routes out of London are being closely monitored."

A shiver runs through my entire body and I feel cold.

"Poh, Cari, good work. This assignment is now complete. Poh will debrief you." Michael smiles briefly and leaves the room. Is that it? Is that all I get? My entire life has changed and that is it.

"So, debrief me," I invite Poh sarcastically.

"I am still your mentor," Poh reminds me, indicating my comment is not appreciated and that there is still a pecking order to respect. "As stated by Michael this assignment is complete and there are no further tasks to undertake. We will continue to train as per normal."

"Is that it? I've ruined a relationship that is important to me, and my friend has fallen for Brett, and I can't do or say anything to stop her. Oh no, is she going to be tracked and possibly picked up tonight with the rest of them?"

"Caitem comes first, and you know that. Before relationships, partnerships and family. Brett will be picked up this evening and I am only telling you this, so you are prepared. You need to be surprised like everyone else when news gets out as to why he is not in the office on Monday, which of course will be a fabrication. Any further information is classified."

"And that's it, it's done? Business as usual until the next assignment?"

"You did your job Cari. You should be happy that you contributed to stopping the operation."

"What about Lita and Craig, are they mixed up in all of this?"

"We are re-working their profiles."

"So what happens now, what do I do?"

"You continue working at Tyn-T, and training with me, until the next assignment."

"As if nothing has happened, business as usual." I say to her. "Getting closer to Brett has ruined my relationship. There is nothing usual about that. Lita is going to be upset when Brett just disappears without telling her, and I will have to comfort her knowing exactly what happened."

"Remember the confidentially agreement," Poh says, as cold as ever.

"Fine. Are we done here? I need to go home, and I don't care what you say, I'm not training now. And yes, I know I overdid it last night, but considering I still did my job it should be overlooked." I sound like a snotty child.

"I have a higher priority now. We will resume training Monday morning," Poh dismisses me. Every cell in my body is relieved that I do not have to train and that this is finally over. I can go home and hide from the world. If only Mr Blue Eyes had not seen that kiss. I check my phone but there are no new messages and no missed calls. This is ridiculous. I am going to his place and I am going to make him speak to me.

His flat is dark and quiet. It is obvious he is not home. My stubbornness sets in, and I sit and wait. It does not take long before the exhaustion and cold hits. I text him again. He must give me a chance.

– CHAPTER 20 –

Saturday, I wake from the deepest sleep feeling much better than I did yesterday morning. My head is clearer, and I replay the Michael, Poh conversation wondering whether the pickups happened last night and who they were. I will know it happened if Brett is not in the office, but will there be others missing too? I check my phone, no texts, no messages, and no missed calls.

Maybe this is it, and Jake's way of letting me know. I have lost Jake. Monday, as awkward as it will be, he will just be my line manager.

I want to stay in bed under the protection of my duvet and never come out.

My thoughts are interrupted by a pesky knock at the door. I ignore it. I am not expecting anyone, or a delivery so it can only be someone trying to sell something. I rebury my head.

The knock continues.

"Go away!" I call out, muffled by my pillow. I then get a text, it is Mr Blue Eyes, "Answer the door".

I bolt upright, my heart pounding, and open the door as casually as I can.

"Let's talk. Can you get changed?" He asks expressionlessly. There is no Mr Blue Eyes. He looks exhausted, but he is here.

"Sure, come in." I excuse myself to change from my

pyjamas and into casuals. He has remained standing, staring out my window, eerily still.

"Hey." I let him know I have returned to the room.

"Hey." He replies as he turns to look at me. I pause to see if he wants to say anything, but there is nothing.

"Jake, I know what I did was wrong and that you think poorly of me right now, but you have to believe me, it meant nothing, it is nothing and I don't want this to end. We had, have, something special. It's strong and I know you feel it too, please? I've been trying to contact you and heard nothing, but I'm happy to see you now. Please tell me we can get past this?" I plead unapologetically. He doesn't respond. "What's the point of coming over here if you aren't going to say anything? The fact that you're here has to mean something. Please don't throw this away."

"I obviously recall a different set of events," he finally responds coldly and turns back to look out the window. He cannot even look at me. I have had enough of this and move myself between the window and him. We are close, not touching but I can still feel him.

I look up and realise I no longer know this man. He has changed. I search for something familiar. Something is not right. I know what I did was wrong, but he is here, so he must have something to say. He is a man of strong opinions and I know he must be bursting to let them out. I never imagined it could go this wrong so soon.

He finally looks at me, moves to the door ready to open it, looks back at me and says, "Cari, you know the drill,

Caitem comes first." Then he is gone.

"What?" I say out loud. "What? He said Caitem comes first, he is Caitem? This can't be, I am Caitem, what is going on?"

I am sure what I heard, but not sure why. I am stunned, flabbergasted. I cannot move from this spot, this spot is where I heard those words, if I stay here maybe something will change. I do not know what to do with myself. I make myself move, pace, think, where is my phone? Maybe I need a drink, that will not help, yes it will.

My heart is racing, my mind is empty, there is a strange nothingness. In this moment I am completely lost. I need to call him, but will he answer? Probably not.

Shit, shit, shit. Now that I am moving, I cannot stand still. I must get out of here. I grab my phone, my headphones, and head out, nowhere in particular, I just need to keep moving. I put my headphones in and decide on a coffee shop. I do need something stronger, but pubs are not open yet, then I remember one of my locals serve Irish Coffees, this is what I need. I take a seat, my body reluctant to be quiet. I reconnect my headphones and open my phone. I stare at the last message, "Answer the door", and recap how I felt the moment I saw the message and how quickly everything has changed. I scull half my coffee and wait for the effects.

Between the coffee, my music and people watching, my nothingness is being flooded with questions coming thick and fast. How did he know I am Caitem? Has he known from the beginning? Was I a job to him? Did he do to me what I did to Brett? Does he know about Brett? Did he know all along? What was his role in all this? Was he my keeper? Was any of it real? What does it mean that he told me? Does he not have a confidentiality agreement? What does he do for Caitem?

I scull the rest of my coffee and get back onto my feet. I need to talk to someone, and that someone is Jake. I try my luck, no answer, no surprise and I do not leave a message. My phone rings, my heart skips a beat.

"Hi Cari, its Shelley, how are you? Have you recovered from the party?"

"Hi Shelley, I feel much better than I did yesterday, how are you?"

"Good thanks, what are you doing? Feel like catching up?"

"Not sure that I do, Jake and I are not talking, I think we may have ended, and I am quite tired from last week, not sure what I need right now."

"I know what you need, meet me at the Albion, it has a great beer garden. I can head there now, see you shortly?"

"Sure, I'll grab a cab."

The Albion does have a nice outside area, and as the pub has just opened, there are not many people around. Shelley is already seated and has purchased the first round.

"Is this an Espresso Martini?" I ask a little too joyfully for this early in the day.

"Yes it is, and as its still technically morning, and it has coffee in it, it's just a different form of coffee, right?"

"That was my reasoning for an Irish Coffee earlier."

"You have started already? You really are not in a good way. Do you want to talk about it?"

"Not really, nothing much to say. He saw me kiss Brett, and he was pissed at me, and now won't talk to me so I can only assume it's done."

"You probably dented his ego, he will come around, plus you work with him so he can't totally avoid you."

"He could fire me, although that would be a good thing." I chuckle, now realising if he did, it would be due to Caitem, not Tyn-T. "Anyway, enough about me, what have you been up to, how are your personal training sessions going?"

"Good, its quite tiring especially if I have several clients in one day. Oh Cari, you are really upset." She claims spotting the tears welling up. The alcohol has opened the flood gates.

"I feel so sad and helpless, and stupid. Kissing one bloke when I'm into another, is not me."

"Babe, its done, you are not stupid, it might have been a stupid thing, but you pushed him away. Jake will come around."

"Nope, it's done, and I need to get used to it, and use the weekend to deal, otherwise Monday is going to be worse than hell."

"You are strong, smart, funny, gorgeous and if Jake cannot see that, then he doesn't deserve you. Stuff him, I'll have you, we can run away together."

"Thanks, I bet I am none of those things right now," I chuckle. "My round. Same again?"

"Yes, and bring a surprise?"

"A surprise?"

"Yes, like a shot." Shelley offers with a contorted smile. "Maybe something to nibble on too?"

"Sure, probably a good idea," I agree and head to the bar.

An afternoon of normality is exactly what I needed, although I wish I could have told her the entire truth. There was a moment when I almost did but did not want to experience a Caitem 'consequence'.

We do not want to interrupt this buzz and decide to keep the day going with a movie night at mine. On the way we stock up on semi healthy and non-healthy comfort food, wine, and vodka.

What is tickling my nose? It stops, it happens again. I open my eyes and it is Shelley's way of saying good morning. She has two mugs of coffee and a bag of chips we did not finish last night, breakfast in bed it is. Having Shelley around has made me feel a lot better, and as the hours pass, we speak less and less about it. I am slowly accepting the recent events, all I can do now is prepare for Poh, Tyn-T and what could unfold.

Shelley leaves early afternoon and I perform a super clean. The more I do, the better I feel. I move onto organising myself for the week, focussing on the positives. I will not have to see Brett and Jake in the same place, I do not have to pretend to be into Brett anymore, I will not have to lie to Lita and all this training has given me the best body I have ever had. I think, cautiously, I might be as prepared as I can be for the week ahead.

Monday morning, the start of the week. The week that will be like no other. I am nervous but excited and prepared for Jake to be my line manager only. My training with Poh was needed. I pushed hard to eradicate the final bits of angst, which surprised Poh.

"How did Friday night go?" I casually ask.

"Good."

"What does good mean? Did everyone get picked up, did Brett get picked up, will he be at Tyn-T this morning?"

"The pickups were successful. Brett will not be at Tyn-T this morning."

"Wow, so what happened? Where is he?"

"That's information you do not need to know." Poh claims as expected.

"You said pickups meaning there were multiple, was anyone else picked up that I might know, from Tyn-T?"

"That's information you do not need to know." Poh reiterates. I get the picture.

"So, what happens now?"

"We continue with our training schedule."

"And?"

"If an assignment presents, we will discuss."

"Is that likely to be soon?"

"It could be anytime. Caitem does not stop."

As I walk through the Tyn-T doors, I know today will be different, but only I will know why, other than Jake. I feel physically good, and I was emotionally okay until now. Now I feel knotted. I can only take today one hour at a time, and I know I will eventually see Jake and need to talk to him, I will keep it professional.

I make it to my desk issue free, there is no Lita, but it is still early for her. I turn on my computer and check my emails. There are no company blasts or his insights on the marketing industry. I will entertain the rumours fabricated by some extremely creative people about why Brett is not at Tyn-T.

As the lie makes it through the teams, everyone will be questioning why so suddenly, my guess will be family reasons, as for today, maybe he will be 'sick' or 'working from home'. Then there will be Lita and how she reacts to his sudden disappearance. All I can do is continue the charade and provide comfort.

While this underlying current is flowing through this vibrant advertising agency, not a beat will be skipped, designs will continue to be crafted, clients will be served, and budgets will be scrutinised.

It is now late-morning and there has been no Jake sightings, emails, texts or phone calls. There is also no Lita or conversations about Brett. I text Lita to see if she is coming in or has a day off. As the day progresses it is proving difficult to not keep one eye on the entrance.

Corey and Sparkles are both here, friendly which is good considering the altercation on Friday, which now seems so long ago. This does remind me I need to setup a meeting with Sheree to go through the Frogman designs and manoeuvre Sparkles away from this project.

I am doing the same work as I usually do, my routines

are the same, people are behaving the same, yet everything feels different. London has changed me, Caitem has changed me. It is nearly the end of the day and there has been no Jake, no Lita, no reply to my text, and no Brett. I feel brave and decide to do some exploring, starting with Brett. As soon as I exit the lift, I can see he is not at his desk. I ask his colleagues about him, but no one knows where he is, and do not seem concerned. How does that happen?

On my way back to my desk I run into Tommy and ask if he has seen Jake, he had not. I ring Lita and receive voice mail. What is going on? My last hope is to find Bill. Bill and Jake are peers and seem to have a good relationship, maybe he knows where Jake is, or claims to be.

"Hi Bill, how are you, did you have a good weekend?"

"Hi Cari, nice to see you, well done on Toadstool, a great success, Alex is really happy with how it turned out."

"Thanks Bill, that is very kind. Can I ask you a quick question?"

"Sure, what's up?"

"I haven't seen Jake today, did he have a day off?"

"Sorry Cari, I thought everyone knew, he was called last minute to one of our sister companies to help with a situation, and he is owed some personal days which he is also taking this week."

"Oh, I did not know that, or maybe he did mention it, but I forgot. There has been a lot going on. How long will he be gone for?"

"Just this week."

"Okay, I expect he is still contactable?"

"Yes, he is, by all the normal means. I spoke to him this morning. But only call if it is an emergency as he does need a break. I am happy to help if needed."

"Okay thanks, and thanks for letting me know." I head back to my desk. He is obviously deliberately ignoring me, and I have no more avenues to pursue. Looks like I have no choice other than to ride this out on my own.

Days go by and no Lita, nothing from Jake, and some Brett gossip is starting to trickle through, but it is not that he has left, people are making comment that they have not seen him or any of his normal email blasts. I ignore it. My concern is about Lita, I still have not heard from her, and she has not appeared at work all week. Apart from this, my world does seem settled. There are no Caitem persons of interest to track, training is consistent, Sparkles is no longer involved with project Frogman, and Corey is still arrogant, but somewhat productive.

It is Friday and I am feeling comfortable with this new normal, but still looking forward to the weekend. From the corner of my eye, I see Lita stroll in, but she is not looking her normal bubbly self. I stop mid-type and watch every step she takes, and move she makes to get ready for her day at work.

"Hi?" I say.

"Hi?" She replies. I continue to watch her.

"Are you okay?"

"Of course. Are you?"

"Of course, shall we get a coffee?"

"Sure." She agrees a little hesitant, but we grab our coats and head out of the building.

"Where have you been, and why have you not answered any of my texts or calls?"

"Um. On leave."

"Um, I don't believe you. You would have returned something. Were you with Brett as he hasn't been here either?"

"Hasn't he, where has he been?"

"I don't know, I thought maybe he was with you, that you finally got together and were in some love bubble."

"Hardly."

"So, you weren't with Brett?"

"No."

"Then where were you?"

"I can't really say."

"Why not?"

"It was weird."

"Weird? You know you can tell me anything and I'd never judge."

"Okay, first let's get another coffee and go somewhere private."

We do just that, and I can't wait any longer.

"So, tell me." I prompt.

"I am not even sure if I can talk about it, or how much I can say?" She claims.

"Why? No one can hear us here, look, there is no one around." I plead.

"Turn your phone off," she demands.

"What, why?" This is making me nervous.

"Just do it."

"Wow, okay." We both turn off our phones.

"It started Friday night, I was at home, on my own and I answer my door to these people who say they need to question me in relation to a recent incident and whether I could accompany them."

"Accompany them where, and who were they?"

"They didn't say specifically, but they alluded to being investigative agents like the FBI."

"You didn't ask?"

"No, as that's what I thought they were, they were convincing and professional."

'Okay, so what did they say?"

"They said they worked for the government, and they needed to question me regards information I may have, unknowingly, regarding a case they have been working on."

"Wow, this sounds like something out of a movie. Then what happened?"

"They asked me lots of questions, and the worst bit was they questioned my relationship with Brett, so I think it has something to do with him. Have you seen him?"

"No, that is why I thought he was with you. And, what happened next?"

"The questioning continued over the weekend, and I had to stay wherever I was."

"Where were you?"

"I had no idea, but I knew I was still in London as we

didn't go that far. But I couldn't work it out as the car I was in had dark windows and it was late evening. I stayed in a room that was like a three-star hotel room, everything I needed was provided. I just didn't have internet or my phone."

"Really? Were you scared?"

"At first I was, but they were generally nice, and seemed genuinely concerned about whatever they are investigating and the way they explained things made sense."

"Why couldn't you have your phone?"

"They didn't say."

"Wow. Were you with them all this time?"

"Only until Sunday afternoon, but they requested me to stay out of circulation until today, so I text Jake to say I was sick."

"You knew where you were when you left?"

"Yes, but that I am definitely not allowed to say as I had to sign a confidentiality agreement and they were serious about that."

"Okay, wow, why didn't you text me to say you were sick?"

"They requested strongly to stay out of circulation and not contact anyone as it might compromise their investigation. I thought they would know if I did, that is why I said to turn our phones off."

"Wow, this is intense."

"It is, and what was even weirder, for a split second, when they were taking me from a room to where I was staying for the night, I thought I saw Jake, or someone that looked like Jake."

"Jake? Really? Surely not. I saw him Saturday, and Bill has told me he is at a sister company for a few days this week. But I haven't seen Brett, did you see him, or do you think he was where you were?"

"I didn't see Brett, but it would make sense if he was there too. As I'm back in circulation now, if everything was okay, he should be too."

"He hasn't appeared at work, and there have been no company-wide emails either. Have you tried to contact him?" I ask.

"Only this morning before coming into work."

"And?"

"And nothing."

"So, what happens now?"

"As far as I know, that was it, there is nothing else, but that was weird, and I have done weird before, but this was the weirdest."

"I am glad you are okay, but next time, try and get word to me somehow as I was getting really worried."

"Sorry, there will not be a next time. I am back, and all is good. I am concerned about Brett though."

"I would be too, what were they asking you about?"

"Just things about our relationship like how close we were, what we did, where did we go, who did we socialise with, I didn't have a lot to say."

"Yet they still kept hold of you."

"I know, they did ask me about different people."

"Like who?"

"Just random people I never heard of, I can't really remember their names either as there were quite a few."

"Anyway, I am glad to see you and have you back in the office. I was getting lonely." I say with a forced chuckle and give her a little squeeze.

"We need drinks after work."

"Absolutely," I agree, and we head back to the office. I am not surprised by this conversation, strangely satisfied to know more about how the Caitem world operates from someone not connected to Caitem. Only two more mysteries to solve.

Sunday morning and time for training. Trainings are mostly performed during the week, but some Sundays have been scheduled. I think it is Poh's way of making sure I behave Saturday night. Poh sends me a text to meet her at the juice bar and not to be late. I might be reluctant at times, but I am rarely ever late.

As I enter the juice bar, I can see our usual table is occupied, but not by Poh, but this imposter is still wearing a FitUs kit.
I head over.

"Hi Cari."

"Hi Jake." My heart is racing. Shit, fuck, shit. I am not prepared for this.

"You look surprised."

"Really, and I wonder why that is." I say at a whisper and loaded with sarcasm.

MONICA RITZ

"I have taken the liberty to order you a juice."

"Thanks, but I think I need something a little stronger than a juice."

"Cari, I am sure I do not have to remind you that we take health seriously."

"Yes, I mean no." I am numb. He is just another version of Poh. "What is going on, where is Poh?"

"She had a prior engagement."

"Poh never has a prior engagement. Why didn't she reschedule?"

"I requested to take your training."

"And she was okay with it?"

"She didn't have a choice."

"Why didn't she have a choice?"

"I am a higher level than Poh."

"Of course you are." I can feel tears forming as I am overwhelmed by all the different feelings in my head, heart and gut. I feel I have been played, am being played, stupid for falling for this man when it was not real, and all the anguish I felt when I was crossing the line with Brett. "I can't do this with you," I say and get up to leave.

"Cari, please sit down," he responds, grabbing my arm. His touch still has an effect on me, so I obey. "I will explain as much as I can."

"Fine."

"Yes, I am Caitem, and I knew you were going through the recruitment process before you arrived for your interview."

"So, I didn't win the job on merit, it was Caitem

placing me."

"Yes, Caitem needed you at Tyn-T, but you had excellent credentials and the other panel members awarded you the role, I did not have to influence."

"You knew that my person of interest was Brett?"

"Yes."

"How much of what I did, do you know?"

"All of it, as it happened."

"And you continued this?" I respond, pointing at Jake and then at myself.

"Yes."

"Why?"

"Caitem comes first."

"That's bullshit, so I meant nothing to you, I was your assignment?"

"No, I was meant to monitor you, but there was, is something about you, and I crossed the line."

"If you knew what was going on with Brett, which made me physically sick, why did you have such a big reaction when you saw us kiss? Was that your way to get out of it, knowing you had crossed that line?"

"No, knowing and seeing are two different things and it was that moment that I realised what I really felt."

"You pretended so well, you really had me fooled that we had something and were building something."

"Caitem is difficult, as you have seen. A constant balance. You were profiled, and I could feel the chemistry and thought this was an opportune way to do my job."

"So I was a job? You are an arsehole. I am done, seeya." I get up to leave and this time make it out the door.

"Wait, I have not finished, we have not finished this conversation, and this is the only time we can. Come back inside and sit down," he demands, darkness appearing.

"Fine. What else do we have to discuss? I know that you are Caitem, Caitem comes first, and I was just a job," I reiterate.

"You were a job to monitor to start with, but I did not pretend anything."

"This has been the hardest time for me, I was so torn up and had no one I could talk to. Poh just toed the company line. And then when you said 'Faitem comes first', you blew my mind. Then you left me to deal with it on my own."

"I didn't have any time to explain, but needed you to know at least the Caitem part. I thought it would help you understand some of my behaviours."

"I take it you were busy with the pickups?"

"Confidentially, yes."

"Then I need to tell you something, but you have to promise there will be no consequences as a result."

"I cannot promise that."

"Fine, then I say nothing."

"Is it important to Caitem?"

"Yes, I think so. It could be."

"Then you have no choice, you must say, you do not get to decide."

"I don't care, I will only say if there are no consequences

as a result of what I say, for anyone."

"Anyone?"

"Yes, anyone."

"Okay."

"Promise?"

"Yes, promise."

"You would know that Lita was picked up and questioned about Brett."

"This is information you should not know," he says, that darkness re-appearing again.

"I know, but Lita is one of my best friends, she told me virtually nothing, no locations, no names other than Brett."

"Caitem will not be happy with this."

"You promised. And this is not the main bit."

"Go on."

"She said that she thought she saw you at wherever she was," I tell him. He has gone dark. I can see him thinking through what this might mean. "Jake, are you okay?"

"What did you say?"

"I said it was impossible, that I saw you Saturday and that last week you were working at the sister site."

"Did she believe you?"

"Completely. Now you can see why I needed to tell you, and she should not be punished, as this was important for you to know."

"Okay, do not mention this again, to anyone."

"Okay. What happens now that I know you are Caitem?"

"Nothing. The only change is that you now know one more person at Caitem, and as comforting as that might seem, it will not be easy."

"Why? I think it makes things a lot easier."

"It doesn't, your behaviour will change, and you will expect mine to change as well. Relationships are difficult in Caitem, you experienced that already."

"Did you know I first met Brett and we had, um, relations in Thailand?"

"Yes, I did, this is why we encouraged you to get closer."

"You encouraged it?"

"To get closer, not the intimacy."

"It was not intimate."

"It was from his perspective. And why would he not, he already had a taste of you, and you do not know how intoxicating you can be."

"Um." My face is burning red. He smiles and I can see some familiarity coming back.

"My feelings are real, and I have missed you, but am glad the assignment was a success. Caitem comes first, and I am unsure if we can balance both in a mutually healthy way. As well as being your line manager at Tyn-T."

"I would still like to try," I plead.

"Let's see," he responds, and for the third time I get up to leave. "Where are you going now?"

"Home."

"We still have a training session to do."

"Are you serious?"

"Completely, let's go."

***

Carrie and the crew will be back.

Find out what happens next in book two, due for release soon. In the meantime, check out some other titles in the Brand Artisans catalogue.

brandartisans.com.au

FROM THE AUTHOR'S DESK...

By day, I am fully entrenched in the corporate world, but I have always considered myself a creative, not once however, did I see myself as a writer... yet here I am.

Growing up, I followed a traditional path. I went to school, graduated, went to university and then worked hard on my career. In 2002, I realised that other than excelling in the workplace, I hadn't explored other areas of my life. So, I decided to pack up my life in Australia and live in London — or at least see if I could.

In 2008, my third job in London felt like I had landed in another world. The people I worked with seemed to speak another language, they played by a different set of rules and they didn't like to share. I was distraught and for the first time in my life I thought I may not be able to continue the work I was doing.

One of my friends, a co-worker, observed my daily trauma and recommended that I download my emotions by putting pen to paper.

I took her advice, and began my daily downloads. I continued these for months, and then my boyfriend at the time said, 'why don't you turn it into a book?'

This turned out to be the only smart things he ever said!!

My book began as an exposé on the Advertising industry, an insider's perspective — warts and all. At the time there were similar books (e.g. 'e-Mail' and '99c') that were popular, so I figured there was a market for it.

I left this job and concentrated on completing a first draft.

After multiple edits, what I was reading was not exciting me, and as such I decided to weave a crime theme through the already established storyline – this excited me and my passion for writing was realised.

In 2012 I returned to Adelaide. It was a shock to return to a place I knew but I now looked at completely differently.

I picked up my book again, and after reading it with fresh eyes, I realised I had two distinct story lines. I felt too close to make the hard decision to turn the story into one.

I found an editor who pulled it apart. I now had a solid, beginning, middle and end and continued to work at it.

A London Affair is the first of a two part series and I am looking forward to seeing where these characters go.

Monica

Want to learn more about Monica? Visit: brandartisans.com.au/monicaritz

310

THE 'STORIES FROM...' SERIES
N.J. EWING

Stories from the City is the debut romance novel from acclaimed fiction writer N.J. Ewing.

Best described as a 'Gritty Chic Lit', the first book in a series of three, hits on hard topics in a sensitive way. Written with so much heart and humour to boot, Stories from the City is fun and easy read despite the heavy subject matter.

Written for an 18+ audience only, this book comes with a trigger warning for anyone sensitive to drug abuse, domestic violence and sexual abuse.

Genre: Urban Romance; Erotic Fiction
Similar titles:
- Fifty Shades of Grey - E.L. James;
- Outlander - Diana Gabaldon;
- Burn - Maya Banks;
- Rachel's Holiday - Marian Keyes

STORIES FROM THE SEA
N.J. EWING

Stories from the Sea is the third installment in the 'Stories from...' series by Perth Author, N.J. Ewing.

A much lighter read than it's predecessors, as the characters rebuild their lives and leave behind the dramatic events that brought them all so close together.

This book introduces two new protagonists as we follow Ritchie Carlton back to the West Coast of Australia, while Ashley and Nathan begin their life down in Cornwall.

Written for an 18+ audience only.

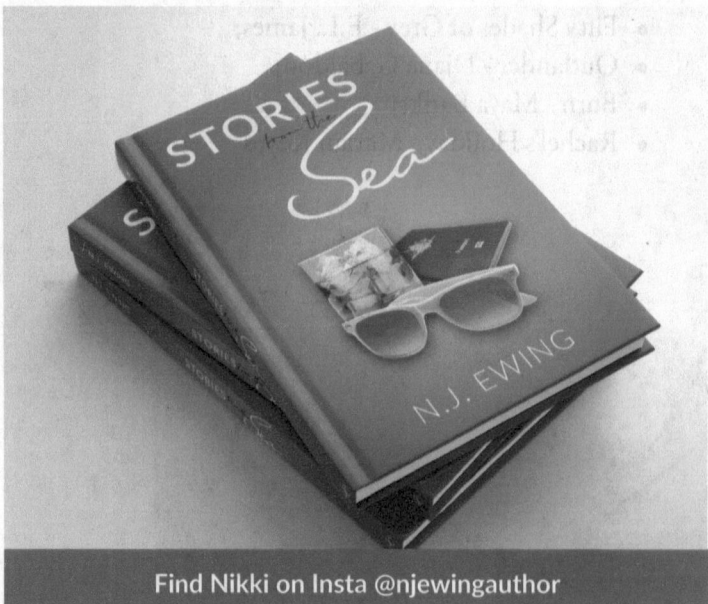

Find Nikki on Insta @njewingauthor